Red Blooms in the Forest

Red Blooms in the Forest

Nilima Sinha

NIYOGI
BOOKS

Published by
NIYOGI BOOKS
D-78, Okhla Industrial Area, Phase-I
New Delhi-110 020, INDIA
Tel: 91-11-26816301, 49327000
Fax: 91-11-26810483, 26813830
email: niyogibooks@gmail.com
website: www.niyogibooksindia.com

Editor: Gita Rajan
Cover Design: Shashi Bhushan Prasad/Niyogi Books
Layout: Sarojini Gosain/Niyogi Books

ISBN: 978-93-81523-99-5
Publication: 2013

Printed at: Niyogi Offset Pvt. Ltd., New Delhi, India

To my father, Late N.C. Srivastava, I.C.S.,
loved and respected,
and mother Nalini,
my husband—Yashwant,
who always encouraged me,
and my children—Sharmila-Ashok,
Jayant-Punita and
Sumant-Vaishali.

1

Champa

There was nothing to distinguish that evening from many others in her young life.

As a glowing orange sun sank behind the tall *saal* trees, village doors closed against shadows creeping ever closer from the jungle nearby. Windows shuttered up and alleys fell silent. The village cloistered itself off from the looming forest hovering at its edges, the silent sentinels of trees hiding the dangers within. The sun dropped into the depths of the jungle, leaving in its wake an unleavened darkness.

Champa lifted the kerosene lamp from its usual resting spot on the shelf behind the stove. Striking a match, she lit the lamp's slender cotton wick and set it carefully on the window sill. The light was not bright enough to banish the shadows from the tiny room; still, it lent a honeyed glow to the girl's dusky skin and was reflected in her large eyes. Champa caught a glimpse of her face in the broken mirror that hung next to the old wooden bed, and remembered her mother's laughing voice comparing her eyes to those of a doe. But that was a faded memory at the edge of her consciousness, and perhaps it had never actually happened.

Kamla presided over the activities in the hut. Plump and middle-aged, she sat on the faded sheet on the cot, fanning herself with the broken reed fan, grumbling loudly, even as Champa hurried through the evening chores.

"Come on girl, don't take all day to light the fire. It is time for your Babuji to return. You know how famished he is when he comes … wants his meal at once. And Gopal too must be starving …"

Champa poked at the sticks in the *chulha* and blew on them to stir up the flames. A small orange streak leapt upwards. "Don't worry, Ma. I'll get it going soon. Gopal, are you already hungry?" she asked, trying to keep her voice calm despite her growing irritation. She waved away the smoke which made her eyes water.

"No *didi*, I can wait," came Gopal's voice from the other room where he struggled to read in the dim light. "But I wish you'd help me. I don't know how to do these sums."

"Yes, I will, Gopu. One moment, I'll be there soon," said his sister.

"Hah! That's all she likes to do–meddle around with books," grumbled Kamla, "Hurry up, will you? And better scrub that black *karhai*, it is so sticky and filthy! Do you want us all to fall ill?"

"I know what I must do …," began Champa when they heard a loud bang at the door. "Wh … what's that?" cried the girl, leaping to her feet. Her eyes sparking in sudden alarm, she rushed to the cot, gripping its edge as the door was battered from outside in a determined manner. Creaking under the onslaught, the frail wooden bar that kept it shut against the world, gave way. The door burst open.

"Who's there?" Kamla's startled eyes grew round in alarm.

Guns! It was the first thing that Champa noticed. The men barged in, not one by one, but all together, like a tidal wave of khaki. They swarmed into the hut, their black masks and brown uniforms overwhelming the room, overshadowing the single wooden cot and the fire now burning fitfully in the *chulha*. The *dhibri*'s light flickered uncertainly at the intrusion.

The guns were pointed deliberately at Kamla and her.

"Jungle folk!" Champa had heard about them from villagers who had encountered the armed men, but had never come face to face with them herself. "They cannot harm women," the thought seemed to lend her confidence. As Kamla's fear impaled her to the solidity of the *chouki*, Champa boldly took a step forward. "What d'you want? Babuji has not returned from the cement factory. There's no one here except us."

"Food! Cook us a meal!" the tall man, their leader, rasped out through the cloth covering his mouth, "And fast. We don't have all the time in the world!"

"But there's nothing in our hut, *sarkar*. How can we feed so many?" mumbled Kamla.

"Don't tell lies. Isn't there the goat bleating in your *aangan*?" The man strode towards the cluster of earthen pots kept in a corner of the hut. His pointed gun flicked the lid off the largest pot. "And what's here? Rice!" He threw off another cover, "*Daal*? That will do. Kill the goat and cook the rice!" he snapped.

"No … o." They heard a sudden, shocked cry from the other room and Gopal rushed out of the darkness. "NO … don't touch Raja. The goat is mine. He is *my* Raja!" he pushed his way through the group at the door and tried to reach his beloved pet.

"Halt!" A gun blocked his way. "Stay there!" ordered the leader. He pushed Gopal back. The frightened boy stumbled into the waiting arms of his older sister. The gun continued to be directed at the trembling women. "One move and you join the goat," spat out the leader. "Vijay, get the animal ready for our meal."

Champa heard the suppressed whimper from the small body tightened against her own. The man named Vijay strode to the broken door, having already drawn a knife from his belt. She could see the goat, tethered to a stake in the hard ground, frantically pacing as if he had understood the sentence. The boy, held in place by the strong arms of his sister, could not move. The anguished bleating of the goat rent the air. The boy struggled, echoing the cries of his pet, but the girl's arms held him tight. In her trembling he could sense not only his own dark fear, but the current of anger that shot through her.

"Don't you hurt Raja!" she screamed, unable to stop herself. The gun was immediately pointed to her head. With a cry, the boy buried his face deeper into her sari. The three stood transfixed. The frightened, frantic bleating was heard once more, and then there was silence.

The man called Vijay walked back in, carrying the chunks of dripping flesh wrapped up in a piece of cloth. He handed it to the leader. The man pushed it at Champa, who recoiled with horror at the sight. "Go on, cook it!" he ordered, jerking his head at where the fire flared.

Champa felt helpless and alone. She knew she must stay silent and obey the men. She had heard hushed conversations and whispered talk about the ruthless 'jungle' people who chopped off villagers' hands or blew men up into bits if their commands were not followed. The jungle folk showed no mercy, they stopped at nothing, she well knew. Yet, she could not move. It was Kamla who took the meat from the outstretched arm as the other two averted their faces. The boy sobbed helplessly. Finally, she picked up an onion and set to cutting it, the tears it evoked masking her real ones.

Drops of frustration, and then anger, dripped into the masala on the grinding stone. Kamla, too scared to utter a word, sliced the onions, her fingers shaking in fear.

Soon the tempting aroma of meat cooking in the earthen pot wafted into the air. At any other time Champa would have flared her nostrils and sniffed at it with pleasure. But now the steam from the simmering curry only made her want to throw up. The men had no such qualms. As soon as the meal was ready they tore off their scarves and fell on it greedily, smacking their lips and burping in satisfaction.

The sound of quiet footsteps made them all look up. Champa caught her breath. It was Babuji, lingering at the threshold, his glance taking in the shocking scene inside. The old man knew. It had happened in other huts in other villages. Only the other day, the Naxalites had raided a pucca house belonging to a contractor in a nearby village. The man had made lakhs of dirty money in the recently constructed village road and no doubt deserved what he got. Though he had a gunman to protect him, he was shot and his house looted and burnt.

There was nothing in his own hut, yet it could happen to him too, the old man feared. It was no use protesting. The men would only slit his throat and go their way. Without a word, he sneaked towards the little group crouching in the corner and put an arm around his son.

Champa's heart thumped in panic at the thought of what the intruders could do to her father. But the men, their stomachs filled, were no longer in a mood for confrontation. In fact they seemed relaxed and in good spirits as they bantered with each other, the grins on their faces replacing the earlier grimness. It was a relief to see them tie the black scarves back on their faces and pick up their guns.

Only Vijay, the man responsible for killing the goat, lingered to take a last look. "Sorry, *bacche*, but it had to be done," he told the boy who still sobbed softly in his father's arms. He threw a quick glance at the girl standing stiff and sullen near the *chulha*, lips sternly set and frown on her brow. "Get him another pet! But not a goat! How about a ... a ... parrot this time?" Pleased at his own sense of humour he stole another look at her to gauge her reaction.

The girl glared back at the man angrily.

The smirk still glued onto his face, he turned to follow the others while Champa, gritting her teeth, watched the killer melt into the shadows outside.

2

She was still asleep when the sun, streaming in through the window, warmed her cheeks and forced Champa to open her eyes. Her brother was all hunched up, snuggling close against her, snoring gently; it reminded her of last night's trauma. For a moment she wondered if it had really happened. But there was no time to linger as other sounds intruded on her consciousness. The tramp of many feet, sharp shouts and orders, combined with the sinister click and clink of metal, slashed the tranquil familiarity of the everyday morning sounds, alerting her to a new danger. Something was very amiss. She ran to the window, her heart racing again in alarm.

Her fears were not unfounded. Champa found the *aangan* filled once again with strangers. The door of the hut was open. Uniformed men swarmed all over their home, tramping in and out of their tiny hut in their heavy boots. The broken door swung crazily on its hinges, ready to crash any moment to the floor. The policemen ignored the inmates of the home so rudely invaded by them. They searched briskly all around, exploring, probing, poking into everything, looking for cues and clues that existed only in their imagination.

Curiosity impelled her to set her fears aside and Champa drew closer to see. Her father sat stiff and silent on the *chouki*, every muscle on his body taut in tension. The twitching of the deeply etched lines on his face revealed his nervousness. Kamla stood nearby. Every few minutes she would wring her fingers helplessly and mutter terrible curses against the policemen; not that it had any visible effect on the rampaging, hardened men, who ruthlessly carried on with their job.

Some picked up pots and pans to examine the contents; others poked and prodded at the family's few pathetically ragged belongings. The faded sheet on the *chouki* was flung to the floor. The garments hanging on the clothes' line strung across the room lay discarded in an untidy heap. Babuji's only shirt, carefully hung on a peg on the wall to keep away creases, lay crumpled on the mud-smeared floor, trampled upon by several pairs of dirt-encrusted boots.

Puzzled and mystified though she was, Champa dared not open her mouth. "You sheltered those men, Ganeshi Mahto. You know they are criminals in the eyes of the law. But you fed them. You even sacrificed your goat to give them a sumptuous meal! We got the information from the villagers, who heard the noises in your hut last night," she got her answer soon enough.

"No *sarkar*, b … believe me, *sarkar*. They came here last night, when the women were alone. They forced them to cook. I was not even there, *huzoor* …," said Babuji with folded hands and a shaky voice.

"That won't do. You must prove it," snapped the policeman rudely.

Champa was never to forget the humiliation of the scene that followed. Her father, though stern and distant, was her protector and guardian. She deeply respected, yet feared and loved him. It was a shock to see him bend towards the policeman's feet in an attempt to touch them, only to be rudely kicked aside. The normally aggressive Kamla grovelled before the uniformed men. Together, the two presented a picture that would remain forever etched in the girl's mind. Her father's bewildered, desperate cry proclaiming his innocence was a sound that would echo and re-echo in the silence of many a sleepless night.

The police remained unmoved and unconvinced. "This drama won't fool us! You well know where those men are hidden. Tell us, and we won't trouble you. But if you keep quiet … we'll arrest you for abetting criminals."

Babuji only shook his head and kept repeating the words, "I know nothing, I know nothing …"

It did not convince the men. "Don't repeat your lies. You do know. We won't hurt you if you tell us. If you don't …," they ended the sentence with a sharp punch on Babuji's shoulder. Champa cringed and closed her eyes. Red hot anger seared her body. How could they be so sure that he knew? He was not even present that evening. Besides, early every morning, he left for the cement factory where he laboured hard all day, returning only after it was dark. "No!" she screamed, unable to watch the humiliation anymore, "He knows nothing! Can't you see that?"

At once Ganeshi turned around to grip her arm. "Quiet, girl. It's nothing to do with you. You stay away … go!" He tried to push her away but Champa remained stubbornly glued to his side.

"Oho, so you are the one who knows, is it?" The policeman now turned towards Champa. His eyes travelled slowly and deliberately all over her body, lingering over the dishevelled sari that barely covered her young curves, in a manner that made her feel uncomfortable, violated. She quickly drew the sari around to cover herself up. The disturbing stare seemed to burn her even through the cloth. There was nothing to be achieved by standing there. Drawing herself up and trying to regain her lost dignity she escaped to the other room. She sat there next to Gopal, hoping and praying the men would soon leave.

The police had obviously made up its mind that Ganeshi was hand in glove with the jungle people. Champa heard Kamla scream loudly. She ran to peep out of the window. The men had forced Babuji into their jeep. It drove off, raising a cloud of dust in its wake. Distraught, Kamla shouted wild abuses, which was all that she could really do.

All day the women waited for their man to return. The minutes dragged on slowly, painfully, until the sun dipped down at last behind the thick trees in the forest. A gloomy, brooding darkness settled around the hut. The two women huddled silently on the *chouki*, staring with vacant eyes at the dark shape of the door.

Night fell, but there were no signs of Babuji's return.

The morning dawned fresh and bright. Kamla, who had not really slept, awoke exhausted and red-eyed. She vented her frustration on her usual target, Champa. The girl carried on with the early morning chores for she knew her mother was in no condition to step out of bed.

The hut and the *aangan* had to be swept and cleaned, the cow fed, milked, the fire lit and the milk boiled, pots and pans scrubbed, the cowdung gathered and the water fetched–the daily tasks must be carried out, no matter how depressed she felt. If Kamla was not up to it she, Champa, must shoulder all the responsibility, as she always did. Wearily, she went through the daily tasks, accompanied as usual by Kamla's strident voice issuing unnecessary instructions.

It was a relief to pick up the big earthen pot and head out to the village pump. Out of earshot of the grumbling older woman, Champa felt her spirits lift a little as she breathed in the cool morning air. She walked slowly, savouring the crispness of a new day.

Their hut was some distance away from the rest of the village. It nestled snugly between a huge rock and low sprawling bushes that hid it effectively, adding to its isolation. No wonder the people from the jungle had chosen their home for barging in that night.

3

The sun, hot and yellow, dazzled overhead driving away the shade. Awaiting her turn in the crowd around the solitary village pump Champa felt its rays reach every pore of her body. The older women were in no mood to give way to her. They were the busy ones, too much in a hurry to stand in line; their homes and fields awaited them. It was for the girls, who had nothing to do, to bide their time. As the women fought and pushed each other, the girl patiently waited.

Filling up the pitcher at last, she headed for home. It was a relief to reach the shade of the jackfruit tree. She stopped a while to wipe the perspiration that dripped down her cheeks. The sweet, sickly smell of the ripening fruit reminded her of the past when she and her friends had lingered there while returning from school. She smiled to see the birds hop about under the trees. She remembered how the friends had dawdled there–teasing each other, chatting, reluctant to return home to household chores. Bold and carefree like those tiny creatures, she had challenged Gouri and Jhumki, her schoolmates, to climb the jackfruit tree. She had beaten them, of course! Not once, not twice, but more times than she could remember, she had reached the topmost branch. The others stared up at her in envy while she triumphantly waved down at them.

It was the same in class. Always ahead of her friends, she was the one who scored in tests. Poor Gouri, poor Jhumki–not once had they succeeded in beating her! Champa tossed her hair back with a proud lift of her head. Yes, she was the best and she knew it.

If only her mother understood. She, who had never been to school herself, could find no justification in letting the girl continue schooling.

After all, she had done eight years there already. Was that not enough for a girl? In vain had Champa pleaded that she wanted to become someone, maybe a teacher or a nurse, in vain had she begged and pleaded. In the end she had run to her father, knowing well that he felt proud whenever she told him about her school results. He was sure to overrule her mother.

Babuji could not face the onslaught from his wife. She turned to him immediately after her daughter finished. Champa heard the loud, complaining voice even in the other room and knew that her mother would go on and on until her father was forced to give in. "Why must she go? You know there is so much to do at home. I am too old to cook, clean, look after the cow ... I have to do it all alone. Why must the girl waste her time doing nothing? No, it is time she stayed home and helped!" And so on, until her father walked out of the room. As usual, her mother had won.

Not that it was any use criticising Kamla. She had arrived one day, all wrapped up in a red sari with a long veil that hid her face. Their hut had been full of relatives gathered there to welcome her. They sang songs and garlanded the visitor. They smiled and told the little girl she need not cook or clean the hut anymore. Babuji had brought the new woman home to take care of them. She was to be her mother. Champa believed them. She did not really remember her own mother, though a smell or a sound would sometimes evoke a faint, vague memory of a warm presence. There was another reason why she was happy when the new woman came. Plump, soft and curvaceous, she made her Babuji laugh again, which he had not done for a long time. Champa was grateful for that.

The two got along well until Gopal was born. Kamla began to leave more and more tasks for the girl to complete. Champa did it all cheerfully, cleaning, cooking, carrying Gopal around with her, even when her mother closed the door of the room, shutting Babuji off from her and the baby. School, home, and later the little boy toddling around her kept Champa occupied and contented. The only time she really resented her mother was when she had forced her to leave school. A year had gone by since then. Even now, when she saw other children walk by or heard the noises as she passed the pink walls of the school, she felt the urge to run there.

Champa shook her head impatiently. No point going back to the past. Her eyes followed the flight of a white crane heading towards the pond far away. She could glimpse the pond's silvery surface through the rolling fields. Tall *sakhua* trees, their leaves fresh, green and gleaming, stood in clumps on the brown and green land. Way beyond, was a mango orchard belonging to a city trader. Beyond it was the industrial area facing the highway to Ranchi, the state capital. Her father worked there as a daily labourer in a cement factory.

With a sigh the girl jumped to her feet. It was no use sitting there and feeling despondent. It was getting hot even in the shade and it was time she was within the cool walls of her hut. She dusted the fallen leaves from her sari and picked up the heavy pot again.

Kamla was waiting to pounce on her. "And where have you been, girl? Does it take that long to fetch water? What have you been up to?" She looked suspiciously at her. Champa knew it was best to stay silent. She sighed as she looked around.

Babuji had not returned.

The two waited for sounds that would announce their man's arrival. Champa lit the *dhibri* and set it on the window sill. She watched the shadows dance as a light breeze through the open window made the light flicker. Surely the policemen would not keep him with them forever, hoped the women. She must light the fire, for Babuji was sure to return. Champa collected the twigs and laid them in the *chulha*. As she groped for the matchsticks, tucked out of sight behind the *dhibri*, they heard a loud bang at the door.

There he was! At last! The women rushed towards the door.

It was not Babuji. Outside stood the group of men in masks who had forced their way into their hut earlier. Champa gasped, staring at them in dismay. Not again! The men swarmed noisily into the hut.

It made Gopal scream and rush into the other room. Kamla stepped hastily forward and muttered in a voice that was almost inaudible, "*Ab kya chahiye*? What d'you want now?"

"Don't look shocked, woman. We liked your cooking so we decided to taste it again," announced the man whose voice they recognised as the leader's.

"But you know there is nothing … you emptied the hut last time you were here … my man too was taken away because of you. Why must you come here every time?"

"Woman, you should be happy we are here. We have not come empty-handed this time. Look!" He gestured to a man standing near with a sack that he emptied on the floor. "*Daal*, rice, vegetables, oil, masala–everything you need and more. So go on, cook us some *daal-bhat-tarkari*. You may eat too. And quick, we are hungry."

Champa knew this meant nothing but more trouble with the police. She shot a furious glance at the tall, slim man, whom she recognised as the goat-killer. His eyes, above the black scarf tied around his face, were fixed on her. It only enraged her further and increased her sense of helplessness.

Kamla stood frozen, though her eyes gleamed at the sight of the food. Their defiance seemed to anger the leader. He raised his gun and pointed it threateningly at them. "Go on, hurry up. Or I will not hesitate to shoot."

Before they could move he had rushed into the other room. The next moment he was back, dragging Gopal out from the corner where he hid in fear. The boy's face was ashen; his terrified eyes darted from face to face. The leader put his gun against the boy's head and snapped at the women, "Now will you hurry up?"

Kamla looked as if she was about to faint. Champa knew she must act quickly before it was too late. "Put the gun down!" she screamed, "We'll cook! But let my brother be!"

Surprised, the man lowered his gun, "Alright, we believe you will, girl. But remember, we're watching. One wrong move, and …" He made a gesture that sent a shudder down her spine. She bent and picked up the bag of potatoes. Kamla crouched beside her to help. She used the curved *hasua* to slice the onions while Champa peeled and chopped the vegetables. She wondered what would happen if she made a sudden move with the knife she held in hand, especially at the man who had so enraged her. But she knew it could not be done.

As soon as the meal was ready the women were hustled off to the next room while the men gorged on the *daal-bhat-tarkari*. They belched loudly when their stomachs were full and prepared to step out.

"Alright ladies, we take your leave now," said the man everyone addressed as "Sir". He glanced around at the almost empty pots lying near the *chulha*. "Don't worry, we've left enough for you to eat. And never say the comrades are not grateful. Here, take this. You've served us well." He took a wad of notes from his pocket and held it out towards Kamla.

"No, don't take it Ma, we don't want their money," muttered Champa angrily, but Kamla was looking at the proffered gift with a greedy glint in her eyes.

"Yes, yes, take the money," said the odious man who had wielded the knife. Champa gave him an indignant look.

The leader pushed the notes into the older woman's hands. She quickly grabbed the bundle and hid it in the folds of her sari. Champa could only shrug her shoulders helplessly. Heart filled with resentment she watched them put on their boots and pick up their guns. It was because of them that Babuji was with the police. How dare they come here, force them to cook and then offer money?

All others walked out except the man called Vijay. He lingered at the door. "Say *Lal Salaam* to my friend, your brother. I see he has not got any pet as yet," he called out.

For the first time the girl glanced at his unmasked face. She noticed the small dimple on one cheek that deepened when he smiled at her. She was in no mood to respond. Instead her brows drew together in an angry scowl. She immediately turned her face away.

Vijay swung around and walked off into the night.

4

Vijay Lall

As a child, Vijay had lived in a big house built by his grandfather, Ganpat Lall, who had retired as a *daroga*. After Ganpat Lall's death the house passed on to Ganpat Lall's two sons, Mohan and Sohan Lall. Vijay was the only son of the younger son, Sohan. The four sons of the elder brother and Vijay and his family lived together in the big house.

Trouble soon began in the joint family. On the plea that her family was much bigger, Mohan's wife extended her living space until Vijay and his parents were confined to two small rooms at the back. Sohan, gentle and mild in nature, respected his elder brother too much to protest. His only wish was that his son did well in school. "My father was just a policeman, but my son will compete in the civil services examinations, and become a Collector or an SP. That is all I want," he told his wife, Mira, and his son.

Life continued as usual in the large joint family until the day Vijay found his cousin standing at the school gate, waiting to take him home. The look on his cousin's face should have warned him, but the boy was too young to notice that something was wrong. "Hurry," said his cousin and he followed as fast as his ten year old legs could carry him.

His mother waited for him. As soon as Mira saw him she burst into loud wails and clung to the little boy. Sohan Lall, Vijay's father, lay dead in the room. He had gone to the bazaar to buy fresh oranges for his brother who was sick. He was standing outside the fruit stall when a speeding truck had hit him, killing him on the spot. The driver had sped off. Passersby, who recognised the *daroga*'s son, brought him home in a rickshaw.

Mohan and his wife consoled Mira and promised to look after her and Vijay. However, not many months had passed when their concern turned into indifference. The compensation for the death by accident became another point to argue about. Mohan's wife insulted Mira whenever she could. Vijay's mother felt unwanted in the big house. She realised that her sister-in-law would be only too happy if they vacated it and left the whole place to her family.

Mira was already a teacher in the local girls' residential school. She tried hard and was able to get appointed as the warden of the hostel. This entitled her to get accommodation on the premises.

Mother and son settled down to a new life. It was quiet and peaceful in the hostel, away from all family squabbles. Mira made sure that Vijay worked hard at his studies. He, too, felt that the only way he could please his late, beloved father was by studying hard and doing well in class. He made no friends. Once he returned from school he rushed to finish his homework. He spent the rest of his time at home reading, or listening to music on the radio. Life was nothing but school, homework and the hostel. But the two were content; they would not have had it otherwise.

Vijay passed school with flying colours, coming at the top in his class! He could have got admission to any college in any city but he decided to join the local institute run by missionaries, the best in town. He wanted to stay close to his mother.

College was an eye-opener for Vijay. He enjoyed the freedom and the chance to discuss subjects in class. He had taken up history and political science as he was told that they would be useful to him when he sat for the Competitive Exams. He listened to lectures avidly, taking down copious notes. It irritated him when Sudhir, one of his classmates, interrupted lectures to disagree with some minor point made by the teacher.

Sudhir argued endlessly, thrashing out points with lecturers until he was fully convinced. Vijay wished the teachers were not so patient; he most certainly did not like to watch precious time slip away in futile argument. He would try to stop the boy by telling him that teachers knew best, but Sudhir only laughed to see Vijay take lectures so seriously.

"Come on, *yaar*," said Sudhir one day, finding Vijay sitting in the old library taking notes, his head buried in a book, "What will you gain from those stuffy old books?"

"What would you rather have me do?" Vijay asked testily, irritated at being disturbed.

"Throw away the musty papers! Come see a film … why not?"

"Don't forget we have an exam," muttered Vijay, reaching for the book which Sudhir had snatched from him.

"So what? Let's talk, if you don't want to waste three hours on a film!" said Sudhir, his teeth flashing white against his pale olive skin.

"What about?"

"Why not about ourselves? Tell me, who are you? What are you?" asked Sudhir, flopping down on the chair in front of Vijay.

"Nothing much to tell," began Vijay, but soon found that there was enough in his short life to tell anyone willing to listen. He felt good about it. Sudhir of course chatted freely about himself. His father was a lawyer who wanted his son to follow in his footsteps.

"But I'll never be a lawyer! What lies must they tell, *yaar*! I find it most repulsive, having to defend the indefensible. I remember once there was a girl, a maid in a rich household, who had been raped by her master. My father was defending the man….he twisted all that she said, making the poor girl so confused she lost the case and the man was let off. I was there and felt she was telling the truth … but … it was so disgusting! How could my father defend him? No, I'll never be a lawyer. Never!" Sudhir shook his head violently, making the thick strands of his black hair fall over his handsome features.

Vijay laughed. "What do you wish to do then?" he asked.

"I want the world to be fair and equal towards all. Why should someone from a rich family get away with a crime, while someone who is weak anyway have to suffer? It is not right. Was it fair to let a rapist go? No, there must be justice for all. All who are born here by the grace of god should be considered equal, whether rich or poor," insisted Sudhir, his pale skin going all red and flushed.

"Well, as a deputy commissioner or a police officer I plan to do just that. Give fair and equal treatment to all," assured Vijay, smiling, trying to calm the agitated young man.

"You wait and see. It won't be possible. Haven't I seen the corruption that exists in government? Everyone takes bribes. You are bound to end up as one of them."

"Of course I won't," asserted Vijay.

"We'll see," said Sudhir.

Vijay was surprised to note that there was a serious side to his new friend. In spite of his wild chatter and sometimes impossible statements he was a man with a conscience.

Sudhir was well up on the latest gossip that did the rounds in their little town. He knew which businessmen had made money illegally and who were the authorities who had turned a blind eye towards their misdeeds.

"The last Deputy Commissioner allowed corruption to flourish. Every time government schemes were allotted to contractors he took hefty sums to pass the projects. And why should he not? After all he himself had paid a neat sum to be appointed boss here!" he said one day.

"But he is a senior officer!" Vijay asked, surprised, "Transfers are routine for them. Why must he pay for it?"

"Come on, don't be so naive! Don't you know, to get a posting of your choice, you must bribe the minister ... after all, he needs the money too, for elections!"

"Don't forget I am preparing for the civil services," protested Vijay, "There are strict rules, you are not supposed to cosy up to politicians ... you must maintain a distance, remain impartial and objective in performing your duty."

"Impartial! Ha, ha, tell me another!" scoffed Sudhir, "If you give me one example of an impartial officer, I will polish your boots every day for a month, I promise."

"Alright, alright, I believe you," laughed Vijay.

He began to enjoy talking to Sudhir and soon the two started to meet often. Vijay took his new friend home. Mira was glad to see that her son had found someone to talk to. She encouraged the boy to come home and often joined in their conversation. She agreed with Sudhir's views. Being in touch with her students and through them their parents, she had heard stories and complaints on almost every aspect of life in their small town.

"I have earned my place in heaven," said Sudhir one evening, picking up his cup of tea and looking smug. "I performed my good deed for the day!"

"Really, and what did you do?" asked Vijay.

"There was this old woman. I found her weeping near the Block Office. I felt sorry for her and asked her why. She burst into sobs. With her husband dead she was entitled to 'Vidhwa Pension' from the government. Her papers were perfect. Yet they made her run from office to office. Finally she was told to hand in two hundred rupees for her papers to be received."

"Just for receiving?" asked both Vijay and Mira together.

"Yes. It made my blood boil. Take me to that man, I told her. At first she was too scared … but then she did."

"And … you bashed him up, like Amitabh Bachhan in a movie?"

"Of course not, *yaar*. This is not a movie. And I am not a hero."

"Then?"

"I pretended I was from the CID. Threatened to make an inquiry against him. It was bound to put him behind bars for corruption. The man looked this way and that and–would you believe it? Offered me two thousand rupees not to tell on him!"

"What?" laughed Vijay, "He tried to bribe you?"

"Yes! I pocketed the money, made him do the job, which he did without any fuss. The old woman got her pension."

"So, where's the two thousand? Are you going to treat us? Or keep the money yourself?"

"Of course not! I gave it to the poor woman. She was so grateful, called me her son and blessed me heartily."

Vijay was impressed by his friend's generosity. He laughed. He felt happy at making a friend he could be proud of.

Mira liked to see him in a happy mood. She had often worried about his leading a lonely life, cut off from his family and other relatives. Several times she had thought about asserting her right over part of the big house, but the memory of the humiliation she had suffered at the hands of her sister-in-law put her off. Nevertheless she remained aware of the fact that her son had every right to live there. She did not forget her father-in-law's fond wish–the families of his two sons would live there in peace and joy forever.

5

Life never runs smoothly for too long. Just when it was all going well and they were looking forward to a promising future, his mother suffered a debilitating stroke.

As days passed Mira's condition began to worsen. Soon there came a time when the doctors began to shake their heads and look grave. She understood, and spoke to Vijay one day, tears in her eyes. "Go back to the big house, son. After all it is your home too. Where else will you live after I am gone?"

Vijay hushed her up. "Don't worry, you'll be well soon," he assured her, holding her frail hand in his. All the same, he prepared himself mentally to face the inevitable when it came.

It was a devastating shock, all the same, for Vijay when the end finally came. His uncle, Mohan Chacha, along with wife and family attended the funeral and participated in all the final rites. Once everyone left, a deathly silence settled over the flat. A few days later a letter arrived by post. Vijay was told very politely but firmly that he must vacate the premises as soon as possible. The flat would be required by the teacher appointed in place of his mother.

"*Yaar*, you must go to your paternal home," Sudhir advised his friend, "They did attend the funeral. They cannot be all that bad. I'm sure they will welcome you if you tell them about your problems."

Vijay hesitated.

"I will come with you if you like. Don't worry, I will wait outside. You go in and talk to them," suggested Sudhir.

Mohan Chacha was warm and welcoming. He enquired after his welfare and sent for snacks and tea. Vijay did not know how to bring up the topic and avoided talking about it. It was only when he was about to leave that he summoned the courage to tell his uncle about the letter and his need for a place to live.

"Of course, you are most welcome to stay here," said his uncle, then continued hesitatingly "But … but I must inform you, it would only be right to tell you … that … that … the property is now ours."

Vijay was puzzled. What did he mean? Did the property not belong to both his father and his uncle? That was what his mother had told him.

"You see, Vijay," interrupted Chachi, his uncle's wife, "The property has been …"

"Keep quiet, woman!" warned Mohan Chacha, "Let me explain. Vijay, you see, both the land and the house are now in my name and in that of your cousins'. We transferred it because we thought your mother would never come back … was not interested … and so …"

Vijay was stunned. Without a word he rushed out, highly agitated. Sudhir was waiting outside. "What happened, *yaar*?" he cried, seeing his friend's flushed face.

Vijay burst into a flood of angry words. It took Sudhir some time to understand. "Obviously your uncle has cheated you! But how?" he asked, "Wait. I will find out. I'll ask my father's friends to ferret out the details."

Sudhir persuaded his father's colleagues and friends to examine land records and was able to uncover the unpleasant facts. Vijay's uncle had used his father's old contacts and had bribed the relevant officers to transfer the house and lands to his own name and to that of his sons.

Vijay no longer had any claim over the property.

"Mean, selfish man!" cried Sudhir, "Didn't I tell you, Vijay, people today are extremely dishonest? They cheat, manipulate, bribe, do anything to get what they want. There are no morals or scruples left … everyone is for himself. But wait …. I'll ask my father to take up your case. We must fight it out. We cannot allow your uncle and the bribe-takers to get away with such a dishonest deal."

Unfortunately Sudhir's father refused to take up the case. There were important people involved, he said. Those who had broken the law for the sake of money were too influential. He would certainly not like to antagonise them, take up a case against them.

"The coward," muttered Sudhir, "Just like him. Takes up cases only of the rich and powerful, even if they are corrupt! It is true, it is an unfair world."

Vijay stayed silent, but not Sudhir. He was furious at the injustice done to his friend. "I tell you they are all the same. Corrupt, from head to toe. And you wanted to become one of them …!"

"No I don't! Not any longer!" burst out Vijay at last, "What is the point of joining those who make rules, only to break them the next moment? That is what the authorities do. I don't want to be a part of that set-up. Hang the civil service! I will not join their ranks … to become as corrupt as they are."

"Well said. You know, Vijay, I've seen the dirty side of life. Don't forget, my lawyer father meets all kinds of people. Thieves, murderers, cheats, criminals! It has made me cynical. But I've always felt sorry for those at the receiving end … of the unclean hands that manage to get away," Sudhir tried to explain.

Vijay nodded sympathetically.

"Recently I met people who felt as I did. They wanted the world to be a better, more just and equal place. I talked to their leader. I have thought long about it. It will definitely be satisfying to work with young enthusiasts like them. What do you say? Would you like to join the group?"

Vijay nodded eagerly. He had decided. There was no point in studying hard and sitting for the competition any more. Why should he work hard? For whom? He jumped to his feet. "Why not? Who are they?" he asked.

"I'll tell you later. Let me meet them first and explore possibilities. Are you sure you're interested?"

"Yes, yes....what else is there for me to do?" Vijay's voice grew bitter, "I am ready for anything!"

"Good! In the meanwhile, Vijay, I know where you can stay. I know of a place where you could lodge. No ... no, don't worry! I'll pay for it. It's not much. Surely I am allowed to do my bit to help a friend!"

Vijay nodded, grateful for the help offered. He shifted immediately from the rooms that his mother had occupied.

A little later the two friends joined the group known as the 'jungle folk' by the villagers, and Naxalites by others.

Vijay happened to be with them when the men barged into Champa's home.

6

Champa

Champa walked glumly out of the hut towards the trees not far from their village.

Another night had passed with no signs of Babuji. What would happen to them if he did not return? It was a fear that sat heavy as a sack of stones on her chest. She shook her head to throw off the feeling of despair that threatened to settle on her. Deliberately, she fixed her eyes on the greenery ahead, the play of light and shade under the spreading trees and the cool, shady depth of the forest.

She had brought the two cows, Kajal and Kajri, out to graze in the forest. Now she followed as the cow and calf walked sedately a little ahead, the bells on their necks jingling gently, soothing her tense nerves. The fresh green leaves on the lower branches drew them on, and soon cows and girl were inside a denser part of the jungle. She liked the peace and silence, and settled down on a rock to rest while the two animals grazed. It was so quiet, so hushed, she could clearly hear them munch.

The sound of a voice singing softly broke into her thoughts. She looked up and saw a familiar figure walking towards her from behind the bushes. Startled, she jumped to her feet. "Gouri, you? What brought you here?" The girl was not a stranger at all; rather she was one of her classmates whom she had not met since she had left school.

"Looking for firewood," replied her old friend, "And you? What are you doing here in the wilds?"

Champa pointed at the animals grazing among the trees. "They brought me here," she said, laughing. She glanced at the *sindur* shining bright in the parting of the other girl's hair, "*Arre*! But when did you get married? And why didn't you tell me about it?" she asked, accusingly.

"There was no time. The wedding was in our ancestral home in Bihar. Though his parents live close by we had to have the wedding there. We could not invite any of our village friends," explained the girl.

"*Achcha*. Oh, I am so happy to see you! Give me all the news! What is your new life like? How do you feel? How is the new family? Are they good to you?" Filled with curiosity, Champa wanted to know everything. Gouri was the first among her friends to have got married.

The other girl was excited too, and eager to chat about her new experiences. "Yes, yes, they are good to me, though they do not have much at home. There is some land, but not enough to feed the family. My man has not found a job as yet, so though he has passed Class X, he must farm the land. I, too, must help at home. But I am happy, for he is so loving and gentle, so kind!" she ended, blushing.

Champa smiled. There was so much more that she was curious about, like … how did it feel when a man touched you? What did they do when they were shut inside a room together? And so on. She remembered how as girls they had giggled and whispered when an older girl had got wedded. But now she had other worries to think about. As the two gathered twigs and picked up the fallen dry branches together, Champa related her own story.

"And Babuji is still there," she ended with a sob, "All because of the jungle people."

Gouri was sympathetic. "Tcha, tcha, *bechari*," she murmured soothingly, "But, *pata hai*, d'you know, the jungle people are not so bad?"

"What d'you mean … not so bad? Is it good to force people to cook at the point of a gun? Is it good to kill a little boy's beloved pet?" asked Champa indignantly.

"I don't know about that. But they did come to our help when we were in trouble. One of their men was in school with my husband. Just after we married, during the sowing season, we needed money to buy seeds. There was nothing left from last year and no money to buy more.

In desperation *he*, approached his old friend who was now one of the jungle folk. And you know what they did?"

"What?"

"Their captain spoke to all his people to help, and they passed around a cap to collect the money. They were generous and we got enough to buy the seeds. Not only that, the captain said we need not return the money. What does it mean? Are they bad people?" asked Gouri.

Champa became thoughtful. She remembered the wad of notes that had been thrust into her mother's hands. Perhaps it was meant well and she need not have felt so humiliated. But how could she agree with the methods they had used? They had shouted out orders as if she and her mother were their slaves. And why threaten with guns, could they have not requested them properly? No, they were hateful tyrants and she would never wish to see them again.

The two girls had to leave before the sun sank behind the trees and darkness enveloped the forest. Champa's path was different from the other girl's and the two parted with the promise to see each other soon again.

The cows walked now at a faster pace, the bells on their necks jingling merrily, reflecting their eagerness to return home. Champa followed, wondering if she would find her father at home when she returned. She pictured a scene that immediately lifted her spirits … her mother happily serving her father his meal while he sat on the *peedha* before the glowing fire.

Immersed in her thoughts she did not hear the crunch of someone's feet until a tall figure loomed close and almost collided with her.

"*Arre*! Look where you go, girl. You must be more alert while walking in the jungle. You never know what you will encounter," she heard a voice she was familiar with. A hand reached out to steady her.

Champa stared at the brown face which had a deep dimple on one cheek. "Oh, it's you?" she snapped.

"Yes, Vijay Lall. You are the one who cooked those great meals for us. I still remember the mutton curry."

Mention of the cooking released the pent up fury she had been nursing the last few days. "You beast!" she yelled, "You criminal! You hurt my brother, you spoilt our life! Do you know, the police have taken my father away? And he has not come back yet? *Bhagwan jaane*, what they are doing to him!"

Vijay's expression changed. There was a guarded look in his eyes. "What did your father tell the police?" he asked in a sharp tone.

"How do I know what he said at the police station? But he kept pleading ignorance. They would not believe him … they just pushed and kicked … and then forced him into their jeep."

"Yes, yes, I know the police can be very brutal."

"Why blame them … aren't you the same?" retorted Champa, fire in her eyes, "You killed the goat, you forced us to work for you at gun point …"

"Shut up, girl!" Vijay's voice was now rough, "We are not brutal, nor are we cruel. We may seem so to those who are against us. But we help those who trust us. If you don't believe me, ask the people in your village."

Champa remained silent, thinking. Yes, Gouri had said they were not always bad. They had been kind to her husband, but then he was an old school friend.

"It is not your fault, nor ours," Vijay fixed his eyes on her flushed face and continued, "The government has no feelings. Their people will harass the poor and the helpless, and suck up to the rich. That's the way the police functions. Why don't they jail the fat *banias* who hoard food and raise prices to make more and more money? Why jail the poor who know nothing and have to struggle just to exist?" his voice was passionate, filled with anger.

Maybe his feelings were justified. Champa remembered how Babuji had returned from the bazaar only a few days ago, looking glum because the *bania* had increased the price of rice and he did not have the money to buy rice even for two-three days. He had pleaded with him to sell the rice on loan, but the *bania* had refused to do it. Yes, life was so unfair.

But why must she get involved with what the young man said? She had enough troubles of her own.

"I must go," she told Vijay, "It is getting dark. I must milk the cow too."

"If you are in any trouble, do let us know. We'll try to help ..." offered Vijay.

"Hunh. I'll never seek help from people such as you!" scoffed Champa.

"Still, do listen. Here, take my mobile number. You can ring me up," said Vijay, his eyes on her face.

"As if we have one of those things ... we are not rich like you, don't forget," Champa's voice was full of scorn.

"I am not rich. But do take this. It is my number, a secret one. No one knows about it. But I am giving it to you. You can use any of the phone booths available. If you ring up, we will certainly help, alright?"

Champa strode off, but not before she had taken the paper chit offered by Vijay and tucked it up in a fold of her sari. Reaching home, she made sure it was kept safe in a place where it would not be seen by curious eyes.

7

Three more long and anxious days followed. The monotonous 'tip-tup, tip-tup' of the rain dripping off and on their thatched roof added to the feeling of darkness and despair. There were still no signs of Ganeshi Mahto's return. The family, swinging between disappointment and hope, kept its eyes constantly glued to the still broken, tottering door. By now Kamla was no longer silent and dazed. Her tongue loosened up, breaking into insulting words Champa was familiar with.

"If only I had an elder son instead of a daughter, he would have helped, gone to the police station, found out about his father. What good is it to have a girl? She can only sit at home. Oh, what kind of kismet do I have ... to keep, feed and care for a girl who is of no use? Indeed I am cursed, yes, it is a curse on me, to have a girl who can do nothing at all, nothing ... nothing at all! Woe betides my fate!" she ranted and cursed as she lay all day on her cot next to the wall.

The words were like sharp stabs that sank deep into her mind. Of course she had heard similar words before, but at this point in time Champa's own mood was as disturbed as Kamla's. In her heightened state of tension, each word was like a knife twisting into her heart. She ran to the pile of newspaper cuttings she had stored in the wooden chest where she kept her treasured possessions–an old faded picture of her late mother, a torn sari earlier worn by her, some of her old school books and a clay piggy bank in which she had dropped a few coins.

The cuttings were about girls who had scored–at games and sports, board examinations, and various competitions. All had done well under difficult circumstances and Champa admired their courage. Secretly, she too aspired to make a name for herself in some field or the other, though she was not sure which.

She would show them! Now was the time. She would show everyone that she was as good as anyone, and equal if not better than any boy.

Quickly she put everything back into the old chest. Now that a decision had been taken, she felt much better. With firm, brisk steps she strode to the wall and pulled down her salwar-kameez suit from the peg. She flung off the sari that only hampered movement and slipped into the more practical dress. She tied up her hair in a high ponytail and looked at herself in the broken piece of glass that served as a mirror. A bit of *kaajal* in her eyes, a final pat to her hair and she was ready.

"*Ab kahan*? Where are you off to?" her mother's voice followed her as she walked to the door.

"To the police station. To find out about Babuji."

"Good. At last she has shown some sense. Go then." said Kamla.

Champa set off on her journey to the police station. The intermittent rain had filled the fields with water, dividing them into little pools. She kept her eyes fixed to the ground, wary of the snakes that could lurk behind the stones or creep across the higher, drier strip. She walked carefully, fearing that she might slip on the wet, uneven land and fall into the muddy water. She soon reached the back of the mango orchard surrounded with its high walls.

Champa could see the high steeple of the temple inside the mango garden. She remembered she had been to the garden, called Aamra Vatika, twice with her father–once to offer thanks to Lord Shiva at her brother's birth, and the next time to pray that she did well in her Class VIII exam. Not that matters had worked out well afterwards–though she had come first in class, her mother had insisted she need not attend school any more, she remembered with a bitter sigh.

Nevertheless, Champa folded her hands and bowed in the direction of the temple, asking the deity to bless her on her mission.

A narrow, *kuccha* path led around the walls to the industrial area on the other side of the orchard. For a moment she hesitated. Should she seek help from the men at the cement factory which employed her father? Then she shrugged her shoulders. Why would they care? Even when he was ill and unable to work, they had been unsympathetic and cut his wages for the three days he had been absent. Her mother had gone to plead for some money to buy medicine for him, but they had turned down her plea for help. They were forced to take a loan from the *bania* again and were still trying to return the amount.

As long as Babuji worked he was useful to them at the cement factory, she well knew. If he got involved in a police case, he would get neither sympathy nor support from his employers. No, she must act on her own; there was no point in seeking help from anyone.

The girl stood beside the highway, waiting for a passing vehicle that could take her to the town. The milestone before her informed her that she was eight kilometres away, too far to reach on foot. Thankfully, she did not have to wait long. Honk, honk, she heard, and a tempo filled with passengers halted to a stop right in front of her. An old lady, two men and three women in brightly coloured saris disentangled themselves from the mass of humanity tightly packed inside the bus and stepped down on to the road.

"Does this go to the muffasil police-station?" she asked.

"Yes, yes," chorused several voices and she was pulled into the tempo by willing hands. The mass of humanity adjusted itself to the new addition and the tempo started again on its journey into town.

Champa clung to a rod at the side of the tempo. Pushed and jostled by the crowd inside, she was almost thrown out of the vehicle every time it bumped over one of the several potholes that littered the highway. The clustering together of the half-complete brick houses on both sides of the road told her they had almost reached town. The tempo honked past rickshaws, and scattered men and women out of the way until at last they reached their destination.

The police station was a large, white-washed building right next to the main highway. The tempo unloaded several passengers outside its gates. Some disappeared into a lane which led from the main road to a nearby village, while a few entered the gates of the police station The building stood within a compound, full of broken down, ancient, rusted vehicles, covered with dust and grime, parked anyhow, untidily, under some spreading mango trees. Hesitantly, Champa walked up to the building and climbed the low steps leading to the front veranda. She stepped through the open door into a hall.

Policemen as well as others crowded the large hall. She looked around, puzzled. Whom should she meet? Someone directed her to a smaller room where a man in uniform sat at the table. He twisted his moustache on seeing the shy young girl enter his room.

Fortunately the man was helpful. "What can I do for you?" he asked warmly.

"It is my father, Sir," she replied, trying to keep her voice steady, "The police took him away three-four days ago. Since then, we have not heard from him."

"His name?"

"Ganeshi Mahto, Sir."

"Village, thana?"

"Nawadih, Bazaartand!" she smartly answered.

The man frowned. "Ganeshi? Yes, I know his crime. Has been in contact with the Maowadis. He knows he must not …"

"No Sir," interrupted Champa, "He did not commit any crime. It wasn't his fault either … he wasn't even there. It was only us, my mother, little brother and me, when they came …" She faltered at sight of the stern look in the officer's eyes.

"So you colluded with the criminals?" asked the man sharply.

"No … yes, we were forced to cook for them. They put a gun at my little brother's head … and … threatened … we had to do it, Sir. Cook for them, I mean … "

"You shouldn't have done it." The man's voice had turned kinder, softer. He pressed a bell. Two policemen entered and saluted the officer. "Where's the file on Ganeshi Mahto? I want to see it … at once."

"Yes Sir."

The men were gone a long time. Champa sat on a chair, nervously twisting her fingers. She watched the officer deal with many others. He was efficient and brisk and this raised a ray of hope in her heart. He would surely be fair to Babuji.

"The file is not there," the policemen, who returned at last, muttered, "Seems to be misplaced somewhere."

"May I see my father?" begged Champa impatiently, "Let them look for their file. In the meantime, please allow me to meet Babuji!"

The officer had become busy with a woman whose child had gone missing. She was wailing, crying, and creating a lot of noise. Her relatives had surrounded her and the officer. Champa realised he was too preoccupied now to notice her. She jumped to her feet. "Can I meet him?" she asked the two policemen who had gone to get the file.

The men nodded and gestured to her to follow them. She looked at the officer, but his face was hidden by the wailing woman and her relatives. Champa decided there was no need for further permission. Quickly she jumped down and followed the men who were now at the door, heading out of the room into a corridor. They would lead her to her father, she knew. At last! At last she would meet Babuji. Thrilled at the thought, she rushed after the two policemen who looked back and nodded to see her following them.

8

The men led her down the long corridor. Champa's heart beat louder in excitement as they walked past the rooms that opened into the passage. Soon she would meet her father. How surprised he would be to see her. And how proud when she told him that she had achieved this all on her own, without help from anyone!

It was dark in the passage. But soon they had come out of the building, and were crossing a courtyard overgrown with grass. There was a small room on the opposite side. It was quiet and silent there, and no one was around. "Where is my Babuji? Is he here?" asked Champa as a sudden doubt crept into her mind. Her heart began to pound faster, louder. Where had they brought her? Surely this was not the place where they would keep him? Her steps slowed down.

"Hurry up, girl. Walk faster. We don't have all day." One of the two turned around to glance at her. A chill ran up her spine as she noticed it was the man who had come to their hut earlier and taken away her father. She had hardly looked at the men, so excited had she been at the thought of meeting Babuji. She remembered now the look he had given her, and shuddered.

"Oh yes, your father is here," said the other man, as he saw her linger behind, "Come on, are we going to eat you up?"

"Of course not!" declared Champa with a confidence she was far from feeling.

"Here he is," they opened the door of the room and, grabbing her by the arm, pulled her inside. One of them quickly reached up and pulled the door close. Champa drew in her breath sharply, realising that she had been tricked. One of the men squeezed her arm. "Come on, you little *gulabjamun*, be sweet to us. We are not going to hurt you," he mumbled.

Champa screamed, and immediately a hand was clamped onto her mouth. Fingers groped around her shoulder and settled on her chest, while other fingers slunk towards her legs. She recoiled in disgust, trying to fight off the fingers that crawled up her bare skin. The hands only pressed harder against her body. One gripped her waist; the other squeezed her breast, hard.

"As stubborn as your father? Come on, be kind to us, you juicy little *mithai*! We'll not harm you if you are good ...," said one of the men, with another squeeze to her breast.

"We'll send your father back, if you let us ... " said the other.

No, no, NO! Her mind screamed. She must fight those hateful, creepy fingers. She struggled with a mad strength, kicking and hitting out. NO! She would not allow them to touch her. She had to fight, she must ... she bit the arm that circled her and pushed away the fingers on her breast. She kicked wildly. And then she remembered ... those giggling friends telling her about spots that were weak. Her wits alert in spite of the dangerous situation she found herself in, she aimed her kick deliberately, and was relieved to hear the scream that followed. A harder kick the next time and she felt the pressing hands loosen their grip. Now. She must escape! She sprang towards the door. While the men still groaned, holding their hands against the injured part, she flung the door open.

The next moment she had made it! She dashed desperately out through the door, down the corridor and into the hall where the crowd still surrounded the police officer. She did not want to face anyone, not now, when she was full of the shame and humiliation of what she had just experienced. She just wanted to get out, away from the suffocating atmosphere of the room filled with men, away from those horrible fingers that had slid and snaked so disgustingly across her body.

It was a relief to get out of the building. Safety! She must make it to safety, was the thought that made her run faster and faster. She found time to breathe at last only when she was in the midst of the crowd and traffic on the road, the police station safe behind her. Somehow she made her way back, finding a bus to take her to the eighth milestone from the town, and walked, fast, to the safety of the fields and forests near her village.

As she walked past the mango orchard, the high dome and steeple of the temple greeted her. She folded her hands in a prayer of thanks. It was because of lord Shiva that she had succeeded in escaping. Otherwise how could she have fled from the clutches of the two powerful men? Yes, it was only because of his blessings … in a burst of gratitude she threw herself down on the rough ground and closed her eyes. Tears of relief ran down her cheeks.

For a long time she lay there–until the rain dripping on her body again reminded her that she must hurry back home.

Silently Champa crept into her hut. Kamla still lay on the *chouki*, staring at the open door. "Back? Did you get to the *thana*?" she asked as soon as she saw her walk in.

"Yes, Ma, I did. But I could not meet Babuji," mumbled Champa, hoping Kamla would not ask any more questions.

"What happened?"

In slow, halting words, the girl tried to explain what had taken place at the police station. The words brought back fresh images of those terrible moments when fingers had crawled across her skin. She began to tremble. She remembered the tightening pressure of the hands against her waist, the hot, disgusting breath of the men on her face, the horror of the whispering voices coaxing her to be calm. Bravely she went on, telling her mother about how the strong arms had tried to force her down, how she had resisted them, and finally how she had kicked them and escaped.

"I escaped only because god saved me, Ma. Otherwise…." she shuddered in the darkness.

"What, otherwise? If you had not resisted, your babuji would have been here just now, right beside us. Ungrateful girl. After all that I've done for you … this is what you do. Instead of helping your father come back, you fled from there!"

The shocking words drummed loudly in her ears, sharp and hitting. Dumbstruck, Champa stared at her mother in astonished dismay.

"After all that we have done for her," repeated Kamla, "This is what we get from her in the end …" she went on.

But Champa had run away to the other room. Her brother was huddled up on the *chouki*, a book by his side. His eyes were closed, for he had dozed off while reading. She snuggled close to him. "*Didi*, when will Babuji come?" she heard him mumble.

"Soon, Gopu, don't you worry," replied his sister, relieved to find him turning over to the other side with a sigh, before falling asleep again.

9

Did her mother actually mean what she had said? Champa's mind was in turmoil. No, it was not possible, she could not really mean it. After all, she was under great strain herself with Babuji being gone for so long. She must have been as upset as she herself was and in her moment of despair uttered those hurting words. Champa tried to put herself in her mother's shoes and decided that she would forgive her.

It was best to get out of the hut. She picked up the water pitcher and walked towards the village pump. She would sit for a while in her favourite place under the jackfruit tree.

"Has your father returned?" asked a villager passing by. The schoolmaster returning home from school asked the same question. Women with pitchers on their heads were clustered up before the pump. "Heard your father has been picked up by the police, Champa. Has he returned?" a woman asked.

"Why is he still in jail? Why doesn't someone try to get him out?" another woman wanted to know.

"I know who can take him out. Only fearless men like those Maowadis. After all he is in jail because of them, isn't it, girl?"

Champa's ears burned to hear the myriad questions. Everyone had something to say, some story to relate, either about the police, or about the jungle folk. But none had any help to offer. None wanted to be involved in an affair and get into trouble. The voices became too much to bear and Champa jumped up to leave. She filled up her pitcher and turned homewards.

Champa could hear them as she reached closer home. Good, her mother had company. It would help her to talk to someone. The voices belonged to men. Was it Babuji then? There was a leap of happy expectation in her heart as Champa's steps grew quicker.

She crossed the front courtyard. Through the open window voices floated towards her. She halted, shocked and surprised. That ... that voice ... surely she would recognise it anywhere? She hastily put the pitcher down and tip-toed towards the open door. Hiding behind the fodder stacked in a corner, she put her ears close to the wall and tried to listen.

"Yes, we'll bring your husband back," said someone.

"That will be very kind of you, *sarkar*. May god bless you, *huzoor*," replied Kamla.

"But you must make the girl listen to us. She must behave with us, in return for the favour we do you. Then only will your *buddha* return. Understand, *budhia*?" said the second man severely.

"She insulted us. We know how to deal with such women. You better tell her this. She should be with us. Tonight. And you will meet your man before dawn tomorrow," said the first policeman.

"Yes, yes, *sarkar*. As you wish, whatever you say, *huzoor*, *mai-baap*. Just bring back my man," pleaded Kamla.

Champa heard the clink of glasses and knew Kamla must have offered the two men some tea. After that they would come out and find her lurking there. Quick! She must hide before that happened. She ran to the cowshed, where she crouched behind Kajal's ample back. She touched the gently heaving flank of the cow and laid her head against its warm skin.

Her mother's words had shattered Champa as nothing had done before. No longer could she make excuses for her, no longer could she explain away the words that hurt. Kamla was her mother, the one who had taken care of her for so many years, the only person whom she could call her own, except for Gopal who was just a kid, and Babuji, who had vanished from their life. All her growing years, she had thought of her as a mother, had accepted her as one in spite of the unfair treatment, and had been dutiful, obedient and affectionate.

Yes, she was her closest relative. But now, suddenly, all good feelings for Kamla melted away. She was not her mother, she could not be; she was just a woman her father had brought home to live with them, a woman ready to sell her husband's daughter to any man who wished to maul her. Champa realised now, she could never think of Kamla as her mother again. The trust was gone, the old relationship broken forever.

Hot, bitter tears spilled onto her cheeks. She snuggled closer to the cow's back and let the tears flow, washing away the shock and sorrow from her heart. As it turned colder and darker inside the shed, and mosquitoes swarmed around her, Champa realised that the men had gone and she had been hiding there for a long time. She wiped the tears that had already dried on her cheeks and rose to her feet. What was she to do now? She could not stay there any longer. She had to escape, or she would be thrown into the arms of those hateful men.

Where could she go? Maybe to one of her friends, like Gouri, but then she lived in her in-laws' home and anyway, they were not so well-off that they could feed another mouth. No, not there.

More than anything, Champa wanted her babuji back home. He would have protected her, she knew. But how was he to come? How could she have him back, without the help of those dirty men? She now recalled the words of the young man in the forest. She hated him, of course, for killing her brother's pet, but he did say they would help, she remembered.

Champa jumped up excitedly. Yes, this is what she would do. Call Vijay Lall and ask the jungle folk to help. After all, it was because of them that her father was in trouble. They had better find him and she would join them in the search. Decision made at last, she walked slowly out of the shed and entered the front room.

"Back at last? Where have you been? I have been looking for you," said Kamla in a sweet voice that did not deceive her daughter.

"To the village to fetch water. Here it is," replied Champa shortly.

"I want you to ... but maybe tomorrow. It is too late," mumbled Kamla.

Champa's heart had missed a beat; but now she sighed in relief. "Yes, yes, tomorrow, Ma, it is so dark ...," she said.

Early next morning, before her mother could say anything, Champa picked up the slip of paper from its hiding place and raced desperately through the fields, past the mango orchard, past the cement factory, to the row of shops that lined the highway, a few rupees clutched in her hand. She made her way to the phone booth and holding the chit carefully in one hand, dialled the number the youth had given her.

There were some strange noises in the phone before she heard a clear voice, "Who? Who is it?"

"Champa ... you gave me your number ..."

"What? Speak louder!"

"It's me, Champa. You said you'd help ... the girl who cooked ..." she tried to explain.

"Yes, yes, what d'you want?"

"Get my babuji out! It is your fault. So get him out now!" shouted Champa over the phone.

"Oh? Alright. Meet me in the jungle then. Same spot. Just as the sun goes down. We'll help, of course," said Vijay and the line was cut off.

10

Champa stayed away from home the whole day. She knew Kamla would be looking for her, but she also knew it would be dangerous to return. She wandered back to the village and stayed with her friend Jhumki in her hut until it was time to meet the young man in the forest.

And now the jungle beckoned her. She liked its leafy greenery, the shade of the thick *saal*, the lingering, sugary smell of the *mahua* and the sound of the koel singing above, along with the chirping of the birds. It was still bright daylight and she knew the jungle was safe at this time. The sun had not yet gone behind the hills in the distance. As soon as it did the whole jungle would be shrouded under a black curtain. But she was almost there by now. There was the rock on which she had sat the last time she was there along with her cows and had met her old friend Gouri. A little further on was the spot where she had met the *jungle* man.

His coming was noiseless or Champa would have heard. Suddenly he was there, appearing out of nowhere, it seemed to her. He put a finger to his lips to warn her. "Shhh. Quiet. Let's get out of here first, or it would be too dark. Follow me."

She took a step, and was immediately stopped by him. Her feet had crunched the leaves noisily. "Remember, no sounds. Come this way," said Vijay Lall, pointing to a pathway that vanished deeper into the forest.

The silent pair walked on. Champa had never stepped beyond the outer edges of the jungle. Now, for the first time, she found herself in a part that was strange and unknown. The bushes crowded closer and closer together. Thick trunks almost touched each other and the leafy branches formed such a thick canopy above that the sun's rays, now fainter and dimmer, could hardly provide the light to show them the way. However, though deep in the jungle, the way seemed to be miraculously clear. Hardly a twig crackled; hardly did a swaying branch brush her cheek. No entangled branches obstructed their way; it was as if feet had trodden the path a thousand times before.

On they walked–Vijay in a brown and green uniform that merged into the jungle background and Champa in her non-descript salwar-kameez. "Hurry, we must reach before we are seen. Hurry, hurry!" were the only words that Vijay spoke. She wondered where they were headed. Was she about to land in a situation more terrible than the one she had left behind? Out here in the jungle she was at the mercy of strangers, for she could never find her way back from this maze of bush and tree.

But then ... Champa shook her head. No, she did not want to return home, not with the sword of fear hanging over her, the sword of being forced to go to men whose very touch was so humiliating, so filthy it made her shiver even to think about it. On the other hand, grasping the hand of one of them–the jungle people–was just as fraught with danger. It was as if she stood between two deep, black chasms, each more frightening than the other. She wondered which was more dangerous. Yet, in the innermost recesses of her heart she felt she did know which direction she would take. It was a path her feet had already set off on, the path that now led her on, inexorably, into the deep, deep forest, into the dark, dense greenery called the 'jungle'.

Suddenly it turned dark. The sun must have gone down behind those hills, she concluded. A fear now filled her heart. It was the fear of the unknown, of walking in strange, unfamiliar surroundings where nothing much could be seen. The man seemed to sense her fear for he turned around and clasped her hand in a protective gesture. "No need to feel scared. I know the way. Just stay close behind. It won't take us long now," he assured her.

He knew where he was going and had probably come there often. The thought reassured Champa, making her steps more confident. They had walked for more than two hours and she was beginning to tire. But there was no point in stopping. They must walk on. Fortunately the moon had now come up, and she could make out the black shapes of the trees and their branches. She realised that they had been walking on a well trod pathway that was clear of obstructions. No wonder Vijay had been so sure of his way.

Before them loomed higher, blacker shapes, which she soon discovered were low hills. As they neared the hills she noticed they were made of rocks and boulders, sparsely covered with low but thick bushes. At the foothills lay huge boulders and more rocks. There was hardly any vegetation there as the ground was dry and littered with stones and pebbles.

The moonlight revealed two or three tin roofed shelters covered with leaves and branches, well hidden behind clusters of rocks.

"Here we are," Vijay told her.

She stood staring at the scene. So this was where the jungle folk lived. Curious now, she stared at the bleak surroundings, at the forest they had traipsed through and which now stood behind her, and at the boulders that gleamed white where the moon's rays fell on them. Once again her eyes travelled to the roofs she could barely glimpse through the rocks hiding them from view. It was the secret hideout, the place from where the mysterious jungle people descended on villagers and forced them to act, from where they ordered their shootings and killings and where probably their leader lived. This was the place about which the policemen wanted to know. About which her babuji was totally ignorant; yet was being pressured to reveal.

"You must meet our leader. We act only on his orders. We can help only if he says so," said Vijay, his voice no longer hushed and low.

They walked towards the largest cluster of rocks. Behind it were low mud walls with a tarpaulin covered roof. The door was a canvas tied up to cover the entrance. Outside stood a guard, gun in hand.

"May I come in, Sir?" asked Vijay.

"Yes, yes, come in," said someone Champa had heard before. She followed Vijay timidly into the room. The leader, a dark, well-built man with brooding eyes, sat before a table, a pistol beside him and a pencil in his hand. He was looking down at a map that was spread on the table and talking to a young man who stood nearby.

"I've brought the girl, Sir," Vijay gave his leader a smart salute.

"Welcome," said the man shortly, giving Champa a cursory glance before going back to the map.

"Salute the Commander, *ladki*. Don't you know how to greet seniors? This is Commander Bhaskar, our great leader," said the man standing next to the table, "Have you come to join us?"

"No, no Sudhir. I told you about her. She wants help to get her father out from jail. After that, who knows … she might!" said Vijay.

"Oh, her father! Yes, yes … but why should we help, unless …" began Sudhir, who, with Vijay, had now become part of the group.

"Enough!" interrupted Commander Bhaskar, "Sudhir, don't overstep your position. It is for me to decide. Alright, girl, explain. What d'you want?"

Champa was staring wide-eyed at the machines and gadgets that filled the room. She had never seen anything like it, never imagined all this could exist in the midst of the wilderness she had walked through to reach this strange place. It was as if she had stepped into a different world altogether, away from the village, hut and fields that constituted her own space.

"Speak up, girl. What d'you want?"

"My father!" she answered promptly, gazing boldly into the Commander's eyes. She saw that he was older than the other two and looked different from them. He seemed more mature, more experienced; there were deep furrows on his dark forehead and a scar that ran down his left cheek.

11

Bhaskar Reddy

Commander Bhaskar Reddy had never belonged to any of the armed forces, but had acquired the title 'Commander', as a senior Maoist leader and the head of a zone. He had a shrewd, calculating, brilliant mind that enabled him to outmanoeuvre his opponents. Not for nothing had he been elevated to the important post, for his plans for armed action never failed to work, invariably leading his men to success.

Years of experience in guerrilla warfare in the jungles of the southern states had honed his skills to perfection. Bhaskar knew when and where to strike, when to withdraw and retreat into one of the camps hidden deep in the jungles, and when and how to please the local population.

Bhaskar Reddy had been a lecturer at a reputable college in the small town of Chinampalli in Andhra Pradesh. His subject was science. As a teacher of physics, he was greatly respected for his knowledge, learning and experience. He was a fine lecturer, albeit a strict one who would not allow any indiscipline in class.

"Physics is a complex subject. One minute of distraction or inattention will cost you several marks," he admonished his students. "If you do not concentrate you will not understand. The whole edifice that I build on a particular concept will collapse. You cannot afford to let your mind wander, no, not even for a moment."

Students respected the professor; at the same time they feared him for his sharp tongue. The highly ambitious aspired to study under him; the professor too showered his attention on them. A few joined not because they possessed the necessary drive to achieve success, but because it was a matter of prestige to be in Bhaskar's class. Raghav Rao was one such student, there because his rich politician father, M.V. Rao, had donated a fabulous amount of money to the college.

Bhaskar often found Raghav disturbing his serious classmates with juvenile pranks and silly questions. It irritated him. When the time came, he failed him in his class tests. No, he had not been unfair; it was just that the boy deserved it.

Raghav's father was outraged. The boy had always done well at school. How could he fail now? He immediately dispatched a warning note to the Principal, who sent for Bhaskar and took him to task, sternly, for failing the student. After all it was a college test. He could have been a little more generous in giving marks to the boy who was so special.

"Sir, ask him to take up another subject. He may do better in arts or commerce ... How can I give more marks when he hasn't even understood the basics?" explained Bhaskar patiently.

The Principal did not agree. Without mincing words he warned Bhaskar. "Look, it is your responsibility to see that he does better. You know his father has supported our institution. Be lenient with the boy. Make sure he does not fail. Or you will lose your job, let me warn you."

Bhaskar's thick, black eyebrows shook in indignant response. The fawning attitude of the Principal made him even more resentful towards the privileged student. It was the beginning of a running feud between the brilliant teacher and the arrogant father and son duo.

"I'll see how my son fails to do well in class," roared M.V. Rao before a bunch of loyal followers, "I'll get that man kicked out from the college. Wait and see. If my boy doesn't get a proper percentage next time, his teacher will not remain in his job."

Bhaskar received a real shock the next morning. Raghav distracted his classmates by aiming paper balls at his back. When a particularly thick ball hit his neck the professor whirled around, black eyes blazing, ready to lash out at the miscreant. It turned out to be the boy he despised. Just in time he remembered the warning given by the

Principal. He controlled himself somehow, merely saying, "I expect all students to concentrate."

The detestable boy sniggered. With superhuman effort Bhaskar restrained himself from slapping him. But it left him fuming inside.

Fortunately his home was a haven of peace. Ever since his parents had passed away in an accident, Bhaskar had been taking care of his sister, Latha, and his old grandmother. The three lived together in the ancestral home. Latha, younger to him, soon joined his College, but in the Arts section.

One day, he was striding down the corridor to his class when he spotted his sister. He was surprised to find her in the company of a boy. Who was he? Was he someone suitable? She was in a lime green sari, the boy in a blue printed shirt and jeans.

Imagine Bhaskar's dismay when the blue printed shirt turned up later in his own class–it was worn by none other than Raghav! He went home determined to warn the innocent girl. But later he changed his mind. Maybe it was just a casual meeting. Maybe it did not mean anything. Why mention the boy at all; she may have forgotten herself, so why remind her?

The solicitous brother failed to see the tell-tale signs on his sister's face, the bright sparkle in her almond eyes and the pink blush on her usually pale cheeks.

Months later, however, Bhaskar noticed that his sister looked somewhat different from her usual, cheerful self. A strange pallor had replaced the rosy, healthy bloom on her cheeks. Her downcast eyes often slid away from his. She did not greet him in her usual cheerful way when he returned home. Instead, she would slink quietly to her own room. Was something wrong? Maybe she needed to see a doctor.

He immediately fixed up an appointment at the civil hospital in town. "Tell Latha not to go anywhere after college tomorrow. We are going to meet the doctor in the evening," he told his grandmother.

But it was not to be.

Bhaskar was deep in a lecture when he heard the commotion outside. He stepped out to see. There was an excited crowd gathered outside the college building. What was the matter? It seemed there had been an accident. He rushed out and saw, to his shock and horror, a crumpled, limp figure lying on the concrete floor.

An accident, he heard the murmur of several voices. Bhaskar parted the agitated crowd aside and hurried closer to see. The figure was absolutely still, its face down on the hard ground. Why did it look so familiar? He stepped closer, a strange fear gripping his mind. His feet refused to move, his body turned cold while his face was on fire. He had to see, he must. He forced himself to go on, though every nerve in his body warned him. Do not look, do not go closer.

But he had to. The small round face was not recognisable anymore, but he knew it. It was Latha–his sister with the bright, laughing eyes, with the chirpy voice that greeted him when he returned home from his battles in class–his dear, precious Latha.

"They … they've killed her!" cried a girl, "They killed my friend!"

The ambulance had arrived. His sister was picked up and carried to the hospital. In a daze, Bhaskar followed the stretcher into the vehicle. The doctors examined Latha and said that the death was self-inflicted. The girl had committed suicide by jumping down from the roof of the college.

Bhaskar could not believe it. Why must his sister take her own life? What had disturbed her so much? What ailed her? He had to find out. He sought out Malathi, his sister's friend.

"No, no, she did not kill herself. I told you … they murdered her!" insisted Malathi, her eyes filling up with tears.

"Who? And how do you know? Tell me," urged Bhaskar.

"They were friends, that boy Raghav and Latha. She told me he wanted to marry her. She was so happy, so thrilled. Who knew … that he was not serious! Never had any intention of marrying … but then she became pregnant …" said the girl.

"What? Latha?" Bhaskar could not believe it. That his dear sister, so young, innocent, had been made a fool of, and that too by the boy he detested, was something he could not accept.

"And you know what he did when she told him? He just laughed … what did she think? His father would allow his only son to marry a professor's sister?"

Bhaskar gritted his teeth, his face darkened as he held his hands against his ears, not wanting to hear more about his sister's sorrow and humiliation.

But Malathi was full of it. "He … he said, his father had big plans for him. Nothing short of a rich businessman's or an influential politician's daughter would do for him! Latha insisted … after all, she had every right to marry him. She loved him, and didn't he, too?" she went on.

"Then?" asked Bhaskar, reluctantly, not wanting to hear yet determined to know everything.

"She was devastated at his refusal … but … she told me she would meet his family and tell them everything. They were sure to agree when they knew. Raghav was furious, said she was never to step near his parents. Never! If ever she did so … but … you … you know the rest," ended Malathi.

12

Bhaskar knew in his heart, as surely as if he had seen it with his own eyes that Raghav, or one of his father's cronies, had killed his sister. The certainty filled him with fierce determination. Justice must be done, the perpetrators of the crime brought to book. It was his duty as a brother to see that the truth was told, the culprits punished. He rushed to the police station to lodge his complaint.

The man at the table ignored the visitor. Tense and impatient, Bhaskar waited until the officer set his file aside at last. He demanded that the police arrest Raghav Rao for his sister's murder.

"You're wrong," answered the officer coldly, "We have already seen the hospital report. The post-mortem proved that it was a case of suicide. Do you know what will happen if you malign a VIP?"

"Malign? What do you mean?" Bhaskar could feel his temper rise, "I am giving you some information. You must investigate to find out the truth. That is all I want!"

The man refused. Bhaskar went to court to file his complaint. Fortunately the court was sympathetic and ordered the police to initiate an investigation. The police was quick to submit its report. In brief, plain words it asserted that the matter had been investigated thoroughly, only to confirm that it was suicide and not a murder. The case was therefore closed.

Bhaskar did not give up. He consulted friends and lawyers and finally wrote to the court requesting it to order its own investigations. And then he received a threat from M.V. Rao. How dare he drag his son's name into the scandal? If he wanted to live, he had better refrain from pursuing the case, otherwise he had better watch out.

As if all this was not enough, his old grandmother, who had never reconciled to the tragic news of her grand-daughter's sudden death, silently passed away.

Bhaskar, already grieving for the death of his sister, could not control himself at the second shock that he had received within a few days.

Why was he alive, he wondered? Why, why? Finally he concluded that the One Above, who saw and knew everything, had let him stay alive for just one reason.

So that he could take revenge.

Bhaskar's mind brimmed with feelings of hate and anger. The target of his hatred was M.V. Rao for his ill-gotten pelf and power, his disdain for others and disregard for rules and laws; and the men in uniform who wielded power but used it unfairly.

For several days he did not turn up for classes, until the Principal called to inform him that he had been dismissed. Bhaskar received the news with studied indifference. Here was another example of the worst kind, a man who lived by flattery, one who favoured the powerful even when they were obviously the wrongdoers.

The erstwhile professor of physics had arrived at a crucial conclusion that would change his life drastically and forever.

Those in power definitely lacked in morals and ethics. They had to be removed, no, in fact, they must be removed, rooted out.

The state of Andhra Pradesh was known as a hotbed of Maoist activity. Their doings so far had remained at the fringe of Bhaskar's conscious mind. He had never bothered about them, though he had read about them in the papers. He also knew of the People's Liberation Front. Their leaders were present in jungles as well as in cities; some of the organisational heads made their plans sitting in big metropolitan towns from where they handed down their diktats to the cadres hiding in the forests. The violence adopted by the revolutionary groups began to appeal to Bhaskar. He understood their fury against an unfair world. Their anger reflected his own anger, their feelings his own.

Bhaskar knew that real action lay with the guerrilla cadres in the jungles. That is where he now wanted to be.

With a cool, deliberate mind he made cautious preparations, careful not to let anyone know about his plans. The professor sold his house with the excuse that he had found a better job far away. He settled all his bills and paid back all loans. He made enquiries and found out ways of contacting the Maoists.

And one dark, moonless night, Bhaskar stepped out of his own despised world and set out to join the world of the revolutionaries.

It was not easy. The Maoists were suspicious. He was asked to explain. Earnestly he told them that he believed wholeheartedly in their philosophy and wanted to make his 'humble' contribution towards the cause. It took many months before he could gain their confidence. It was satisfying to learn that M.V. Rao was already on the hit list of the Maoists for his greedy, unscrupulous ways.

Plans to kill the man were made and Bhaskar given charge.

Three days later, the hated man's cavalcade drove over a *kuccha* road that passed through a dip between two rocky hills. It had been laid with mines. Hidden behind rocks on the slopes of the hill were gunmen ready to target those who attempted to flee when the vehicles blew up. Four of the best combat men were positioned near the road to strike anyone still left after the bullets had done their job.

Everything went off as planned. Bhaskar watched the whole scene from his vantage point on the hill slope, where he lay behind a boulder, his eyes on the scene below.

As soon as the first vehicle drove over the mine laid below the surface of the *kuccha* path, there was an ear-splitting bang. The car was blown up and came crashing down, shiny white metal in the midst of orange flames. Figures were thrown into the air and then flung, twisted and broken, onto the road. Cars that followed screeched to a halt and figures holding guns in hand sprang out to take cover in the ditches behind the boulders.

The white Ambassador car in the centre of the cavalcade halted and tried to escape the ambush. With a loud screech it hastily reversed and tried to speed away. But it could not. Boulders had been quickly rolled down the sloping hill by Bhaskar's men hiding on the slopes. The car was forced to halt. The portly man in the back seat was seen ducking low in his seat. The younger figure beside him tried to jump out and find cover, but the combat men hiding nearby immediately aimed their pistols at him. Both men soon lay sprawled, one inside the car, the other on the dusty road, their bodies spattered with blood.

The last two vehicles in the procession managed to turn around and speed away. The attackers swiftly vanished from the scene. Silence lay over the gory scene as the injured struggled to get up and the killed lay sprawled in the dust.

When the police arrived soon after, it counted seven injured and five dead. Among them were the businessman-cum-politician M.V. Rao and his only son, Raghav.

At last Bhaskar felt vindicated, as if he had somehow made up for his sister's shame and humiliation. So what if the police could not punish the killers? He, Bhaskar Reddy, had done it! He felt a rush of gratitude towards the men who had helped him make it possible and restored his peace of mind.

Several raids, all successful, were carried out under Bhaskar's leadership. His reputation for strategising and planning grew. He rose higher in the hierarchy of the organisation.

Soon Bhaskar was sent as commander to a new region. Jharkhand was not very different as far as the terrain was concerned. The thick forests, rocks and hills provided shelter to the Naxalites. Natural resources like lakes, ponds, tumbling streams and nullahs provided for further needs. At first, however, he had problems of communication, for the language spoken there was unknown and unfamiliar. With his usual aptitude for mastering difficult subjects Bhaskar was able to learn not just Hindi but also the local dialects. He was soon at home, eating the food the locals ate, and making himself familiar with the problems of the region. He explored the area and made his own detailed maps based on its features. He soon knew every rock, ditch, village, and forest path as well as the back of his hand.

Bhaskar loved his new assignment. He loved the simple village folk, enjoyed their songs and learnt to play the *dhol* and the *mandar* exactly the way the santhals and other tribals did. During festivals like the 'karama' he danced away the night, and for 'sarhul' he worshipped the *saal* tree with them to celebrate nature's bounty.

There were several girls in their camp. Usually they cooked and cleaned, but Bhaskar encouraged them to train in rifle shooting and the handling of weapons. He wanted them to be tough and self-reliant ... unlike his sister Latha–gentle, meek and submissive–who had never learnt to protect herself, and so had lost her life. Teaching girls to become strong and independent made him feel better. It somehow made up for his neglect in taking care of his little sister and assuaged the feelings of guilt that constantly rankled in his mind.

His experience told him that girls made not only good followers, but disciplined soldiers too. Bhaskar planned to recruit many more in the future.

13

Champa

Champa realised she had been staring at Commander Bhaskar. Embarrassed, she quickly lowered her eyelids and mumbled, "My father was caught by the police. They jailed him for helping you, when, as you well know … we were forced to!"

"Hmm. We'll see about that. Now that you are here, be our honoured guest. Look around, meet other girls. Talk to …"

"I don't care about others. I want you to rescue Babuji. Will you do it or not? Just tell me that!" No longer diffident and hesitant, Champa interrupted to ask.

The leader seemed surprised at her boldness. A strange look–was it of approval, encouragement–flashed into his eyes. "We'll try to. But no promises, alright? Vijay, take her to the women's quarters," he said.

The girl felt a stab of disappointment. The hopes that had made her leave home and family to walk into the wilderness had been rudely destroyed. The man had dismissed her with just a few words and no assurances at all. Tears sprang to her eyes. She tried to brush them away, hoping they would not be visible in the dark. But the moon's rays picked up the teardrops on her cheeks, turning them into gleaming pearls.

"Don't feel bad," said Vijay who had seen the tears shining on her cheeks.

"Isn't he going to help?" asked Champa, searching Vijay's face for signs of hope.

"You never know with Commander Bhaskar. If it suits his plans, he will. But it may take time. Don't worry. He has welcomed you here. Stay and enjoy it."

"Enjoy? Hunh, what is there to enjoy in the jungle? In this remote, lonely place?"

"Oh. There is plenty to do. Come, meet everyone. You'll like it here, let me tell you," said Vijay in a tone that was confident.

The words were reassuring. Champa's steps lightened as they crossed a clearing and reached another group of large boulders. Hidden behind them were long, low walls covered with tin sheets well camouflaged with leaves and branches. A roughly hewn wooden door led inside. Vijay stopped at the door and gave a low whistle, which was answered by two soft whistles from inside. The door opened and the two entered.

By now the visitor's curiosity was fully aroused. Champa was eager to see how the jungle people lived. Her eyes slowly took in the rolled up beddings on the floor, the faded green and brown uniforms folded and kept neatly on one side, the guns resting against the walls and the ammunition belts hanging on a chair. There were about twenty females in all. They were of all ages–several as old as her, a few middle-aged and a couple of women who were much older.

"Comrade Rekha, this is Champa. Commander Sir wishes her to be our guest. Look after her. I must leave now," said Vijay, giving the older woman a salute. He turned on his heels and marched off, leaving Champa alone with the women. For a moment the girl felt her heart go cold with alarm. She had come to depend on Vijay and he had walked out on her. The next moment she shrugged. Who was he? Why must she take him as a friend? He had escorted her there, now it was up to her to stay put there or flee, if she did not like it. Of course leaving the place would not be easy, and she was prepared to wait and watch. Meanwhile, it was exciting to be in the midst of the jungle people who had forever been a mystery to villagers like her.

The woman called Rekha was the only one there in uniform. The other girls wore saris or salwar-kameezes, or shirts and trousers. A few had skirts on as well. Rekha wore the green and brown shirt and trousers worn by the men and had her hair cut short like a boy's. If it had not been for her feminine curves and delicate features, she would have been mistaken for a young man.

"Why are you here? And where do you come from?" Rekha asked.

"From village Nawadih," replied Champa, choosing not to reply to the first question.

"I asked you why you are here!" snapped Rekha, "Didn't you hear?"

"Don't know. I was brought here," Champa was still reluctant to tell them about her mission.

"Alright, don't tell. Open your bag. I'll take a look, then you can put it there. That's your corner," and she pointed to an empty space in a row of odd-shaped *jholas*, bags and sundry other belongings of the girls. Champa allowed the woman to rummage through her few belongings and walked towards the place pointed out to her. She felt the eyes of the women follow her and was quite self-conscious as she walked stiffly back to face Rekha.

"Relax, we are not going to eat you up," said the woman. "Here, let me introduce everyone ... this is Comrade Usha. She is from a village in Odisha. And this is Comrade Ganga from Chhattisgarh. And she is Comrade Munia from Gaya in Bihar ... " she went on, pulling the girls forward, some of whom giggled shyly while others stared at the newcomer with expressionless eyes.

"Have you eaten?" asked Rekha after she had finished. Champa shook her head and told them it was alright, she was not hungry.

"Sleepy?" Rekha's voice had turned kinder now and Champa nodded. She wanted to be alone so that she could absorb her new experiences in peace.

"Munia, will you take the visitor to her place in the corner to sleep?" asked Rekha.

"Yes, Commander, madam," answered Munia.

Champa followed the girl, who seemed to be her own age. She was darker than her and a little shorter too. But there was a certain charm about her. Her features were attractive, with a pert, pretty nose which had a sparkling gold stud embedded on one side, and a mouth that smiled easily. Champa felt she could be friends with her.

There was no *khatia* or *chouki*, but, exhausted after the long walk, Champa was happy to flop down in a corner of the clean, mud-smeared, rocky floor. "You may sleep now," said Munia, giving her hand a little squeeze, "And don't be afraid of Comrade Rekha. She is the commander of the girls' group and actually quite kind. I was also afraid of her at first, but soon grew to like her. Sleep now."

The girls all settled down in their places. The kerosene lamps were turned down and soon the room was silent except for an occasional snore and a sigh here or there.

The darkness was soothing to Champa. For a few minutes she remained awake, wondering at the strange situation she found herself in–sleeping with so many unfamiliar women in a jungle that was miles away from home. She missed her brother Gopal and wished she could hear him snore nearby; and wondered where and how Babuji was. Soon her eyelids drooped down on her cheeks, the singing of the crickets in the distance faded away and she was lost in a deep, dreamless sleep.

14

"Wake up, wake up!" the insistent voice, unfamiliar for a few moments until she remembered where she was, woke up Champa. The new surroundings stood clearly revealed, with the rays of the dawning sun banishing the darkness from the room. Bare, stark, and perfectly clean, with not a speck of litter, the neatness startled her. She remembered the comfortable clutter of her own hut and wondered. More than twenty females in a room, and nothing to show for it … How was it possible?

"Stop staring. Get up and prepare for classes. We'll have to leave soon, so hurry up!" Munia, who had been trying to wake her up, informed her.

Classes? Like in school? And so early? Champa stood silent, gazing at the others who were busy preparing to leave the room.

"Hurry up. You will find all you need outside," explained Munia. She guided the girl to the makeshift toilet dug a little distance away and showed her the nullah where they washed themselves. The water was clear and cool. Champa splashed it liberally on her face and arms and felt refreshed.

The other girls had put on their uniforms and were ready to leave. They stood together in two straight rows, and as soon as Commander Rekha gave the orders they marched forward. Munia ran to join them, pulling Champa along with her. They soon reached a grassy plot surrounded by tall sheesham trees. Obviously this was where the classes were held. Several rows of boys had already settled down on the grass. The girls were asked to sit next to them, with their leader, Rekha, facing them in the front.

Champa looked around her with interest. It was just like school, except that there was no friendly chatter, no talking across to the boys and hardly any smiles or jokes. Faces were grim and solemn and many had no expressions at all in their eyes. Soon they heard the crunch of footsteps and Commander Bhaskar, followed at a respectable distance by Sudhir, the good-looking young man she had seen last night, and Vijay Lall, strode into view.

The Commander stepped briskly and purposefully towards them. Rekha jumped up and saluted him smartly. She rasped out an order and the boys and girls sprang to their feet. They saluted the three men and remained standing until Commander Bhaskar ordered them to relax and sit down.

The proceedings began with a speech from Bhaskar who spoke crisply in a commanding voice meant to be heard. It was no longer a professor addressing a bunch of students in a science class; now it was a persuasive leader calling on his listeners to build a new society by destroying the old one, through arms and violence if need be, so that fairness and justice could be ensured for all. He began by introducing the new person present and the reason why she was there. Later he spoke about the atrocities of the police and the iniquity of the existing system. Champa listened for a while, but soon lost interest. He spoke about matters that were too distant for her, far from her little world of Ma, Babuji, Gopal and the village which she had left behind. She let the stream of words flow above her head, catching a few words here and there.

"The police beat up the poor and the illiterate and let the rich be. Is that fair?" asked the Commander and his voice rose to a higher pitch, "No!"

Champa looked up when she heard the words. How right he was! Babuji had never gone to school and did not know how to defend himself against the unfair treatment meted out to him by the wily policemen. But then … what about her? Her father had struggled hard and seen to it that she went to school. Even if she did leave her education incomplete she was well able to read papers and magazines. She should have been able to help him. But again … how? Look what happened to her when she went to Babuji's rescue. Was it because, being a girl, she was of no use, as her mother had complained so often?

She now hung on to the Commander's words. He was addressing the girls, his eyes moving from face to face. "You are Durga! Just like the goddess you worship, you too have power in your hands. Take up the gun. Fight those who attempt to harm you. Learn to be tough, and never think you are weak or helpless. You have the strength, and I promise we will give you the skill and the knowledge …!"

The words stirred up feelings she never knew existed in her heart. Yes, how right he was. She must learn to be strong and show them all, she must. It was good she had come to this place. She would join the other girls and show the world what a simple village lass like her could achieve. She began to pay more attention. Eyes fixed on Bhaskar's face, she followed his every gesture, every word. His words inspired her, made her eager to grab a gun that very moment and follow him wherever he led.

His talk ended soon after. It was time for someone else to speak. Champa sat back again, the moment of excitement and inspiration gone. Listlessly she listened to Sudhir, who spoke about rules and regulations and how they were of no use to the poor. Champa's thoughts wandered off again, and she wondered if they would get anything to eat.

It was Vijay's turn after this. He stood up to address them. Immediately Champa straightened up. Was he, also, one of the speakers? Vijay's eyes wandered to hers. For a fleeting moment their eyes held each others, before he gave a distant smile and turned to the rest. "Comrades, I was a student at the Missionary College and doing well in class. I wanted to sit for the Competitions and become an IAS officer. But …" He went on, but his words did not register in her mind. Champa watched his face, waiting for the dimple to appear on his cheek as it did each time his lips widened. Her intent gaze seemed to have disturbed the speaker. In the middle of a sentence he paused to glance quizzically at her. "S … so, you … see," he stammered, looked away and began his sentence again.

Champa felt pleased. She had the power to make the man flustered. She felt good about it. But no, she would not disturb him again, or he would lose his stream of thought. She withdrew her gaze and turned her eyes towards the hills and the rocks that studded their slopes.

"You are not listening, girl!" The sudden remark startled her, making her glance at Vijay again. "Pay attention," he said and continued with his talk.

So what was he saying? Something about it being time young people like them thought about the less fortunate and came forward to help. "Look around. What do you see everywhere? Hungry villagers, pathetically poor, living from one day to another, trying to eke out an existence somehow! Wrinkled women, old before their time, trying to feed their malnourished children by remaining without food themselves! Famished farmers labouring hard with hardly any returns! And what about the landless worker? Always in debt! Does he get enough to feed his starving kids? No, no and no! Not with his meagre wages! ..."

Oh, but was she not one of them? There was no need to look at anyone else. Her own, dear Babuji struggled so hard at the cement factory–the very cement factory which had bought their land and promised to compensate for it. Compensation indeed! A bit of cash that did not last very long, and employment there on daily wages–that was all.

"They take away their land, and let the people starve! Is that fair?" continued Vijay.

How right he was, thought Champa. The people at the factory had given her father employment but the payment was never enough. Often they had no money to buy food. If they did not have the cow and sold its milk they would have starved too. So what could he tell her? He had probably lived in the city with a proper roof over his head, not one that leaked every time it rained. What did he want folk like her to do? Pick up the gun and go fight? That was what the Commander had said and Vijay was only repeating his words, but did they think it was practical to go around shooting people? Surely it would only lead to imprisonment!

"Alright, thank you," Vijay ended his speech, turned around and walked away. The other two had already left. The classes were over, and the girls could go back to their shelter. Champa was relieved, for by now she was so hungry she could think of nothing except food. Each girl was now handed over the *chura* and *gur* that constituted their breakfast. She ate the *chura-gur* with great relish, gulping down three glasses of water to make the dry meal go down her throat.

There was no time to rest for they had to hurry back for the drill and practice session, held at the same spot where they had assembled earlier. Champa was only a spectator. With wide, startled eyes she watched the girls pick up weapons she had never in her life touched. Obviously, the others had been training for some time. They handled the dangerous weapons with confidence and ease, and were good at target practice. Munia seemed particularly adept at handling the revolver. Champa could not but admire the dexterity with which she aimed it at targets placed at a distance. Rekha, their teacher, was just too good. Her instructions were clear and precise, making Champa eager to try her hand.

Lunch was a leaf-plate of *khichri* cooked by the older women on a wood fire. After that the girls were free to relax. A few went to sleep, tired after the early morning start and the rigorous drill and practice that followed. Being a newcomer, Champa was soon surrounded by girls wanting to know more about her. She was curious too. Why had they joined the Maowadis? What had made the girls, many of them young like her, give up home and family to take up guns and fight the world?

15

The stories that Champa heard were both moving as well as fascinating. She discovered that the girls had led troubled lives and fled only when they could stand it no longer. A few had been forcibly picked up by the Maoists and made to join the Front.

Munia had stolen away from her home in Gaya, Bihar, when she found that her parents, too poor to give a decent dowry to the groom's side, had betrothed her to an old widower with three grown-up sons, one of whom was married. "Ugh, the very thought of old, wrinkled, rough hands fumbling against my skin was hateful. I could not stand the idea." She had fought against her parents' decision, but they refused even to consider her pleas. There was no other option except to escape home. A girl friend told her about the Maowadis camping in the jungle not far away and had arranged a meeting with them through a friend of another friend who knew their leader. "And that's how I'm here," ended the girl with a smile.

Comrade Usha from a village near Cuttack in Odisha was about to be sent as a maid to a rich trader in Delhi. She had hated the very idea. "Just think, working in someone else's home–scrubbing their *jutha*, used utensils, and washing their filthy clothes! I would rather starve on the street than become someone's slave. Here I am a free bird, to shoot and kill if I want to," she declared triumphantly. The girl had fled home and was found wandering alone at the town railway station. She was seen by one of the members of the Front who invited her to join them. She had accepted–and here she was.

Sita and Uma were from a village nearby. Their parents had nine daughters whom they found difficult to feed and clothe. They succumbed to pressure from the jungle people and parted with the girls in return for a few hundred rupees. "But we are quite happy here," said the two girls, "At least we get to eat every day and don't have to go to bed hungry."

Then there was Ganga, from Chhattisgarh, the eldest of seven siblings. She had never been to school for her labourer parents needed someone to care for the little ones. She had stayed home, looking after them, until the fat and old landlord next door began to 'cast his evil eyes' on her. "I think he bribed my parents. They just shut their eyes and closed their ears whenever I complained. And one day, when that bloated beast stole in … I … I just picked up the *chakoo* and stabbed him. And then I ran! Somehow … but that's a long story … I came here and joined the other girls. I mean to kill that animal … some day!" cried Ganga, her voice rising again in anger.

As they related their stories Champa felt her heart reach out towards them in sympathy. Many had suffered worse fates than her and faced heartbreaking lives. Molested, exploited and hurt by both near and dear ones as well as those in authority they had set out to make new lives for themselves. She felt good in their company. Before she knew it she found herself blurting out her own story. She told it all, from the forced entry into their hut to the attempted rape by the policemen, ending with the shocking offer that Kamla had made to the men.

The murmurs of sympathy that followed her disclosure melted all Champa's doubts and resistance. Hot tears began to spill down her cheeks, though she tried her best to prevent them from doing so. Munia squeezed her hands and cried, "Don't go back, Champa! Stay here with us."

The warmth of the words and the clasp of the hand made the girl break into a fresh flood of tears. She meant it with all her heart when she squeezed Munia's hand back and murmured, "I will, I will, comrade Munia!" As Munia smiled back at her Champa wiped away her tears and said loudly so that all could hear, "I want to be friends, I want to stay … But can I?"

"Sure, you can … if you want to!" said a voice from the other end of the room. It was Commander Rekha who had been listening silently to the girls' chatter, "You will have to talk to Commander Bhaskar, of course, but I am sure he will be happy to welcome you."

Later that evening Rekha led Champa to the leader's room. He was there with Sudhir and Vijay, discussing something. He looked up questioningly as the two women entered the room.

"Yes?" he asked.

"The visitor wishes to talk to you, Sir," said Rekha.

"About?"

"She wants to stay on. If you permit her, Sir. I brought her here to meet you … "

"Hunh. So you wish to be with us?" asked Bhaskar.

"Umm, yes. But please, will you help find my father?" Champa would not miss the chance to plead, now that she was face to face with the leader again.

"Is that the reason for your wishing to stay? To put pressure on us?" the leader's voice was stern.

"N … no. I like it here. The girls are friendly. Besides, I have no home now. If Babuji comes back … "

"You will return home?" the question caught Champa off guard. She found the man watching her closely, as if trying to read her mind. She hesitated for a second before replying truthfully, "Umm … maybe. I don't know."

"There are no maybes here. If you stay, you stay. Understand? There's no going back for those who have lived with us. We don't allow it." His voice had gone cold and stern and Champa knew that he meant it.

For a long moment the girl remained silent, weighing the Commander's words in her mind. The statement seemed like an order, and she well understood that this man, who seemed to see through her into her heart, would not take it kindly if she changed her mind later. Doubtful now, she lowered her eyes. Was she taking the right decision? Would she regret it someday? Confused, she stared back at the leader.

Just then, to her great surprise, Vijay stepped forward. "She won't go back, Sir. She'll stay, I am quite sure."

What did he mean? How could he speak for her? For a long moment Champa stared at the young man, puzzled and confused. His eyes held hers in a mesmerising grip. It made her heart go thump-thump so loudly she feared the others would hear. Shaken by the strange, unknown emotion she was feeling, she quickly looked away and said in a voice suddenly gone weak, "It's alright Sir. I'll stay."

"Good. That's settled then. We welcome you as a new member in our camp," said the leader. She noted a touch of relief in his voice, as if he was hoping she would agree and was relieved to hear that she did.

"Thank you, Sir. But what about my father?"

"Yes, yes. We'll see. Go now!"

He dismissed them with a wave of his hand and there was nothing to be done except to return to their own shelter. Munia was waiting eagerly to meet Champa. Her big eyes sparkled happily as she hugged her new friend close. "I'm so glad you'll be with us now. There's so much I want to talk to you about. You see, the girls here don't always understand … they are from different backgrounds and cultures. Some cannot even read …"

"Can you?" asked Champa.

"Yes, I went to school. But could not finish … they wanted to marry me off while I was still at school … I had finished my seventh …" said Munia, shrugging her shoulders with a resigned sigh.

"My mother took me away from school after the eighth. Said she wanted me to help at home," interrupted Champa.

"But I am learning so much here. About politics, about social change, about history … Marxism and Mao. About China too. Subjects never taught at school. Very interesting, I find them." said Munia enthusiastically.

"I wish to learn too," agreed Champa.

The two girls chatted for a long time, discussing their tormented, troubled pasts and their dreams for the future. Slowly the talk veered around to men and what they felt about them. Munia was quite free with her thoughts. “I think Comrade Sudhir is just like a 'fillum' star. Isn’t he?” she giggled.

Several girls agreed with her. “Commander Bhaskar is so grim. He hardly ever smiles. But how well he speaks! We love his speeches!” murmured several.

Champa was told about Rekha too. She was from Bengal. She had studied medicine and got married into a reasonably wealthy family. At college, however, she had got interested in politics and had become a great admirer of Mao and other Left leaders. She agreed with their thoughts and felt that revolution could not be brought to the nation through democratic politics as practised in India. Only violent revolution could usher in change and empower the poor. She had finally broken up with her capitalist husband and his family and joined the Maowadis, using the contacts she had made earlier as a student.

“I think the two Commanders get along well. They should marry each other!” giggled Munia in Champa’s ears.

Amused, Champa was in a good mood that night. It was the first time that her mind was not dwelling on the persistent thoughts that haunted her whenever she was alone. When would Babuji return? How would Gopal manage without her to help? What was happening at home?

Instead, the chatter of girls filled the space once occupied by the nagging worries. As she drowsed off to sleep, she found her thoughts turning towards Vijay and the words he had suddenly burst out with in front of the leader. She remembered the wild somersaults her heart had taken when she had looked into his eyes. She hugged the experience close and tried to relive that strange, magical moment. It filled her again in wild ecstasy, which was joy and pain at the same time.

What did the feelings mean? And, most important of all, was he also going through similar emotions?

16

Vijay Lall

It was not that Vijay was unaware of the girl he had helped induct into the Maowadi fold. He remained conscious of the disturbing presence of the young, spirited girl whom he had noticed the very first day he had barged into their hut. Champa evoked mixed feelings in his breast. He liked her boldness and high spirits and remembered the way her large eyes flashed at him when she was angry. The tears that glistened on her smooth, honey brown skin that moonlit night had aroused tender feelings in his heart and made him want to protect her.

However, the new emotions also made him cautious and wary. Vijay was about to begin an exciting new life in an environment absolutely unrelated to anything he had experienced before. Since the day he felt so furious at having lost all, he had given up his aim of following the straight and direct path towards a steady, secure career in the bureaucracy. His aspirations now led him in a direction exactly the opposite of the one laid out by his father, Sohan Lall. There was no point in being gentle, patient, and undemanding like his late father. To succeed in life you must know how to protect your rights, nay, even fight for them if the need arose. The policeman's grandson had swung to the other extreme. No longer did he have any respect for authority, no longer did he believe in the rule of law as laid down by the strong against the weak.

Commander Bhaskar Reddy's ideas on changing the nation's social fabric impressed the young man tremendously. At college he had attended classes on the different political philosophies propagated by leaders and thinkers. But at best his knowledge was still very basic and half-baked. Now it was Bhaskar who was his teacher, mentor, guide;

not just that, the Commander had replaced his father in his thoughts. It was his ideas that influenced him, his goals that he aspired for–indeed, Bhaskar was the ideal he wanted to follow in every way.

Sudhir and Vijay enjoyed the discussions they had with Bhaskar. They found him well-informed and knowledgeable, and what is more, always ready to share his learning with them. Obviously he too enjoyed their company, for he spoke long and passionately on subjects that he had mastered almost as well as the physics he had taught earlier. They were the ideal students that he may have missed in his lonely life in the jungle. As usual, Sudhir argued with him on several points. Disliked by his earlier teachers for his argumentative nature, Sudhir became an instant favourite with Bhaskar, who seemed to appreciate his enthusiasm in discussing a theory threadbare before embracing it heartily.

The two friends found plenty of literature there to explore. Bhaskar carried with him a chest-load of his favourite papers, books and documents, which he made available to his eager students. Sudhir depended more on the spoken word, but Vijay soaked himself in Maoist literature. The more he read, the more impressed he was by the revolutionary philosophy of Mao, Lenin and Marx. He spent his free time educating himself by reading the books he found. He learnt that the Maoist Communist Centre of India (MCC), the Communist Party of India (Marxist-Leninist) and the People's War Group had recently merged together to form the Communist Party of India-Maoist (CPI-Maoist), uniting all the Left Wing extremist groups, or the Naxalites, in India. The aim of the united groups was to overthrow the 'bureaucrat bourgeois' and big landlord classes who controlled state power, and to establish in its place a new state under the leadership of the proletariat, which, in other words, meant socialism and communism. The annihilation of class enemies, with extreme violence if need be, was the goal of all groups, who were committed to Mao's strategy of 'protracted armed struggle', leading to the seizure of power. In great excitement Vijay read the document, "Hold High the Bright Red Banner of Marxism-Leninism-Maoism", along with other papers that were outlined by the Central Committee of the Maoists, and dreamt of a bright future for the people once they were in power.

The thought of having a Communist Liberated Zone covering the entire stretch of territory from Nepal, Bihar, Jharkhand, Chhattisgarh and Odisha, down to Andhra Pradesh, under the revolutionary rule of the Naxalites was a dream that elated the two friends. In great excitement they would talk and discuss the idea, often arguing about the possibilities but always confident that someday their dreams would come true.

At this crucial juncture in his life when he had set out on a new path and was on the threshold of an exciting new world Vijay could not afford to get distracted by a girl. All softer feelings that arose in his heart had to be ruthlessly suppressed. So, though his heart leapt every time the girl's face appeared before his eyes, he did his best to prevent it from straying in her direction.

It was a matter of great pride to Vijay and Sudhir that they were often invited by the Commander to discuss various problems that worried him. They were thrilled when Bhaskar asked them over one evening. For a change Vijay found him sitting away from the table with the open map. Instead he crouched on a blanket spread on a cot and looked tense and worried. Vijay and Sudhir squatted on the floor nearby and waited for Bhaskar to begin. For a long moment, however, he remained silent, while the others wondered what he had in mind.

"There is a problem," Bhaskar said at last, "And I want your help in solving it."

Vijay's heart beat in anticipation. The words showed how much confidence the leader reposed in him and Sudhir. He looked up eagerly.

"What is it, Sir? We are ready to help wherever we can. Just tell us, Sir," said Sudhir.

Bhaskar gave them a searching glance, perhaps wondering how much he could confide in the untested young men. "The organisation has grown stronger and bigger. I am glad to note that it is spreading its hold over a much larger area than earlier. Our activities have increased tenfold and our membership has increased too."

"That is great news, Sir. You must keep up the good work," said Sudhir enthusiastically.

"Our work amongst the poorest of the poor is well appreciated by the locals, whatever the government might say," continued Bhaskar.

"Yes Sir," Sudhir agreed quickly, "You are right, Sir."

Finally Bhaskar came to the point–it was necessary to find funds to support their activities and he wanted suggestions on how it could be done.

The words led to a thoughtful silence from the two listeners. Vijay wondered how they could contribute. Financing the organisation was an aspect he had never dwelt on, filled as his head had been with the lofty ideals propagated by his leader. But he wondered now. How did they find money for the weapons, food, clothes and other necessary stuff required? The practical aspects were a mystery to him.

Sudhir seemed to be better aware of mundane, material matters. "Loot a bank? Ask for levy from contractors working on government projects? Isn't that how we collect funds?" he asked, hesitant, wondering how frank he could afford to be. Vijay stared at him, shocked at such open mention of activities he knew to be wrong.

Bhaskar took the suggestions in a matter-of-fact way and merely nodded. This brought home to Vijay the fact that there was an unpleasant side as well to the new life he had taken up so spontaneously and readily, without thinking of the consequences. He, the grandson of a police officer, must now take up activities he once would have considered not only illegal but also immoral.

"We must think how best the money can be raised. The government is quite dead these days. There is no construction–no roads, no bridges, even the railway project seems to be stuck. There is no longer any money in development work, I feel. Nothing much can come out of levies on projects, for there aren't any," said Bhaskar.

"Looting a bank, then?" suggested Sudhir.

"It is a possibility. But we'll have to plan it carefully. With all the security these days ..." Bhaskar paused, became thoughtful.

"How about kidnapping someone for ransom?" asked Sudhir brightly.

"Who? Do you know anyone?"

"A rich man's kid, of course. I know there are many businessmen in town who have so much wealth they don't know what to do with it," said Sudhir.

At once Vijay remembered his uncle, Mohan Lall. He could seek sweet revenge by kidnapping one of his four sons. The next moment he shook his head. No, he would not like to hurt one of his own cousins. However wicked his uncle had been, he had nothing but pleasant memories of the four kids he had played with as a little boy.

"I know who is the richest of all," said Sudhir enthusiastically, "Also the most undeserving. He built a palatial bungalow down the road from our house. And you know how he made his money? By selling coal illegally. He was part of the coal mafia. Later one of his sons got a license for selling liquor. Here too the scoundrels cheated. Sold country liquor in Scotch whiskey bottles at high prices! He made pots of money selling it to ignorant customers."

"Sounds like just the right man to me, a typical example of the criminal bourgeois we need to annihilate," said Bhaskar approvingly.

"Oh yes! I know because my lawyer father helped him get out of several problems that he faced. Of course everyone has now forgotten. And why not? He is a rich man, after all! Everyone respects the rich. All crimes are forgotten once he starts living in a huge bungalow with uniformed sentries at the gate, gleaming cars in the driveway and smart clothes bought abroad," explained Sudhir, bitter and sarcastic.

"All that is very well, but does the man have any kids?" asked Bhaskar.

"I remember some boys playing outside on his lawns. Probably his grandsons, about the same age as I was. I used to look at them over the wall. But then they went away–to some big school in another city and I lost track," answered Sudhir.

"What's his name?" Vijay wanted to know.

"Ram Prakash Gupta."

"Oh, him? I know! Not just money, he has acres of land as well," added Vijay.

"Right. He is the owner of the big mango garden on the Ranchi highway. He has developed it into a beautiful resort. It is used to entertain important officers and politicians so they may bestow their favours on him. My father attended several parties there," Sudhir seemed to know everything about the rich man.

"We must find out more about this man. Whether he is really rich and whether he has a family with kids who can be held for ransom," decided Bhaskar.

"Leave it to me, Sir. I'll find out everything," offered Sudhir.

17

"Our other great need is for arms and ammunition. We are running out of rifles, bullets ... other sophisticated weapons," to their great delight Bhaskar continued to confide in the two young men, "I plan to raid one of the police *chouki*s to secure more arms for ourselves. I know there is one in the village the other side of the hill. At Bhelwasa. It won't be difficult to raid that *chouki* ... we could do it on a dark night."

"Yes Sir, it's a good idea," Sudhir nodded sagely, as if he had carried out raids all his life and knew what must be done.

Bhaskar got up with a satisfied shake to his head. "Good, I am glad you both agree with me. So it's decided. We must carry out both these missions soon–one, to kidnap a member of Ram Prakash Gupta's family, and two, to raid the Bhelwasa police *chouki* to capture whatever ammunition may be stored there. You may leave now. Thank you."

With a slight nod and a wave of his hand he dismissed the two. As soon as they were out of the room Vijay looked at Sudhir. "What will happen now, Sudhir? Are we to get involved in all this? I had never imagined that we'll have to go this far!" His thoughts went back into the past. He remembered his father, a real gentleman, who would never have allowed him to stray from the straight and well-trodden path. Vijay sighed. That was long ago, he tried to tell himself.

Sudhir laughed and thumped his friend on his shoulder. "Come on *yaar*. Don't be such a wet rag. Just think of the fun and excitement of carrying out the two tasks! I'm sure I look forward to it. It will be great to see Gupta's face when he hears that his kin has gone missing. Just remember the various crimes that man has committed. I'm sure he deserves what is coming to him!"

Vijay still felt doubtful, though he tried not to show his feelings. Now that he had chosen the path, he must cast aside all his fears and learn to stride along it with confidence. Besides, as Sudhir had just reminded him, Gupta was no saint. He had heard about him, of course. He was known as the local coal mafia lord, who had made his riches by stealing coal and selling it at high prices. His son had inherited his criminal nature and gone many steps further. He sold spurious liquor which had killed many, he had heard. No doubt the two deserved what had been planned for them.

As the two walked back through the darkness, they saw a shadow flit across their line of vision. It was a woman and she seemed to be walking towards the Commander's shelter. Sudhir touched Vijay's shoulder and whispered in a dramatic hiss, "Know who it is? Commander Rekha. Do you think she is going there to discuss plans with him?"

Vijay was puzzled, but shrugged off the question. "Who knows, and why should we care, anyway? There must be something to discuss."

"Why discuss so late at night? No, I think she has other important matters on her mind. I have heard whispers. You know what? I think there is something brewing between them," Sudhir seemed to be enjoying the thought.

"The Commander does not seem to be the type," began Vijay when Sudhir thumped his shoulder again.

"What d'you mean, he is not the type! Is he gay or something? He is only normal, like you or me. I am glad he is not that deadly serious, after all. We don't want him to be deprived of these small pleasures, do we? Oh no! I am glad he has company. Good to know he is human," laughed Sudhir.

Sudhir's words brought back the image Vijay had been trying to stop from sneaking into his mind the past few days. He allowed himself to remember the face that appeared before his mind's eye time and again. It was the last image he dwelt on before he fell asleep that night.

Sudhir was as good as his word. In just a few days he brought back enough information to enable them to plan the kidnap in detail. The good news was that Gupta had a grown-up grandson who had studied somewhere in Delhi and was to come soon to meet his grandfather.

"That's the person we need to target!" said Sudhir excitedly, "And you know what? He is to stay at Aamra Vatika … that green heaven they've built … for his holidays! It makes it so much easier. We need not even enter the crowded town. We can whisk him away quietly from their haven … before anyone gets to hear about it … before a hue and cry is raised! He will be far away and within our territory before anyone realises he is missing! What luck, *yaar*!"

Vijay laughed to hear him make it so simple. He could see further towards other details they would have to think about and consider. Of course there would be a crowd at the orchard too. There would be relatives, servants and staff, perhaps even security men to protect the precious grandson. Surely the great and wealthy Ram Prakash Gupta would not allow his children to stay unprotected in the garden, however beautiful it might be.

"How is he to come? When?" he asked.

"Soon, I am told. In a few days," replied Sudhir. He stopped, for they could see Commander Rekha walking towards them. They waited for her to reach.

"Comrade Vijay, Comrade Sudhir," said the lady when she came near, "I've been planning to talk to you. The Commander wishes me to include girls in the various activities planned. He has informed me that you will … er … kidnap somebody and … also raid a *chouki*. He feels that girls need to participate in such … daring … activities. They need to shed their fears and learn to be courageous, face dangers. It should be part of their training."

"Sure, we agree with him fully," nodded Sudhir, "But what do you wish us to do?"

"Include them. Take them along. Some of them are pretty good. They can shoot, run, handle weapons. All that the men can do, in fact," Rekha informed them proudly.

"You've trained them well, sister," laughed Sudhir, "I can see that. Do tell us who you want to send. Anyone in mind?"

"Yes, certainly. I know my girls well. There is Munia. A good shot. She will do well in the raid that you plan," suggested Rekha. She named a few others. Vijay wondered if she would mention Champa, and sure enough her name came up, though almost at the end, when he had given up hope. "There is also Champa, the new girl, who has turned out to be a surprisingly smart and spirited young person. Very observant and intelligent, though she is not so good with weapons as yet. But she will pick up soon, I'm sure. You may take her for the kidnap mission. Her quickness of mind and other qualities will prove useful," ended Rekha.

The remarks made Vijay feel as proud as if he himself was the person she spoke about. His heart had begun to pound in excitement at mention of the name. Wondering if his face reflected his emotions he quickly turned the other way. But of course none had noticed, not even Sudhir.

That evening everyone, including Rekha, met at the Commander's shelter. In front of the others Rekha and Bhaskar were distant and formal with each other, but Vijay could not help remembering the slight shadowy figure that had flitted across to the leader's shelter in the darkness of the night. Somehow it made him feel good to remember that incident, as if it gave him the liberty to come closer to a member of the other sex, even in the disciplined, strict environment of the camp.

18

They made their plans that night. It was a proud moment for both Vijay and Sudhir to be a part of the decision makers, the core group, as the latter termed it when they recapitulated their experiences later.

It was warm and cosy inside the shelter. Bhaskar sat on the cot instead of at the table while the others spread themselves in comfort on a rush-mat on the floor. The lamp cast its soft glow over the scene, hiding the harsher shapes of the rifles and guns in the background. Vijay sighed with satisfaction. He was a part now of the whole outfit, a member of the family as it were, which gave him a sense of belonging. For long he had lived in the company of just one woman, his mother. Tender and loving though she was, and though he cherished memories of her with all his heart, he had remained deprived of a masculine, nurturing presence in his life. He felt Bhaskar made up for what he had missed all his growing up years. He gazed at him in gratitude.

"Let us decide on the two teams for our missions. Sudhir, I want you to lead the raid on the police *chouki* at Bhelwasa. Here is a map of the area. Memorise it well, for you will need to hide in your posts before dark. Once all is quiet; the villagers safe in their huts, you can begin your raid. Try not to hurt the villagers. I don't want that, for they are friendly towards us and I wish it to stay that way," said Bhaskar firmly.

"Yes Sir," Sudhir listened attentively for a change and nodded his head from time to time. Bhaskar also called out the names of the team members. The *dasta* was to consist of twenty members, including two women, Munia and Usha, whose names were suggested by Rekha.

Next, Bhaskar issued quick, detailed instructions to Vijay. To his delight and excitement, Champa's name was included in his team, along with another girl's. The two were told to meet their group members and explain all details to them. Finally Bhaskar wished them luck and allowed the two to leave.

Vijay left Bhaskar's room feeling thrilled and elated. Not only had he been assigned an important task, one of his companions on the mission was to be the girl who was beginning to occupy more and more space in his thoughts. In spite of his determination not to mix work with pleasure he found himself looking forward to meeting her again.

She came accompanied by others. Vijay looked with approval at the girl he had brought to the jungle not so long ago. She seemed to have taken well to the training and her new jungle life. No longer wearing a crumpled sari she was clad smartly in the shirt and trousers that was their uniform. She had tied up her hair neatly into a high bun. How different she seemed now from the girl he had first seen in her village hut. She was then an untidily dressed village girl bent meekly over her domestic chores. Now she had an air of confidence about her. Her head was held high, her shoulders set straight, and an expression of eager expectation shone in her large eyes.

The two greeted each other politely. "Hope you've begun to like it here," he enquired formally.

"Umm, yes. I am learning many new things. And have made many friends too. Like her, this is Munia," said Champa.

"Oh, we know Munia. We've heard lots about her from Commander Rekha. She has nothing but good words about you girls," said Sudhir, smiling. Vijay was impressed. His friend certainly had a way with girls, charming them with his smile and flattering words.

They outlined their plans to the boys and girls and allotted tasks to all, so that each person knew exactly what was expected of him or her. At the mention of Aamra Vatika Champa's eyes lighted up. "Oh, the orchard with the temple? Why, I know the place so well. I've been inside it to pray at the temple. Are we to go there?"

Vijay nodded. "Have you been inside?" he asked.

"Babuji took me there to worship at the temple. If we go, we can find out about my babuji too!" She looked excited at the thought, but Vijay well knew it was impossible to meet anyone then.

"We can't say that! Don't build up such hopes," he said.

"Did you meet the folk living there?" asked Sudhir, trying to change the subject.

"Oh no! We never met the owner, or his family. They must be good people to have built a temple where all are welcome. The village people go there to perform puja at festivals. No one stops us," said Champa.

Sudhir laughed to see her enthusiasm. "You don't really know them," he explained, "That's exactly what the rich like to do. Build temples to exonerate themselves from their sins and show everyone how religious and therefore honest they are. Hah!"

Vijay saw Champa staring at his friend in disbelief. Poor, innocent village girl! What would she know about the wily ways of the rich? "So you have been there. Tell us, is there a road leading to the orchard? Is it in a lonely area or is it situated right on the highway?" The questions gave Vijay an excuse to look directly at the girl which he had been shy of doing. Once again their eyes met, sending a wave of pure rapture through his body. He was pleased to notice the quick lowering of her eyes, the blush that spread on her cheeks.

Meanwhile, Sudhir was answering questions on the raid that he was to lead. The girl, Munia, had asked several questions which he answered with his usual good humour. The questions and answers were soon over and the others left to join the practice sessions that they had been engaged in before they came.

Sudhir soon received more information about the grandson's visit to Aamra Vatika. He had got the exact date. There was great excitement in the camp when news came that the boy would arrive at Ranchi by plane from Delhi exactly three days later. He would drive down straight to the garden. His family was to gather there to await his arrival. Through relatives of Gupta's driver Sudhir managed to get a complete description of the vehicle that would bring the boy home, including the number of their car.

Vijay was nervous but also excited at the thought of the difficult task assigned to him. He hoped there would not be any security around the boy when he travelled, because that might trigger off some firing, which he certainly did not want to resort to. He wanted to carry out his job safely without the shedding of any blood. The thought of spilling blood was still abhorrent, for he was not yet a fully conditioned Naxalite. Of course, if the need arose, he would face it squarely, but in the meanwhile why injure anyone if a job could be accomplished without it?

19

Manas Gupta

The flight landed safely and in time. Manas Gupta stepped down the plane ladder with light, eager steps. How fresh and sparkling everything looked. The sky was a clear blue, the sun shone warm and the breeze that ruffled his hair was cool and fragrant. It felt good to breathe in the fresh, clean air, especially after the rush and crowd of dusty, hazy Delhi. He walked excitedly towards the gleaming new airport building, admiring the bright colours of the dahlias and roses that lined the path. He remembered the building was just a small, grubby place when he had last been there. How much it had changed since then! Like other airports this too was a sign of the progress made by the country.

The feeling of pride continued as he strode towards the car park. Again, the well-tended garden with its pebbled pathways, the rock garden and the bright colours of flowers splashed against the green grass pointed towards change and development in the new capital of the state, once only a summer capital.

His grandfather had sent him the car. "Hasn't anyone else come?" Manas asked, surprised.

"They are all waiting for you at Aamra Vatika, Sir," said the driver, smiling, "They are planning something special, I think. That is why they sent just the two of us to receive you, Sir." He pointed to his companion on the front seat.

Manas felt a little twinge of disappointment. But then he reconciled himself to travelling alone. He would be able to savour the homecoming in peace. He wanted to be alone with his thoughts and expectations for he had come after many years, after all. He looked out with curious eyes as they drove into the city. The place had definitely changed. Cars, honking noisily, jammed the streets, trying to push aside the rickshaws and pedestrians jaywalking in the middle of the street. Tall concrete buildings pushed aggressively upwards where there had been lush greenery earlier. Brand new shops flashed their gleaming glassfronts proudly at him as they drove past.

Manas was not sure if he liked the modern Ranchi with its new found prosperity that showed stark against the ramshackle poverty, existing side by side. He missed the relaxed charm of the old town as he had known it earlier. Not that prosperity had brought order or cleanliness. If anything the town looked dirtier with plastic bags and wrappers blocking its drains and lying scattered in untidy heaps along the roads.

The drive out of the city was slow and tedious. They went past half-constructed buildings, unplastered brick-work, bustling shops crowded with stuff, the new military park with its beautiful garden, past the Apollo Hospital–and at last into the open countryside. It was good to be out of the crowded city. The sight of the green and brown land rolling right up to the low hills in the distant horizon was a pleasant contrast after the city with its concrete eyesores.

Manas sat up straight when they reached the *ghaati*. He loved the twisting road through the hills, their slopes verdant with dense vegetation. The valley down below was a pleasant patchwork of green, yellow and brown. They passed several men with sack-loads of coal slung on their bikes, huffing with the effort of pushing the heavy burden up the slopes. The coal was lugged all the way from the coal belt on the plains to the town high on the plateau where it was sold for a profit hardly enough to compensate for the hard labour put in by the carrier. Poor creatures, what a struggle it must be to lug the heavy stuff up the road. No wonder the men looked so weak and thin. But then, poor souls, what other alternative did they have to earn a living, sighed Manas, in a burst of sympathy towards the huffing men.

They soon left the *ghaati* and entered the crowded town of Ramgarh. After that Kujju, Mandu, Charahi, and then there would be another *ghaati*, with dense greenery on either side. Manas had always found it fascinating to peep into the jungle as they drove past. How he wished he could walk deep into the densest part. He remembered how, earlier, his childish mind would derive a thrill by dwelling on the mysteries of the jungle, inhabited by animals he had read about in his story books. His imagination would run wild about adventures he would have in its mysterious, dark depths.

Now he smiled at those romantic, childish memories. Actually, the family had lived in the town, an overgrown village surrounded by hills and forests. It had its own lake in the middle of the town, where he had gone boating with family and friends. And then his grandfather had bought a mango orchard a little distance away from town. Bit by bit, the place had been developed into a garden resort, embellished with a pond and a temple dedicated to Shiva. During the mango season, the whole family shifted to Aamra Vatika, as it was named by his grandfather.

The kids would spread out under the trees, gorging on the delicious, juicy Maldas, the bitter-sweet Dussaharis, and the good-to-suck-at small Bambaiyas picked up straight from the branches above. It was fun competing with cousins to see who could pluck the fruit from the tallest tree and who could eat the highest number, even if it resulted in upset stomachs and surreptitious visits to the toilet.

Soon his parents had shifted to Delhi to provide the kids better education, but the family returned to Aamra Vatika every summer to meet grandparents and to enjoy the mangoes. Except for the last so many years, thought Manas, when he had been unable to leave Delhi. He sighed with regret. His father had wanted him to study even during holidays so that he could do well for his board and other exams. Tuition, coaching, training at sports, did not allow him to return. Being a rich businessman's son did not mean he could get easy entry into an already flourishing business. His father insisted that he acquire the best education possible in the finest institution abroad. He must be a perfect finished product of the best training available in the world. Not for his son the making of dubious money by selling stolen coal or spurious whisky–as he himself and his father before him had–no, he must be a highly respected business magnate owning a multinational company with branches spread worldwide.

Manas did not let his father down. He got into Delhi IIT where too he scored well. His father took him to Europe and the US so that even at a young age he became a widely travelled and aware youth. And then he got admitted to a prestigious college in the US, which boasted of the best management teaching in the world.

He had already finished his MBA course at Harvard. And now he had returned to India to spend his summer vacation. It would be a good break for him before he joined the coveted well paying job he had already been selected for. Before leaving finally for his new job, Manas was going back to his childhood home to renew old memories and to meet his grandfather whose company he always enjoyed.

Lost as he was in his nostalgic trip down memory lane, time flew fast and they were almost there before he realised where he was. It was the last *ghaati* they were driving through. Manas sat up straight, trying to peek into the jungle that so fascinated him. Around the bends they drove, each turn, each twist offering him a fresh view of the mysterious forest.

20

The car slowed down as it passed a temple devoted to Hanuman. Drivers had made it mandatory to fold hands in homage as they swung past the temple. The small, red-brick construction perched on a jutting hill was said to be lucky and ensured their safety as they manoeuvred the curves and bends. Manas too bowed his head as they drove past. The car took a turn and a twist. Just as it did, he noticed the jeep parked to one side of the highway.

"Another breakdown," thought Manas. Then his eyes fell on the two girls standing near, their thumbs up to ask for a lift. "What's happened?" he asked out aloud.

"Nothing, Sir," muttered his driver, "We need not stop …"

"They seem to be in trouble. Look like city girls. Wonder what they are doing here," thought Manas. The girls wore jeans and T-shirts and definitely did not look like locals. It was dangerous to be stranded on a lonely road miles away from town in the midst of a jungle, probably infested by Naxalites. Imagine getting stuck in this wild stretch, where anything could happen. He had better help them. The thoughts passed swiftly through his mind.

"It is alright, Sir. Their driver is with them. Look," his own driver pointed towards a man bent over the open bonnet.

"Still … oh …! Stop, driver! Stop! We must help," insisted Manas.

Their car screeched to a halt near the jeep. The girls ran up to them and peeped through the window, relief lighting up their eyes. "Please help us," said the taller of the two, an attractive, dusky skinned girl with large eyes, "Our jeep has broken down and night is about to fall. We don't want to be stuck here in the dark."

The other girl nodded, casting nervous glances at the lonely road ahead, the stationary jeep and the thick forests behind her. Manas knew the stranded girls needed help. Dusk was approaching fast and the lonely spot would soon get converted into a danger zone for the unprotected. He swung one leg out of the door.

"Don't, Sir," his driver entreated, "Let's drive on, we don't know who they are ..."

Manas had already jumped out to look at the girls' vehicle. Their driver had the bonnet up and was peeping into the machinery.

Being a mechanical engineer from IIT, Manas felt confident he would be able to correct the fault. "Let me see," he said, walking over to the front. As soon as he bent down, he felt a sudden, sharp whack over his head. Stars arose before his eyes and he slumped over the vehicle. He had fainted. The driver of the jeep had hit him hard on the head with a blunt weapon.

Suddenly, a group of masked men who had been hiding behind the trees rushed close and surrounded his car. After all, the heist was planned well by Vijay, who had left nothing to chance! The driver and the man beside him on the front seat jumped out to tackle the attackers, but they were met with a revolver pointed menacingly at them. The driver quickly drew back and ducked low. His companion tried to pull out his own weapon. He did not see the man who had crept up close and before he could move, he was hit from behind. Within moments the masked men had overpowered both the driver and his companion. The latter was bound up, gagged, and thrown onto the back seat.

"Now go! Before you are shot dead!" one of the ruffians hissed in the driver's ear. The driver was lucky that Vijay, never in favour of shedding blood unnecessarily, was the brain behind the planning of the ambush. Why harm those they did not need and were not interested in? And so the man, along with his companion, was allowed to drive off.

Manas was carried up by the men and dumped unceremoniously into the back of the jeep. There were six others inside who shifted to make place for the unconscious boy. The men who had suddenly and silently appeared from the jungle vanished just as quickly and quietly. Now it was the turn of the occupants of the jeep to carry on with the job. They tied up the boy's hands at the back and bound his legs with quick, deft movements. The driver, along with the two girls who had sought Manas' help, climbed in at the front and the jeep drove off.

It went at great speed, jolting the man lying on the floor of the vehicle. Manas lay there stiff and unmoving. He did not know that his chauffeur had been driven away and he himself had been carried off in a strange vehicle into the unknown.

The jeep soon slipped into a pathway that led into the jungle. It bumped and rolled over an uneven, *kuccha* track that disappeared into the depths of the jungle that had fascinated Manas so much. For almost an hour it roared through the forest, the track penetrating the thickest and densest parts. Trees locked branches overhead and bushes blocked their path as the track threaded its way through, twisting and thrusting ever deeper into the heart of the jungle. Soon the sun withdrew below the horizon and pitch blackness enveloped the forest. The jeep's headlights cut a swathe of brightness through it, picking up shining, filigreed outlines of the bushes and branches that crossed their path.

The gloomy darkness pressed heavy on him. But even through the dense haze he felt the bumps and shakes of the moving vehicle and groaned softly every time the jeep drove over a rough surface, or swerved suddenly to avoid a pothole. Much later, he began to surface from the deep stupor under which he lay. The sound of the jeep now prevailed over the silence that had blanketed him; he felt the sharp roughness of the jeep's floor. The vehicle was slowing down. A sudden jolt of the jeep as it bumped over a rough patch woke him up. Still in a daze he stared around. For several moments his mind did not function. Where was he? What was happening? He tried to lift himself up to look and a terrible pain shot through his head. Groaning, he tried to probe his scalp, only to find that his hands could not move; they were tied tightly together at the back. Neither could he move his feet. He cursed softly in amazement, puzzled. Fortunately his eyes were not covered. He peered through the darkness. At last he realised that he was in a vehicle that was hurtling through a thick jungle. "Shit!" Who had brought him here? His thoughts flew backwards and he remembered the girls on the roadside and the warning given by his driver. He had ignored his words and now something terrible had happened. Was he kidnapped, then? It seemed he was.

And now Manas was filled with remorse and regret. Why had he not listened to his driver? Why had he been so foolish as to have succumbed to the professed helplessness of the scheming girls? Why had he been so stupid? Why, why?

"He's awake!" somebody called out. Manas lifted his head and stared at the dim but solid shapes of the six crooks seated at the back. So these were his kidnappers; how cleverly had they managed it. Craning and stretching his neck, he glimpsed the driver and the two girls who sat beside him. The rogues! They had managed to make a fool of him. He clenched his jaws in anger and frustration. He who prided himself on being a brilliant student from the prestigious IIT had allowed a gang of criminals to trick him. The thought was galling. Now he must use his intelligence to find a way to escape. Think, think, find some clever idea to become free and run away. He must not panic. His mind worked at breakneck speed, trying to conjure up a brilliant idea to escape the criminals' clutches.

"Oh, is he? If he shouts, somebody may hear. Maybe he should be gagged," suggested a male voice.

"Who will hear him? We are already far from the main road and the jungle is empty ... we are in our own kingdom now."

"Yes, where we are the rulers!" said one of the girls.

"We are the kings and queens of the wild, wild jungle!" laughed her companion.

"Hush, this is no laughing matter. Now for the next step ... we must abandon the jeep and walk. The track will not go any further," said the male voice again.

"Yes, but let's eat something before we begin our journey. Aren't you all hungry?" asked the girl who had spoken first.

"Now that you mention it, yes, I am," replied the male voice. "Let's finish that task."

They behaved as if he did not exist, thought Manas, who had never before been ignored like this. The jeep had halted. The crooks opened some packets and began to eat. They talked to each other in low voices. None bothered to address him, nor did they think of inviting him to share the food. Not that he was hungry. Who could think of food in the midst of a crisis? This was followed by shuffling, pushing and jostling, for the men were jumping out of the jeep.

Were they going to leave him there to die? Suddenly he realised the gravity of the situation confronting him and, heart sinking, pictured the terrible fate that awaited him. By now he well understood that he had been kidnapped by the Naxalites he had heard so much about. They were a violent lot and could go to any extreme–kill, shoot, behead, chop him up bit by bit and torture him–if he did not do what they wanted. Only a few days ago he had read the shocking news about a villager whom the Naxalites had tried and killed on suspicion of his being a police informer. They had first cut off his ears, then his fingers, and then his hands to extract his confession. When the poor innocent did not utter a word of the 'truth' they wished to get out of him they had finally beheaded him.

Remembering the incident, he was filled with panic and a desperate fear that sent his heart pounding loudly against his chest. Tension gripped his mind making his head throb with pain. The idea that this could happen to someone like him–protected and pampered, who had travelled all over, was educated and refined and had lived a life of luxury–was a thought that was totally shocking and unbearably painful. Yet it had happened, he realised, and a moan escaped his lips.

"We are forgetting our prisoner," spoke a girl, "He must be hungry too."

"Hey you, want to eat?" asked a man.

Manas shook his head. How could he possibly think of food at such a time? On the other hand maybe it was better to conserve his energy. He must devise a strategy to pull him out of the absolutely unbelievable situation he was in.

"Why do you ask? Give him something." Before he could nod his head in reply one of the girls spoke for him.

"Untie his hands then. Free his legs too. Mister, we have you covered!" rapped out a voice.

A weapon was pushed against his back before Manas was untied. He was given a plastic bag containing some spicy chana. He found himself eating it without any hesitation. He was hungry, after all. A bottle of water was thrust at him. He drank the water in great, thirsty gulps.

"Let's go," said the male voice who seemed to be the leader of the group.

"Go on, walk!" The pistol was thrust deeper against his back. Reluctantly, slowly, Manas rose to his feet and began to walk, closely surrounded by the goondas who had kidnapped him.

21

The men kept him inside a tightly closed circle, nudging him when he did not move fast enough. The girls kept pace. The group seemed sure and confident, marching swiftly towards its destination. Manas opened his eyes wide, trying to examine his surroundings, trying to note down landmarks to be used later. It was almost impossible to do so; not only was his view obstructed by the men surrounding him; the night was too black to pick up shapes against the inky sky. His ears, however, remained acutely aware of the sounds in the jungle. The rustle and murmur of the leaves set off by the light breeze sounded eerie and ghostly in the darkness. At times he could pick up the solemn cries of the owl and at other times the chorus of crickets would suddenly break the silence of the night. And did he hear soft footfalls of the animals that must lurk behind bushes and trees?

Once again Manas remembered the excitement and romance of the jungles of his childhood, peopled by exotic animals like the lion and the panther as well as the lovable rabbits and bears he knew as characters in storybooks. For some inexplicable reason his mind reached back to dwell on his favourite toy–the cuddly tiger he had carried around with him as a kid and hugged close when he went to bed. He could not sleep unless he had his cheeks buried in the soft fur of his beloved tiger. And now here he was–right inside the tiger's home, though the animal he had loved and found comfort with no longer existed in its habitat. Instead, human beings, far fiercer and more dangerous than any beast, roamed the jungles.

"*Chalo, badho aage*! Move fast! We don't want to walk all night!" snapped one of the ruffians, giving a rough shove to the man they had kidnapped.

"*Kaise chalega*? He has probably never walked in his whole life! How can he do it now? He's always been driven around in a grand car," laughed another rudely.

Manas itched to punch the man's face. How dare he speak to him in that rough way? With great effort he held back the angry words that sprang to his lips. No, he cautioned himself, keep calm. For heaven's sake, don't get provoked. There was absolutely no knowing what reaction his words would evoke from this group of crude, uncouth, illiterate men.

"Lal Salaam. What is your name, comrade?" asked a voice that sounded more civilised to Manas. He turned eagerly towards the man. He remembered it was one of the voices he had heard earlier, belonging to the one he guessed to be their leader. He noticed, in the dim light, that he was a tall, slim man, dressed in shirt and pants, with straight, thick hair that fell on one side over his forehead.

"Manas. Manas Gupta, and I am not your comrade!" he answered shortly, indignantly.

"I am Vijay Lall. Sorry we had to trouble you, but there are some things that must be done."

"Why have you brought me here?" burst out Manas angrily, unable to control himself any longer.

"You'll know soon. For the present you must follow us and obey our commands. If you wish to remain alive, that is," warned Vijay.

"So what else am I doing? In any case do I have any alternative?" muttered Manas, his words revealing his resentment.

"No comrade, you certainly don't. So just keep your mouth shut!" Vijay seemed to have lost patience.

Manas could hear one of the girls giggle and another joining her. He felt angrier than ever. He shrugged and clenched his lips. Let me concentrate on walking, he warned himself, let me not get involved in an argument. Keep them in good humour, or the consequences could be grim. By now his legs were beginning to feel heavy. His feet, in their smart city shoes, hurt badly. If only the men would halt for a few minutes. They must have already marched for more than two hours, he guessed. His face felt hot and perspiration dripped down his forehead. The others in the group, used to the jungle, walked briskly, fast, and he had to keep up. It was a good thing he had done all that physical training and gym to stay fit and trim. His body would not let him down, he was sure.

"Are we almost there?" asked one of the girls another hour later.

"Not yet. Are you tired, Champa?" asked Vijay, concern in his voice.

"I am beginning to," replied the girl.

"Couldn't we rest for a few moments?" her companion asked.

For a moment Vijay hesitated. "Alright, if you girls need rest, we'll have to stop. But you know it is getting late. Commander must be waiting for us."

"Just five minutes," pleaded Champa, "My feet are hurting ..."

"All right, comrades. Let us find a suitable spot. Where we can all sit down a while to wet our throats," ordered Vijay the group leader.

Champa had already found some rocks jutting out above a grassy patch. "Look, doesn't that place look comfortable? We can sit there."

Manas felt relieved at this opportunity to sit for a while. He felt grateful to the girls for suggesting that they rest.

The moon, rising above the trees, had banished the black gloom of night. Its silvery beams filtered through the trees and danced on the rocky surface. The moonlight lent a silvery glow to the faces of the young girls. His eyes caught a flash of diamonds sparkling against teeth as the girl called Champa smiled at the young leader. The man's face softened immediately and his eyes grew tender as his gaze lingered on her. Manas realised that there was some understanding between girl and leader. So the jungle brutes did have a softer side, he thought. Good for them!

His captors pulled him towards the rocks. He sighed with relief as he threw himself down on a rock. The short rest was enough to lift his spirits and he began to think once again about an escape plan for himself. No longer would he walk like the proverbial lamb to the slaughter house; he was determined to break free from their clutches. Now there was enough light to find a way out through the forest, once he had somehow escaped his captors. But first he must get out of the tight circle in which they held him. The only way it could be done was by following the old method–of excusing himself on the plea that he needed to relieve himself. Once out of sight he would make a dash for it and, God willing, he would be far away by the time they began to chase him.

Manas agonised over his plans for a long time. He wondered what it would result in, whether it would succeed. The more he thought about it the surer he felt. Of course he could do it. After all the men were just a bunch of uneducated hoodlums, they could never be a match for a sophisticated person like him, who had secured a place for himself in a foreign university known for attracting the world's best minds. It was just that he must make his plans with utmost care, working out all details thoroughly and systematically, he told himself.

The next second his heart was filled with doubt. So what if he had a brilliant brain? Of what use would it be when faced with guns and rifles? He must not forget that the ruffians were armed. Not only that, he was alone, while they were a gang of ten–six around him, one leading them, one driver, and finally, two females! Did he have a chance?

No, he did not, not really, but then it was up to him to create the chance. Only the brave win in the end, the coward die their own deaths, he remembered reading somewhere. He must be the courageous one, the hero who got away, the man who had escaped the clutches of the monsters known and feared as the Naxalites. Surely he was not destined to die just yet. He was a young man whose life still lay before him, he had ambitions to fulfil, dreams to make true … how could he possibly die a violent, sudden death before time?

As they walked on, Manas began to dream his escape. Finally, Nature took over and decided the matter for him. He realised he could not hold himself in any longer, he had to relieve himself. He turned to the leader and asked politely, "If you allow it, I would like to …" he indicated it by raising a finger. Fortunately the man understood, as Vijay, though he had received an incomplete education, had attended a good school, and knew what the sign meant.

He issued quick instructions and Manas was allowed to step out of the circle of guards who surrounded him.

"Don't go too far," he was warned.

Manas walked away, his mind still debating furiously. He chose a shadowy place between trees and bushes which hid him from view. He finished his job and stood there for a while, uncertain and undecided. Should he make a dash for it? He stole a glance at his captors. Two of his guards were also making use of the opportunity. Vijay had his eyes turned in the direction taken by the girls, who had decided to step aside too. Four men watched Manas closely, hands on their weapons. They were the ones he had to look out for.

It was a difficult decision. The flash of an image that suddenly appeared before his eyes helped him make up his mind. He saw before him his old, wrinkled grandfather, his eyes full of expectation and searching for him, surrounded by his anxious father, tearful mother and the rest of his worried family–all awaiting his arrival at Aamra Vatika. It brought sudden, unwanted moisture to his eyes. The next moment, Manas had decided–he had to, indeed he must, take the risk. Quickly he stepped behind a tree and shot a sharp glance at the men. Taken aback by his sudden disappearance, their eyes were searching for him. Before they could locate his figure in the shadows, Manas had dashed towards some thick bushes. The men peered into the shadows, looking for the elusive figure. But Manas was now behind a stout trunk. He stole from one shadowy hiding place to another. And at last he made a dash!

"*Pakro*! *Bhaag gaya*!" Voices screamed out at once. He scurried off from the spot where he hid and sprinted across to hide behind a thicker tree trunk.

"You fool!" shouted Vijay. "We'll shoot! You're not going to make it. Come back!"

Manas did not care by now. It was too late, anyway, and he must either continue running or get caught. He preferred the former. Leaves crunched under him as he raced through the darkness. Run, run, you have to make it, don't give up, he urged himself. His feet crashed noisily through the bushes and branches, giving away his position.

Sudden, sharp cracks rang through the forest. At the same time he felt a searing pain shoot through his leg. A bullet had found its target. No, he would not let the pain hamper his movements. He sprinted faster, though he could feel the warm blood trickle down his leg, wetting his trouser, dripping down into his shoes. He heard the shouts and screams of his pursuers, but it only made him pick up pace. Before long the injury was dragging him down, his leg heavy as stone. He clenched his teeth together, determined not to give up. Limping, groaning, muttering words of encouragement to himself, he forced himself to carry on. Somehow he continued to scramble through the bushes, clutching at the lower branches of trees to prevent himself from falling down. But he could feel the exhaustion seep through his body. With a great sigh, he tried to pull himself up. The pain made him faint. His breath came now in gasps and he swallowed great gulps of air in an attempt to keep going. It was not much use. With a loud groan he finally crashed to the ground.

22

Champa

"I had to do it. Commander's instructions," explained Vijay, a rueful, apologetic smile on his face.

Champa stared at the pistol in the now limp hand. Her eyes travelled to Vijay's contrite face and then peered into the clump of trees that hid the fugitive. "Where is he?" she cried, hoping he was not lying dead out there in the bushes. It was the first time she had seen any human being shot and the sight had left her stunned, bewildered and deeply disturbed.

"Go on, search for him. Bring him over!" ordered Vijay, trying to assume control over the situation.

"Is … is he dead?" Champa asked, her voice subdued.

"Of course not. My aim was not to kill, certainly not. He is just wounded…," muttered Vijay, and the girl let out a sigh of relief.

The men tramped back soon enough, for it was not difficult to trail the wounded fugitive. Champa felt reassured to see the youth walk on his own feet, though unsteadily, supported by men on both sides. His white face, the dragging feet and the barely suppressed gasps and groans revealed the depth of the injury. The man's lips were twisted in pain, his fine eyes hidden by the thick black lashes that drooped against his pale cheeks. A sudden wave of sympathy and concern smote her. She ran forward with a cry, "Are you alright?"

The wounded man turned his face away, not so much in pain as in anger and scorn. Of course, she realised, he had no reason to be friendly towards her, one of the two girls who had conned him into capture.

"Look what you made us do," Vijay accused the captured man. Manas glared back at him without a word in response. Vijay shrugged his shoulders and turned to issue instructions to the driver of their jeep, who had accompanied them. He produced a bandage and medicines from a bag slung over his shoulder. Obviously trained in First Aid he deftly and with practised hands tended to the injury.

Before long the procession was on its way again, wending its way silently through the now moonlit jungle. Champa remained quiet, her mind once again in turmoil. She had been there almost a month now. She had gained a lot, acquired new skills and knowledge and imbibed many new ideas. Not just that, she was being trained to use guns and rifles. Shooting bullets at targets had been just a sport so far to her, a means to demonstrate her skill and intelligence, and score over competitors. She had known, of course, that the weapons could spout death and destruction, but it was the first time that she had actually seen them in deadly action. Now when they actually did destroy, spilling precious, human blood right before her eyes, she felt an uneasy, disturbing sense of disquiet fill her mind.

Thoughts she did not want to dwell on, doubts and anxieties once again assailed her. One day those agents of death could be pointed at her, if she enraged the jungle folk or did not carry out their bidding. She remembered the words of the Commander who had warned her the day she joined them. "There's no going back for those who have lived with us–we don't allow it." It meant that she must stay on, forever, under the command of the leaders, or she was doomed to death. What did that mean?

No longer did she have the freedom to live life the way she wanted to; she was under someone's authority, a slave for life.

The realisation struck her with full force as she stared once again at the injured man. As if to reassure herself she glanced at Vijay. He strode straight ahead, leading the men with a confidence that made her feel better. If he could be comfortable leading this life, surely she would be, too. No, there was no reason for her to feel uneasy; she had nothing to fear, she told herself. She had chosen to live here just as he had done, and she was sure it would end well. Life here was so different, so bizarre compared to her earlier life in the village; also, she missed her father and brother and longed to see them when she sometimes lay awake at night.

But, on the whole, it was exciting, challenging, and stimulating to be with her new friends.

The low hills that rose in silhouette told them they were nearing their destination. The group walked faster in anticipation and Champa too could feel her steps quicken with the excitement of reaching the shelter. It was home now, she realised. Munia, Usha, Commander Rekha–all would be there, waiting to hear if they had succeeded in their mission. As they drew near, the rocks and boulders were clearly seen, the tin roofs of the shelters glistening through their camouflaged cover. Champa's heart beat in anticipation. Yes, this was home. Behind those mud walls hidden between the rocks were the people who really mattered now–the girls, the comrades, her friends.

Vijay led the group to meet Commander Bhaskar, leaving Manas and his guards outside to await the leader's instructions. Manas, almost collapsing by now, sprawled on the ground, eyes shut, half conscious and gasping for breath.

Champa followed Vijay into the Commander's room. He was in the midst of a discussion with Sudhir, who rose excitedly to see the two enter. "How was it, comrade?" he asked, his eyes searching their faces. Vijay gave him a triumphant thumbs-up before saluting his leader.

"We completed our mission satisfactorily, Sir. Unfortunately I had to shoot, he tried to escape. There was no other alternative."

"Did you kill him?" asked Bhaskar in a sharp voice.

"No Sir, it's only a leg injury. But he needs medical aid. Immediately, Sir," said Vijay.

"Sudhir, get it arranged. Ask Commander Rekha to come here at once! We need to keep him alive. Did you send the ransom letters?"

"Yes Sir. We put them in the car, stuck one in the pocket of the driver and the other in his companion's. They must have reached the old man by now," replied Vijay.

"Good job, comrades! You and your team have done well. The girls too have done a superb job."

Champa gave him a smart salute to acknowledge his words of praise. Bhaskar returned it with a nod and one of his rare smiles, which transformed him into a warm friend and guide rather than the feared and respected boss he normally was.

Sudhir rushed to get medical aid for the injured man lying outside. Commander Rekha arrived soon, and ordered them to move Manas to the shack for medical care. Champa, full of concern, asked for permission to follow the group and rushed after her. She was relieved to see that the place was equipped with medicines and other material that would provide relief to the injured youth. Rekha, doctor to the Naxalites, removed the bullet and treated the wound with medicines, tying it up with a neat bandage.

"Comrade Champa, I am glad to note your concern. I give you the responsibility of caring for the injured man," said Commander Rekha, patting the girl as she hovered around the patient, "You are an intelligent girl. You'll be able to follow my instructions and give medicines at the right time and in the right manner. Alright?"

Champa saluted the boss and listened attentively as detailed instructions were given to her by Commander Rekha.

After everything had been taken care of, the girl was at last allowed to retire. It had been a long, exhausting day, but Champa felt satisfied. She had received appreciation from the Commander for the task they had accomplished. Besides, she had enjoyed working with the man who had this strange effect on her–of sending her heart a-flutter, at the same time making her so shy that she could not meet his eyes. Every time she did, waves of bliss swept through her entire being, suffusing her with a warm, pleasant feeling of happiness. Working together had often resulted in physical contact.

An arm had brushed against her shoulders or a hand had touched hers in passing. Was it accidental or deliberate, she wondered. Blushing furiously in the dark, she hoped his actions were conscious and wholly intended.

"How was it?" Munia snuggled close and pinched her arm, "Don't go to sleep just yet. I have something to tell you!"

Lost in thought, Champa did not welcome the intrusion; besides, she was tired and all she wanted to do was to sleep. But Munia was too excited to let her do so.

"Are you listening?" she whispered anxiously.

"Yes, what is it?" murmured Champa.

At once Munia got launched on a long story about how she had manipulated to get close to Sudhir whom she admired greatly, as she had once confessed to Champa. "And you know what? He teased me and seemed to enjoy talking to me–as much as I did! And–listen to this! We are to meet each other alone tomorrow evening. Oh, I am so excited!" chirped the girl.

Champa smiled to herself and closed her eyes.

"And I am really looking forward to the raid!" continued Munia ecstatically, "I am on Comrade Sudhir's list. Just think, Champa, we'll be together in that exciting raid! It is just three days away. I can't wait for it!"

"Hope you enjoy it," replied Champa sleepily, sinking immediately into the land of dreams.

A surprise awaited the two friends. Sudhir outlined an exciting plan the very next morning. "Tell you what, everybody! Today is Karama, a day of celebrations for the tribal folk. Why don't we join them for a spot of fun?" he suggested brightly.

Vijay looked doubtful. Would the leader allow them to go?

"Why not, *yaar*? I for one am really missing our old town life, the music, the movies, the cricket, and even our classes at college!"

Vijay made a face. "Oh those … don't even mention them, I don't care for that past … we are serious about the cause now. How can you even think of all that bourgeois stuff?"

"Yes, yes, I am just as committed to the movement, you know that. Don't forget, I was the one who started it all. And I still feel we took the right step. But … once in a while we can have fun … why not?"

"Well … " Vijay still hesitated but as usual Sudhir brushed aside his objections. "Agreed we are revolutionaries. We have led the austere jungle life for long enough, don't you think so?"

"What d'you mean, long enough? It's to be forever! You forget we have sacrificed our old comfortable lives for the sake of an important cause. It's a cause we strongly believe in, and are absolutely committed to. Or don't you believe in it any longer?" asked Vijay, amused by Sudhir's perseverance.

His friend hastened to assure him that he was a serious, hard core revolutionary. "But come on, Vijay, just for one day … you need not feel so guilty about it. I'm sure the topmost bosses will not mind."

Once again Sudhir steamrolled Vijay's doubts, who soon succumbed to his friend's persuasive tactics. "So? What exactly do you plan? I think you already have something up your sleeve," he asked, grinning at Sudhir.

"Right! Listen then. There's to be a fair at the tribal village nearby, to celebrate the festival of Karama. You know how those folk make merry during festivals. There will be singing, dancing, drinking … it will be fun, after days of the strictest discipline and austerity! Let's join them," said Sudhir.

The two set out, a little nervously, to seek the Commander's permission. Fortunately the leader was in a good mood. "Yes, why not? Take others with you. Let them enjoy the festival!" he agreed wholeheartedly.

The news spread like wildfire through the jungle community, making the younger members especially excited. Soon there was quite a crowd, all dressed in their best civilian finery, waiting to trek three miles to the nearest village. Champa wore her old salwar-kameez, discarded since Commander Rekha included her as a member of the fighting squad, the girls' *dasta*, and now her holiday dress. Sudhir looked dashing in his black T-shirt and jeans and even Vijay had on a red shirt. Munia, for a change, was clad in a bright pink nylon sari glittering with sequins. She had smeared a dash of red lipstick on her lips, making her look as if she had consumed paan leaves. Champa smiled; she well knew why she was all dressed up. Usha, from Odisha had taken out her old Cuttacki sari while Sita, Uma and Ganga wore their somewhat faded kurtas and salwars.

The holiday mood of the party infected Champa. She hummed under her breath as they set off for the fair. Yes, life here was full of surprises and excitement. From being confined to a life of *chulha-chouki*, with the overbearing Kamla's shrill nagging as accompaniment, to celebrations and adventurous expeditions in the jungle–it was not a bad change at all. No longer did she regret it. All her earlier doubts melted away. She decided she had done well to take this momentous step forward in her life

23

The girls were like a flock of excited birds, chirping gaily amongst themselves as their feet flew over the winding path. The young men strode ahead trying to exhibit an indifference towards the girls, though from time to time one or the other would turn back to fling a bantering comment or a good humoured joke at the girls' expense. It was answered by either a giggle or an aggressive reply from one of the bolder girls, like Munia. With the elders, the sick and the injured left behind in the camp, it was with a sense of freedom and gay abandon that the others walked to the village, looking forward to a good time.

The falling dusk had painted the sky in glowing orange and grey shades by the time the group reached its destination. As they drew closer the beat of drums and the singing floated to them on the wings of a light breeze. Champa absorbed eagerly the sounds and smells that pervaded the air, feeling nostalgic, for she had missed them since she had left her village. She breathed in the air, full of the sugary fragrance of the *mahua* wine combined with smells that spoke of frying spices and cooking food, with growing delight. The smoke from burning cowdung, carried across to them with the wind, evoked memories of her home which she had almost forgotten.

Soon they could see village women sitting under the trees in groups, selling the little silver trinkets, brightly coloured ribbons, bangles and garments that they had brought all the way from Ranchi town. Older women, with wizened, wrinkled faces, crouched before heaps of vegetables or herbal medicines used by the locals, offering them for sale. A few village youth in their tight trousers with plenty of pockets and buttons to decorate them, wearing electric bright T-shirts, preened themselves before some giggling girls. But the biggest cluster of villagers was gathered under a huge, spreading banyan tree from where arose sounds of singing and merry-making.

"Look, they have already planted the Karama tree! Come let's join the dancing!" cried Munia excitedly, pulling Champa and the other girls along. While the men wandered off in pursuit of higher pleasures, the girls ran towards the circle of dancers. Lanterns hanging on the branches of the tree lit up the scene and shone on the faces of the row of dancers, clad in white saris with traditional red borders. Red flowers or red ribbons blazed in their neatly coiled, shiny black hair. Their song, sweet, soft and lilting, rose into the air, lifting the visitors' spirits. Reaching closer, Champa caught the words of the song.

"Jhaka-maka kare, ringa-binga kare re
Goriya ker,
Murhe jhabralai genda phool,
Goriya ker, goriya ker, goriya ker...."

It was the *mahua-patai* (*mahua* leaf) song, Champa recognised. They had done it at school once, long ago, it now seemed.

The dancers invited the newcomers to join them and the girl stepped forward excitedly. Munia hesitated, for, coming from a different region, she was not familiar with the dance. The beat of the drums, however, was so vigorous and persistent that she was able to fall into rhythm easily. The girls held each other's waists and danced around the drum-beaters, going clock-wise and then anti clock-wise, dipping and swaying, dipping and swaying gracefully in smooth, rhythmic movements.

Not much later, the young men, having enjoyed their glasses of the heady rice and *mahua* wine, joined the dancers. Some took over the drums, beating them vigorously and dancing with gay abandon.

"Kon-kona barasalai,
Rimi-jhimi paani!
Hai re, rimi-jhimi paani!
Kon-kona badari charhalai, hai re,
Lavke bari jor.

Bhado mahina me,
Karam garhai gelai..."

They sang of the monsoon clouds gathered above and the planting of the karama tree. The young men offered the wine to the girls, amidst much laughing and giggling, protests and denials. It energised the dancers, who fell into a faster, more frenzied rhythm. One by one panting couples dropped off and vanished into the darkness beyond.

Champa could feel the effects of the wine as it filled her guts. A feeling of gay irresponsibility flooded her. She was floating in the air and nothing could bring her down now to the level of the ground. Neither the thought of her family back in the home she had left, nor the fear of the leaders in the jungle could bring her to earth. She saw Munia break into giggles as Sudhir pointed his drum in her direction and beat it vigorously with a mischievous, suggestive smile. Fortunately Vijay was more sober. He stood to one side, clapping his hands and swaying in rhythm with the dancers.

The night hours flew past. The dancers slowed down and the drummers retired. It was time to leave for camp. Vijay, who did not seem to be as wild as the others, took the lead to guide his flock back. He shepherded the now swaying girls and boys away from the scene of merriment.

Laughing and in a gay mood, Champa followed the others. As soon as they were some distance away from the village, the cool, fresh air hit her, clearing her brain of the after-effects of the wine. But another kind of madness had taken its place. She stared at the back of the lean figure that walked ahead of her, wishing with all her heart that he would turn and look at her. Perhaps her gaze had pierced his subconscious mind for, to her great excitement, he suddenly swung around and called out her name.

"Why do you lag behind, Champa? Can't you walk faster?" he asked.

"I will, I will!" Champa cried out silently and ran to keep pace with Vijay. As she drew near, his hand stretched out and clasped hers in the darkness. For a long time they walked thus, hand in hand, minds and hearts locked together in silent acknowledgement of their love. Heart soaring to the sky, she felt she was walking through a dream full of shining, glowing clouds, with stars crowding close and beautiful, enchanting music playing all around. She clung to Vijay's hand which was the only stable, steady object around, for everything else was afloat.

His voice pierced through the mist that enveloped her. "Will you walk like this with me always? Always and forever?"

She nodded vigorously, failing to realise that he could not see in the dark and forcing him to repeat his words, a little more sharply this time.

"Yes, yes! I will!" she cried and felt her hand being squeezed tight in reply.

"It has been a difficult life for me. D'you know, I lost my father when I was just ten, and my mother, who supported me and looked after me, when I joined college," Vijay told her.

A feeling of great sympathy surged towards him. She remembered that her own experiences were no less tragic. Vijay carried on, baring his heart before her. She was drawn into his life, his world and his problems, forgetting her own.

"And now I have you, someone I can call my own, to love always," he concluded.

They walked on, the others in the group treading silently, in twos or threes, some already tired and lagging way behind, while others, having walked faster, far ahead of the two. Champa had no idea where her friend Munia was, nor could she see Sudhir anywhere, but it did not seem to matter any longer. Wrapped up in her own world of warmth and tenderness, she had no thought to spare for anyone else.

The path, often vanishing into scrub and bush, wound through the jungle and at last entered the narrow valley, through which the now almost dry nullah leading to their camp flowed. Rocks and boulders littered the sand on either side of the trickling stream. Still, it was easier to walk here now that they had left the denser areas of the forest behind them. Their shelter was now only a few furlongs away. The travellers hurried to cover the last stage of the journey.

Champa, who wanted the journey to last forever, lingered behind until Vijay pulled at her hand. "Are you tired?" he asked.

"Of course not!" she declared.

"I know you are a strong girl. It was the first thing I noticed about you when I met you that night, in your hut. Strong in spirit, I mean," he explained.

She did not really understand what his words meant, but she was content to note the admiration in his voice. "I hated you then! I was so angry!"

"I knew it. But it was you who rang me up later and asked for help. Your dislike had evaporated by then?" he asked, in a teasing tone.

This reminded her of her own horrifying experience at the police station, but she did not want to spoil their mood by talking about it. "I will tell you later!" she said and laughed, trying not to make it sound like a snub.

"You must! Come this way," he drew her into the shadow of a boulder. The sand below was moist and cool, soothing to her tired feet. "Let's sit a while." The others had already passed the two by, and were perhaps home by now. She wondered about Munia and remembered she had not seen her for a long time. A similar thought had probably occurred to Vijay for he peered into the darkness to comment, "And where is Sudhir? Surely he hasn't stayed back at the village to have a fling with the girls?"

As if Champa cared! She stood back against the rock to look up at Vijay, noting his sharp, pleasant features, the hair falling against his forehead, and, last but not the least, the dimple that deepened on his left cheek when he smiled, as he was doing now.

"What are you looking at?"

"You. I have wanted to do it for a long time," she lifted her hand and stroked his cheek, thrusting her finger into the little dip that had always intrigued her so much. He lifted the hand, patted the fingers one by one, and then buried his lips in her palm.

Time stood still for the two of them. But actually it was only a few seconds, for Vijay soon remembered his responsibilities. "I must see if everyone is safely back home. You must go too, or Commander Rekha will worry her head about you." Reluctantly the two parted company and she turned towards the shelter where the girls slept. It was dark inside. She groped her way to her sleeping area and dropped down onto the mat.

"Is it Champa? Are you back?" murmured a relieved voice, that of Rekha's.

"Yes. And Munia?" asked the girl, stretching out a hand to feel the space next to her.

"She came just a few minutes ago. You are the last. Good, now I can sleep," said Commander Rekha, with a sigh of relief.

24

The trip to the village may have been great fun but they could not afford to forget their duties, Commander Rekha reminded them as soon as the girls were ready in the morning. She sent everyone off for drill and practice, asking Champa to stay back. Had she forgotten the task assigned to her? She had not, and the girl hurried to follow Rekha as she strode towards the medical shack.

The wounded man was laid on a ramshackle camp cot, covered with a torn sheet, a horde of flies and mosquitoes buzzing around him. One of the younger boys, a tribal from the village they had visited last night, was swishing a branch, along with its leaves, over him, trying to keep the flies from settling on the sticky, sweaty face. Rekha placed a hand over the man's forehead and made a face. "High fever! In spite of the medicines I gave. What can I do? Everything is not available here in the jungle. I do my best." She instructed Champa to rub a wet cloth over the man's hot forehead and moved over to look at another patient, a girl lying on a *chatai* in a corner. "This one has malaria. She's been having fever off and on. But she will be alright. I am prepared for this … malaria is to be expected, of course."

A third patient was hunched up next to the girl, holding his knees close to his chest and groaning. "Stomach cramps, along with diarrhoea. I told him not to drink the water without boiling it. I ask those women to boil the water … just the little that is drunk. But they don't always. One can understand … it is not always easy to find dry twigs. Of course they are already immune, but … not everybody is." Rekha muttered to herself, obviously worried and concerned.

Champa knew neither she nor anybody else in her family had ever boiled water. After all, where was the fuel? But they had never fallen ill because of it. Rekha opened her medicine box looking for pills for the patients. "You will have to boil his, of course," she said, gesturing towards the boy who had been shot. "Part of your job. When he wakes up give him the *khichri*. Stay around. And call me if I am needed."

It was a new experience, for Champa had never cared for or nursed patients earlier. Unless one counted the time her little brother had fallen sick. Waiting there, impatient and restless, the girl's mind went several years back to the days when she had sat by the bedside near her brother, who was stricken by the pox. She had caught it from him later. In fact the whole family had succumbed to it. No doctor had visited them, but the villagers had come, one by one, to bring a pot of rice gruel, or some chapattis, to help tide over the crisis. They had brought branches of neem leaves which the sick had brushed over themselves, and later put into the water they bathed in. Afterwards there had been a 'puja' to 'Sheetla Mata' and only then had they become pure enough to lead normal lives. It was all that she remembered about sickness and caring.

"How is the young man?" she heard a voice and Bhaskar, followed by his two aides, Sudhir and Vijay, entered the room.

Hiding her delight at meeting Vijay again Champa rose hastily to salute the leader. "He is sleeping, Sir. Commander Rekha said he has high fever."

"He'll be well soon," Bhaskar nodded to her and turned to Vijay, "Comrade, are you sure you put in the two ransom letters? We haven't heard from his relatives yet."

"I am sure, Sir," confirmed Vijay emphatically. "But maybe the driver and his man did not pass them on. What would you like me to do, Sir?"

"We cannot bank on it. Search the boy's pockets. There may be a mobile somewhere. Find out a number to ring them up!"

Vijay looked a trifle guilty as this had completely escaped his attention. It had never occurred to him that he should search the kidnapped person's pockets. Both he and Sudhir rushed to undo the mistake, fumbling in their haste. They pulled out a mobile, a pen, a wallet with the boy's credit and other identity cards, and some five hundred rupee notes from the pockets of the sleeping prisoner. There was some change as well. Everything was handed over to the Commander.

"You've forgotten the watch!" he reminded them and the two hastened to remove the expensive watch from the man's wrist. The fumbling and the tugging at last woke up the half unconscious boy who fluttered open his eyelids and moaned softly. "What's happening?" he asked, "Who … where …?" He struggled to sit up, his bewildered gaze flitting from face to face until they settled on one that they recognised, that is, Vijay's. He passed a hand over his eyes. "Oh, now I remember … so you brought me here? Where am I? What do you guys want from me?"

Sudhir rushed forward to say something, but was silenced by Bhaskar. He had been scrutinising the contents of the pockets, turning over the cards and papers one by one to examine them. "No, Sudhir. Let me handle this. So you are Manas. Manas Gupta. Young man, you should have guessed by now. I see that you studied in the IIT and are now in Harvard?"

"So? How does it matter to you guys?" In spite of the weakness, fever and the grogginess due to the medicines he had been given, Manas raised an aggressive voice.

"Students from IIT are said to be brilliant. And you are not just IIT … but Harvard as well! That's why I expected you to have guessed why you are here," said Bhaskar.

"No, I can't. I don't expect to meet unlawful and violent gangsters like you," spoke Manas resentfully, before sinking back on the pillow with a groan.

The rude tone and the hostile words did not go down well with Sudhir who sprang angrily towards him. "Don't you dare speak to our Commander in that disrespectful manner! Do you realise who you are addressing? Our great leader himself!"

"Yes, yes. A violent Naxalite, of course," mumbled Manas weakly yet defiantly.

"You'll soon know how violent we are!" cried Sudhir heatedly.

"*Bas*, Comrade Sudhir, that's enough. Let him be. We must do our job. Let's go," ordered Bhaskar, "Now that we have his mobile and his family's phone number we'll ring them up …"

Champa was relieved to see them go. The conversation disturbed the young man. He turned over to the other side, babbling something incoherently. He was greatly agitated. She gave him some water that she had taken care to boil and made soothing sounds to help him fall asleep again. A gentle snoring told her that he had.

All that day and the next, she remained busy caring for the sick. Rekha had directed her to do the job as part of her training. She hardly saw Vijay though she longed to meet him, with an ache that became unbearable at times. At such moments she resented the sick folks and would speak roughly to them, immediately regretting her words, then trying to be extra attentive.

It was a relief to see Vijay enter the shack later on the second day. "Oh, you are here? I've been looking for you. Are you on duty here?"

"Yes, Commander Rekha has ordered me to stay with the patients. I am looking after these sick people."

"How is our patient?"

"Oh, awake at times. Sleeping the rest." She gazed at Vijay, her eyes soft and tender, wishing he would talk about themselves rather than about her patients. He gave her a rueful smile and she understood that he could not say much in the presence of the others. Instead, he clasped her hands for a few ecstatic seconds, and the two smiled at each other wordlessly, eyes clinging to each other's. "And what about you? What have you been doing?" she asked him.

"Commander has kept me busy. Sudhir and his team are to go on raid tomorrow. We've been preparing for it."

"The raid? Oh, I had forgotten all about it. Munia has been so excited … is she going?"

"Of course. You know it was decided long ago. And with Sudhir there she is bound to go!" laughed Vijay, "He has been preparing hard … they are ready with arms and ammunition and will use them if the need arises. There may be firing …"

They were interrupted by moans and grunts from the cot on which Manas lay. Whirling around, Champa saw he was awake, struggling to raise himself on the bed. She ran to help him, but he shrugged off her hands. "Criminals and rogues …!" he muttered, "Buzz off! I'd rather not have anything to do with crap like you!" He pushed away the helping hands.

Champa was indignant. "Look at him! What an ungrateful man! After I waste so much precious time attending on him, this is what he says!"

"It only shows he is getting better, Champa. Your efforts are bearing fruit, you should be satisfied," Vijay laughed good-naturedly and hushed her up, then spoke to Manas. "I have come to inform you that we have spoken to your family. They know now. Until they send us the money, bear with us."

"So I guessed right. It's ransom. Naxalites are not there for any ideology, only for money," commented Manas scornfully.

"Such rude remarks will not deter us. If we do not get the money you will be dead. I advise you to keep your mouth shut, or else!" warned Vijay, his voice controlled and soft, and Champa could see that he was trying not to respond too harshly. She liked his restraint and gave him an approving smile. Vijay nodded. To stop himself from saying more he walked out of the room.

"You can keep your precious advice to yourself," Manas shouted after him, but his voice was not strong enough to reach the departing man. It was left to Champa to respond. "Shh … sh," she warned him, "Shouting will not help. It will only weaken you!" She was glad to note that he became wiser and calmer after this, probably concluding that strength as well as safety lay in being calm and prudent.

Her patient was looking a little better, so Champa went out in search of Munia whom she had not seen for some time. Her friend was still full of Sudhir, whose company she had enjoyed at the village fair. They had laughed and flirted with each other, shared each other's stories. Was that all, asked Champa, disappointed and brimming with curiosity. But Munia would not reveal any more. Instead she giggled, dropping her long lashes over her eyes demurely. She was more forthcoming about the raid that was to be carried out the next night.

"Commander Sir has explained everything. You know, we are twenty altogether, including Comrade Sudhir and me. We are to leave early, while we can still see. It will be a long walk. Five kilometres. We will hide outside the village. And then, when the villagers have gone to sleep, maybe around midnight, we'll strike. Suddenly! The policemen will not even know what hit them. Our success lies in the secrecy and suddenness of the attack," she explained.

"Good luck to you. Will you shoot?" asked Champa, a little fearfully.

"Of course, if the need arises. I've been trained to. Why d'you think we've been practising all these days? But this is my first real action. To think I will have a filmi hero by my side!" Munia sounded enraptured.

She was much more serious and strangely silent when the time came to leave. The guerrilla squad was lined up in the practice field under the sheesham trees. A little group, which included Champa, stood around to wish it well and to see it off. Sudhir was the leader. He gave the boys and girls last minute directions and then hurried to invite the Commander to give them his instructions, if any. A few minutes later Bhaskar strode up to the field where the troops awaited him, Vijay in tow. He surveyed his guerrilla army, his grim, penetrating gaze sweeping over the girls with their loaded pistols and the young boys with their guns and rifles. All had solemn, grave expressions on their faces, their eyes staring intently ahead. Champa wondered what passed in their minds. Were they afraid, or were they too excited to feel anxious or nervous? It was difficult to guess from their bland, stony faces. Bhaskar, meanwhile, had finished examining his little army.

"Comrade Sudhir, I know you will do a good job. All luck to you. Lal Salaam!" said the Commander.

"I will, Sir. Thank you!" replied Sudhir, a grin on his face. His eyes shone in excitement, for this was to be his first raid. At the back, Munia nodded and smiled at Champa, as eager as her hero, Sudhir. Champa could feel the tension in the air. She muttered good luck. For a moment a feeling of apprehension stole into her mind.

"I am so glad for Sudhir," Vijay, standing next to her, whispered, "He has been looking forward to it. He looks good, doesn't he? And so excited! Hope it goes well for him!"

"I'm sure everything will be alright," Champa mumbled, forcing herself to smile.

Bhaskar stepped forward to rasp out an order. Sudhir saluted smartly and the men wheeled around to face the opposite direction. The troop marched, single file, down the narrow, almost invisible path that led away from the hideout. Weaving its way around the trunks of trees and through patches of bush it soon disappeared into the shadowy depths of the forest.

Champa turned back with a sigh of regret. The apprehension had turned into a feeling of pride as she watched the group march off. Now she wished she too could join them instead of staying behind with the sick and the injured. How smart the girls looked, striding in rhythm, shoulder to shoulder with the boys. How fortunate Munia was to march side by side with the man she loved. If only she could have done the same with Vijay Lall.

25

Preparing for drill the next day the girl donned the brown and green uniform with a sense of pride. She tightened her long braids and put them up in a high bun, before fixing the cap smartly on her head. It felt good to be in uniform, like a soldier marching to battle. She raised her head high and straightened her shoulders with a newly acquired air of confidence.

It was a clear, cool day, with the fresh morning breeze gently caressing her cheeks. Champa sniffed the bouquet of fresh forest fragrances that wafted in with the breeze–the scent of the wet earth and the crushed leaves combining with the tantalising fragrance of the eucalyptus. From somewhere far away the call of a wild rooster mingled with the harsh crowing of the crows perched on the sheesham and teak trees. The wild, untamed beauty of her jungle surroundings enthralled her once again. She realised how much she had begun to enjoy the challenges and excitement of being one of the jungle folk.

The girl relished her new found freedom and release from her mother's bullying. How proud she felt to be able to handle guns and pistols instead of the earlier brooms and *belans*. Her skill in shooting and quickness in grasping matters never failed to impress her trainers. The sparkle of approval she had often glimpsed in Commander Rekha's eyes told her she was good.

Commander Rekha? Champa's hands flew to her face–she had forgotten the responsibility given by her–to look after the patient! She rushed to the sick room. The wounded man lay with his eyes closed;

calm under the effect of sedatives. The malaria stricken girl and the man with stomach cramps had left. The boy was alone. As she busied herself cleaning and tidying up she heard the familiar footsteps and looked up with delight. It was Vijay. "How is he?" he asked.

"Sleeping," she said, smiling. Vijay took her hands in his and gazed at her with a look that set her heart beating wildly. He turned towards the patient. "I need to talk to him," he said. The two leaned, together, over the wounded man. "Hey, are you awake?" Vijay laid his hand on the boy's shoulder and saw him open startled eyes.

"What's wrong with your folks?" questioned Vijay, "Don't they want you back? We have not received any response from them."

Manas was now wide awake. He gave Vijay a hard stare and turned over without answering the question. Frowning, and with a grim expression on his face, Vijay gripped his shoulder to shake out a response from the prisoner. "Have you quarrelled or what? Isn't your family interested in getting you back?" he enquired.

He was greeted with more silence. Champa could feel the tension that thickened the air. Vijay raised his voice and asked in a louder, angrier tone. "Well, what d'you think, Mr Smart Guy? Don't you have any answer?"

At last Manas turned over to face his interrogator. In a slow, deliberate and firm voice he replied, "If you really want to know … I think they will be cowards if they give in to the threats of a bunch of crooks."

Taken aback by the unexpected response Vijay blinked his eyes in shock. "Oh, is that so? How brave of you! You really don't wish to be rescued?" he asked with exaggerated surprise. He glanced at the girl and made a face, to which she responded with an amused smile. He decided to change his tactics. He spoke now in a softer tone as he tried to explain. "Now listen, young man. We are not really criminals, as you insist on calling us. We have a mission, a cause that is dear to us. Let me tell you, whatever we do is for the sake of the poor! They have no voice …"

"Hah! Tell me another!" interrupted Manas, with a bitter laugh, "Kidnapping and ransom to help the poor? Don't try to fool me!"

"Seems you know little about our philosophy," said Vijay, still patient, though Champa could see the sparks of anger in his eyes. She wished the sick man would listen to Vijay and not be so belligerent.

"Forget your philosophy. Just tell me what you want from me, now that you've brought me here," Manas retorted.

"Yes, Comrade Vijay," Champa added hastily, "He is not interested in what you're trying to explain. Just tell him what you want!"

"Alright. We want him to ring up his family and plead … beg … to be rescued. Commander's orders. He has already spoken to them and asked for ransom. But they have not responded," explained Vijay.

"Well, OK, if that's what you want. Where is my mobile? How can I speak if you have taken it away?" asked Manas.

"Here, use this. Your mobile is with the Commander," Vijay offered another instrument to the patient.

"So you have confiscated mine!" Manas threw him an indignant, accusing look, but accepted the offered mobile. He pressed some numbers and waited, frowning, until the phone was picked up at the other end. "Hello, hello! Yes, it's me, Manas," he shouted, "Yes, yes, I am OK … no, not really, but as much as it is possible under the circumstances … I'm a … alright …!" It seemed to Champa as if his voice was about to break but with supreme effort he managed to control the tremble.

"No need to take so long," interrupted Vijay in a sharp voice, "Come to the point!"

Manas shook his head and continued, "I … I'm perfectly alright, Dada. No, you can't come … you don't know where I am … no, I can't tell. I have no idea. Somewhere in a deep, dark jungle, Dada …" he broke off and handed the instrument back to Vijay. "There! Hope that satisfies you?"

"NO! You never said what I told you to. Go on, ask them to send the ransom money. Immediately! You want to live … tell them that! You fear you will be killed … if they don't respond at once. Understand?"

Vijay was terse and angry as he repeated his instructions before handing the phone back to Manas.

"D … d … don't worry, Papa! No, Mamma, don't cry … I … I will be alright," Manas's voice shook as he spoke into the instrument once more. Champa knew he must be trying to soothe his anxious and upset parents at the other end. She could well understand the trauma that the family was passing through. "Yes, Mamma, I am f … fine …" He was saying when the line went dead.

"So you won't do what we tell you to?" shouted Vijay losing his temper at the boy's stubbornness, "Plead … not alleviate their anxieties. We want to instil fear in their hearts. Only then will they rush to send the money!"

"What makes you think I will act exactly according to orders? Am I one of your cadres?" asked Manas, sarcastic and openly defiant, though he spoke softly. Champa could sense the wariness in his eyes as he searched Vijay's face for his reaction.

"Say that to the Commander, friend. I am going to call him." Flinging the words threateningly at him Vijay abruptly walked out of the room.

Champa was dismayed to see the patient's defiant attitude. She knew it could lead to swift punishment for the young man. It seemed to her that he did not understand the danger he was in and hurried closer to warn him before he made it worse. "Shh … don't refuse! Just do what they say. Do you want to die?" she hissed, lips close to his ears, her voice full of concern.

Manas raised thick straight lashes revealing eyes that were red and suddenly moist at the hint of kindness in the girl's voice. His mouth twisted to reveal, just for a flash of a second, the suppressed emotions of terror, stress and anxiety that he was attempting hard to hide under the bravado. He nodded mutely and turned his face away, reluctant to reveal any weakness before the girl.

Champa felt her heart turn over in sympathy towards the poor victim. She wished she could help him, but knew it would be taken as gross indiscipline and would be followed with some dire punishment, perhaps the worst that was possible. She dared not even think about it.

She heard the steps and at once left the bedside to busy herself with bandages and scissors. The next moment Bhaskar strode in, Vijay at his heels. Champa looked up fearfully, wondering what lay in store for the stubborn prisoner. To her surprise she found that the Commander had a smile on his usually stern face.

"Dear IIT-Harvard boy, you must follow our instructions. Haven't you learnt any discipline at those famous institutions?" asked Bhaskar, sounding amused, his tone that of a professor admonishing one of his students.

"Yes, Sir. I did. But what must I do?" Champa was relieved to find that Manas was acting on her advice and maintaining his cool.

"Ring up your people. Tell them they must send the promised ransom immediately. That is what we expect you to say, dear boy. Don't you see, otherwise there is a strong chance their precious son will be eliminated? See?" said Bhaskar, sounding absolutely amenable and reasonable, like a kindly teacher.

"But send the ransom where? Have they been told?"

"Of course. I have given them detailed instructions. They must follow them. Soon! Understand?" Bhaskar's eyes, now gone cold, seemed to pierce into the boy's.

"Alright. Where is my phone? Can I have it back?" Manas seemed to recapitulate.

Bhaskar handed the phone over to the boy. For several minutes Manas fiddled with the mobile, before attempting to ring up, only to give up in frustration, for the instrument would not work. The connection was broken, all communication cut. Suppressing the slight flicker of satisfaction that gleamed in his eyes, he handed the phone back to the Commander. "I can't reach them. The phone is not ... working ... something seems to be wrong," he commented, shrugging his shoulders.

Bhaskar stared at him, his black eyes turning darker in suspicion though he refrained from passing any comment. "Alright, we'll try later.

The sooner you contact them the better for you, see?" His tone was cold and menacing.

"I can't help it … it isn't working," repeated Manas, looking helpless and returning Bhaskar's searching gaze with an innocent expression in his eyes.

"You seem like an intelligent boy," conceded the Commander finally, his voice now relaxed, "You did not tell me, which branch of engineering did you take up?"

"Mechanical."

"Myself, I am a professor of physics. You and I will have a longer talk later. We'll discuss a few things. In the meantime you must contact your people. It is very important for you, you know that, don't you?" asked Bhaskar, his voice hard. His eyes searched the boy's face intently. Manas nodded, his face blank and expressionless. "I'm warning you, understand?" The older man's voice was icy, his eyes penetrating. He ended the interview by turning around briskly and marching out of the shack.

Vijay had remained behind, perhaps at the Commander's behest. He approached the patient again, this time with a friendly smile. "You should be happy … the Commander seems to be impressed by you," he said, "He likes intelligent, bright young men, being a professor in his earlier life. In our organisation we can do with talent … in fact we need well qualified youth. But if you don't listen to him … " his voice trailed off. They had heard some sounds outside. Champa jumped and stared at the door. "They're back!" she cried. Vijay left his sentence mid-air and rushed out, shouting, "You're right! They're back from their raid! Sudhir and the others! Let's go and see!"

"I'm coming too!" cried Champa, leaving Manas gaping in surprise at their sudden exit as she followed Vijay out through the door.

The excitement the two felt soon vanished when they saw the grim, unmoving group that waited outside the Commander's door. "What … what's happening?" Champa whispered. Her steps slowed down in astonishment. There was none of the jubilance that would have been expected at the return of a triumphant group of jungle guerrillas. Instead the girls and boys standing there were silent and glum. Their eyes remained fixed on their feet and their rifles and guns pointed downwards. The straight, proud figures that had left with such confidence earlier were now limp, weighed down with a heavy hand that pointed clearly towards a humiliating defeat. Champa found Munia standing alone in the far corner, the uniform on her bent back and sagging form all torn and muddy. Her hair had come loose and fell over her cheek in thick, untidy strands. With one hand she rubbed her eyes and with the other tried to push the hair off her cheeks. Her eyes were downcast but there was no mistaking the lines of tragedy and grief on her face. Something terrible had happened.

Champa crept close to her friend and caught her arm. "What is it, Munia? What happened?" she asked nervously, alarm bells ringing in her mind.

"They … they were there … the police. They attacked and surrounded us from all sides. We just managed to escape, but with losses …"

"And Sudhir? Where is he?" asked Champa anxiously.

"Shot through the head. Dead. They are bringing him … you know we don't leave our dead …" answered Munia in a calm, toneless voice, "He is coming on a stretcher. The handsome soldier who marched so smartly and gallantly … he is returning on others' shoulders. He was so brave. He saved the rest of us … me … got killed himself."

Champa could feel her legs weaken. But she knew she must be strong for her friend's sake. She steadied herself and stroked the hand that rested in hers, one arm holding the girl close. She was the only one who really understood how heartbroken the girl was. She tightened her embrace. Munia remained stiff and grave, but Champa's heart ached and she desperately wanted to cry for her.

26

Vijay Lall

His friend was dead, killed in the raid by the guerrilla squad. Vijay's heart wept in unbearable pain. His mind refused to accept the fact, though he went, stoically, through the formalities that followed as his closest and only friend was consigned to the flames with all the honour and respect a martyr's death commanded. The Commander, shocked and full of anguish at the loss of his favourite follower, ordered full ceremonial rites for the valiant fighter. Inspiring speeches were given about the courageous youth who had performed the ultimate sacrifice for the cause he believed in. Vijay spoke briefly but his speech, full of the sincere, heartfelt emotion that only a very close friend could feel, moved his listeners to tears.

Sudhir was the hero, the martyr, shining way above the two others who died that day. Bhaskar hailed him as a luminous star, the brightest in the firmament, inspiring and motivating them all. "Let us learn lessons from this great revolutionary's life. He left the luxuries he was used to in the city, left his wealthy lawyer father, left his riches and home ... why do you think he did it? Let me tell you, he left everything so that he could devote himself to working for poor villagers such as you. For the sake of people like you who live in abject poverty, for you who have no land, for you whose land has been taken away and for you who toil so hard in the fields yet are left with nothing to eat! Yes, he gave up everything he had–for your sake. We will not allow his sacrifice to go in vain. We will continue our fight against those who exploit us. Those who become fat on our lands, our forests and our labour–they must be destroyed. Removed from this earth, completely annihilated, only then can we think of building a new world, a just society. An equal society. Come! Let us take a vow today. We will not rest until we avenge the killing of a fellow traveller, the death of a brilliant young man who gave up everything he had to join us here in the jungle! Will you vow to continue the fight?"

A deafening roar of approval rose from those who had gathered on the sand near the nullah. It was late evening and the stars, spilling out into the black sky, smiled their approval, twinkling down on the excited crowd below. "Yes, yes, we will fight!" the cry struck the rocky hills and echoed and re-echoed, reverberating again and again, strongly underlining the crowd's call. Vijay felt hot tears prickle his eyes for the Commander's call had moved him greatly. He wanted to pick up a gun immediately and rush off. He wished to avenge his friend's death, to uphold the ideals Sudhir and he had together taken up that day long ago, when both had vowed to fight against injustice, corruption and inequality. "Don't grieve for him, act according to his wishes. That will be your greatest tribute to him," thought Vijay and repeated it to himself. It made him feel a little better.

Vijay's mind could not dwell on any other subject except the loss of his friend. Even the thought of being beside the girl he loved, of being fortunate enough to have his love returned, failed to divert him. Happiness lay only in the company of the one man who appreciated and acknowledged the greatness of his friend–Bhaskar. The Commander grieved as much as he did. He was as much in need of his presence. The two comrades spent long hours together, silently sharing the grief they both felt.

"It is time we became active ... do something about the loss," concluded Bhaskar at last. "We lost a most valuable, precious life. We must get to the bottom of the mystery. How did it happen? How is it that the police got the better of us? We had planned it so perfectly. There was no reason for things to go wrong."

"I fully agree, Sir, we must!" cried Vijay wholeheartedly. The commander was right, they had planned for days and every eventuality had been anticipated and taken care of. Then why?

"I entrust you with the responsibility. Find out what happened. Talk to the men and women who were in the raid. We must understand, so that it does not happen again," ordered Bhaskar.

"Yes Sir," said Vijay, "I will find out exactly what happened that night."

He felt duty bound to solve the mystery and discover the reasons for his friend's death. It occurred to Vijay that Munia was one person who could give a good account of the tragic incidents that took place that day. He searched for the girl but she was not in her shack. Even Champa, busy in the sick room, did not know where she was. At last Vijay found her sitting, sad and forlorn, on a rock on the sand beside the nullah, not far from the place where he himself had spent those pleasant moments earlier with Champa. She raised large, tearful eyes towards him when he approached her.

"Comrade Munia, you have had a terrible experience. But can you tell me what happened that night? Were you caught by the police?"

Munia's eyes glistened with the tears that she was trying to hold back. Words would not come to her lips. "Were you ambushed? Or did they attack after you were already inside?" he enquired gently.

For long, tense moments the girl struggled to calm herself and find her voice. Then the words came tumbling out, as if a dam had broken. She sobbed and spoke at the same time, her words unclear and difficult to understand. "See, Comrade, th … this is where we sat that night! The day we walked to the village for Karama! Such f … fun it was … who was to know that he'd be gone just a few days later? Look, even the moon hides its grieving face behind those dark clouds. That day it shone so bright … " she mumbled on for some time.

Vijay listened, astonished, for he had not realised that she was so seriously and deeply interested in his friend. He had presumed that she enjoyed Sudhir's company for the amusing, charming ways he had, especially with girls. He let her pour out her feelings, a gentle, sympathetic ear turned towards her. Once she was done he softly prompted her. "And then … when you went with the squad to the *chouki* … ?"

"Oh yes! I was so excited. He was, too. We waited outside, crouching low behind the bushes, so as not to be seen. And after it was dark … it must have been about one in the morning … we sneaked out and crawled towards the *chouki*, a small, two roomed house. We could see its yellow walls gleaming … a soft low light from a *dhibri* inside showed us the way. It was too easy … we should have guessed it then. Instead we felt so good; triumphant … we thought we had made it! Two or three men slept there on chairs, their weapons standing close by. They woke up, but faced with our guns, they could only stare back at us. In astonishment, we thought at the time. But it was not so. As we gathered up their arms and ammunition … we heard the shots …"

Vijay could understand the rest. The police had surrounded the *chouki* and advanced upon them.

"They were so many it was difficult to count … firing began immediately from both sides, but soon we knew it was no use. They were too many …" continued Munia.

"Run, all of you. Escape, wherever you can! I will hold them … Go!" Sudhir had yelled, pushing Munia and a few others out through a door at the back. He had caught hold of a policeman and yelled, "I will kill this man. Let my men out!" This had created confusion in the police ranks for a few moments. Taking advantage of it some of Sudhir's soldiers, including her, had managed to escape, explained Munia. She had scrambled through the bushes and somehow managed to flee.

"But how long could he hold on? The firing from both sides continued for more than an hour. There were too many … I hid in a ditch and waited for the others, especially for Comrade Sudhir. We were surrounded by fierce firing from all sides … still, many of us managed to flee. All because of Comrade Sudhir. But he couldn't save himself! Two others who stayed by his side were killed too."

Vijay frowned. There was something he could not understand in her story. The policemen were well prepared to face the attack; despite the secrecy and all their plans to take them by surprise.

"But how did they know?" Vijay asked, "Obviously they were well aware that the *chouki* was going to be raided. But how, I wonder."

"I have no idea. I only know he is no more, my dashing soldier, my brave hero …!" cried Munia, with a fresh burst of tears. She broke down and had nothing more to say. Vijay pounced on the important fact that had emerged–that the enemy was fully prepared. They knew. But then … who let out their plans?

He had to find out. The grieving girl was in no mood to say more but he probed and questioned gently. "Try and remember, comrade, you must. Don't you want to know how you and your friends fell into the trap? Somebody, somewhere, must have talked, don't you think so?"

Munia nodded. He could see that his words had set off a train of thoughts in her mind. "Think, comrade!" persisted Vijay, "Who let out our plans? D'you think it was any one from your squad?"

"No, of course not. We have been trained to keep secrets. We quite understand it can be fatal if plans leak out. No, no, it could never be one of us!" cried the girl emphatically. Vijay could see that he had succeeded in diverting her mind. She was thinking hard. She rubbed her eyes with both her hands and frowned deeply. What was she thinking about? Patiently he waited, for he knew she was trying to remember something.

"That day, comrade, when we celebrated at the village, we had all taken a wee bit too much. Hadn't we? And Comrade Sudhir was in a specially good mood." Munia smiled at the recollection. "I remember he was boasting … I will show these corrupt policemen! For years they have troubled helpless and poor people. Now is the time to punish them. Yes, he was looking forward to the raid. To confronting men he felt were the worst kind of human beings … people who misused their power and office to make money!"

Vijay could well imagine how Sudhir, talkative, casual and free with words, would have boasted about the coming raid. Could he have slipped out the information inadvertently, while lightheaded from the *mahua* drink? It could be. Someone in the village heard and informed the police, conjectured Vijay. It was an idea that would have to be followed through. Maybe he should go to the tribal village to make a few enquiries.

Before embarking upon the mission Vijay decided to inform Bhaskar about the conclusion he had reached. He walked back to the Commander's room. He was there, the map before him. How often had they sat, discussing plans and possibilities together, the map spread out before them! The older man was a picture of tragic despair. Vijay wanted to rush to comfort him. But the man looked up and rubbed his eyes. "Yes, what is it? Have you found out anything?" he asked, rolling up the map and putting it aside. He raised his eyes expectantly.

Vijay was sorry. There was not much to report, except to say that the police was well aware of the coming raid. Perhaps someone from the village had picked up some hints from their own people, blurted out in a weak moment. His words made the Commander sit up straight, his eyes alert. "You are right. That is probably what happened. I don't blame our people for having their bit of fun. And if they let slip our plans inadvertently we can excuse them. What cannot be tolerated is that a villager should take advantage of the mistake and report the matter to the police. I will not allow it. We don't want any informers around. What will they report next? No, no! It will have to be stopped!" he said vehemently.

Vijay nodded, realising that the Commander was correct. He waited for him to continue. "Arrange a People's Court. Bring the villagers there. We'll interrogate them. Find out who is in contact with the police. We will not allow the informer to get away."

Vijay' heart sank. He knew what it meant. The villagers would be tortured and abused until the 'guilty' confessed. And, to ensure that none would ever dare to contact the police in future, an example would be made to put fear into their hearts. He longed to avenge his friend's death. Yet, the thought of innocent villagers being tortured along with the guilty ones distressed him. The inquisition would be followed by the ultimate punishment–death, he well knew. He could only pray that the person actually guilty was discovered and punished, the hammer of death not strike the innocent.

Bhaskar, watching him carefully, understood the doubts and hesitation that passed through Vijay's mind. He gave a grim smile and rose to tap him on the shoulder. "Don't forget, Comrade, he was your dearest and closest friend. The person you turned to when you were in trouble, the one who cheered you when you were sad. Come on, for your friend's sake, learn to be tough!"

Vijay nodded dumbly and turned his face aside. He quickly brushed away the moisture that had filled his eyes at the mention of Sudhir. The gesture did not escape the commander's sharp eyes. He gave a short laugh and thumped his back. "Alright, alright, I understand you are already in pain at the loss. I don't want to add to your suffering. If you don't want to, don't. I'll ask someone else to carry out the job. Or wait. I will go myself! Just make all the arrangements," said Bhaskar in a soft, sympathetic tone, which was quite unlike him.

A variety of emotions surged through Vijay's heart–gratitude at the understanding displayed by the leader, devotion towards an elder who cared for his feelings, and admiration towards one who had the courage and strength to act when he himself was too soft to do so, to avenge his friend's death. Full of gratitude and humility, he impulsively bent to touch his leader's feet.

Bhaskar pulled him up and patted his shoulders. "We have another important matter on our hands. What happened about our demand for ransom? Nothing has been heard from the boy's people. What is happening?"

Vijay had to confess that all was silent on that front.

"You take care of it. I will see to the informers," instructed the Commander. Vijay was relieved he had got an alternate task to carry out. He would talk to Manas and persuade him not to delay the matter anymore. If he wanted to stay alive he must see that ransom for his release was provided immediately. It was up to him to manage it somehow.

Vijay stayed away from the village. Later, he learnt that two men had been beheaded for acting as informers to the police. Their bodies were thrown into the stream that trickled down from the tribal village upstream towards their camp. The water in the nullah, usually a muddy green, was coloured a pale pink the next morning. Vijay saw it bubble past through the rocks and the sand and knew that the deed was done.

The Commander had done what he could not do–punish those responsible for the loss of his closest friend. The heavy burden of grief lifted and his heart felt lighter. The leader had taught him a valuable lesson–it did not pay to be too soft.

27

"You can do what you like. I can't help you," muttered Manas when Vijay approached him later. The colour was back on his face and pain was no longer reflected in his eyes, noticed Vijay. He glanced at Champa who was hovering around the patient, every bit the nurse she seemed to have become. He found the air of professional authority that she had assumed rather amusing. It made him smile as she warned him, in a low voice, not to be harsh on the patient for he was still very much a sick man. "I know, I know," he mumbled, "But I must do my job."

"Go ahead!" offered Manas who had heard the whispered exchange, "I can take it. What d'you want?"

"We still haven't heard from your people. Why?" Vijay emulated the Commander in keeping his voice gentle.

"No idea! But if I know my grandfather he is not the type to succumb to pressure tactics. Not even when it involves me," explained Manas.

"What about your parents? Aren't they anxious to get you out as soon as possible?"

"Well, they will not act on their own. They respect grandfather … if my guess is right, they must have reported the matter to the police."

"Even though Commander Sir has specifically warned them not do so?" Vijay asked sharply, sternly. How could the Gupta family defy his leader, didn't they realise that their son's life was in grave danger? How could they trifle with the Commander's wishes?

By now Manas had regained his strength and therefore his courage and spirit of defiance. He gave a derisive laugh. "He is your Commander, not theirs! They don't have to obey him!"

"But it is all about their son's life, not the Commander's!" Vijay replied in the same tone. "Don't you see the danger you face? We can execute you, as the Commander told you the other day."

"I know," the boy's voice had turned low and grave. For several moments his eyes focused on Vijay's face which he seemed to be examining closely. "Why do you do it?" he burst out at last, "Why do you indulge in violence, kill people, attack the police, blow up roads and bridges ... why? I see that you are a young man about my own age, maybe well-educated ... yet you live in the jungle, killing and destroying ... why?" His words came out in a rush as if he feared that if he stopped to breathe he may not have the courage to continue.

Vijay stared at him, astonished. He had never heard anyone question his leaders and their policies. He had arrived there, already convinced that the Maoist philosophy was the answer to the people's problems. Sudhir was his friend, philosopher and guide and he had blindly and trustingly followed his advice. The Commander had but to sow the seeds for his ideas to find ready acceptance, taking deep roots in his mind.

Here was someone who questioned the beliefs he had come to hold so dear. He shook his head, puzzled, wondering how best to explain his ideology to an unbeliever, thinking of the most effective way to convey his ideas. It was Champa who blurted out a reply in her simple, direct way. "To stop the rich from troubling us!" she cried out emphatically in a heated voice, "You have no idea about the poor ... what they must go through!"

It gave Vijay an opening to begin his explanation. "I don't have to answer ... but since you ask ... let me tell you. For centuries the rich have exploited the poor. But there are some good, unselfish, thinking people who wish to make their lives better. They care for the unfortunate; their hearts bleed for the hungry and they want to improve their condition. They do not care for their own comfort, understand? They are prepared to spend their lives in the jungles, trying to help those who have no voice. What would you know of their sacrifice?" asked Vijay, his voice growing bitter as he remembered the sacrifice made by his dearest friend, Sudhir, "You are so used to your own comfortable life you become blind towards the problems of others."

"I see," said Manas in a serious voice, "And by living in the jungle and denying themselves the comforts of the rich, these unselfish, thinking guys will save enough money to give the have-nots?"

It took Vijay some seconds to grasp the sarcasm behind the remark. "Of course not!" he declared, "Our aim is to fight the bourgeois, the rich, those who exploit the down-trodden. We want to get rid of them altogether, create a totally different world–one where there is no exploitation, no inequality, where everybody is at the same level ..."

"Ah! Utopia! I understand!" interrupted Manas, an amused smile on his lips.

"You do not believe us!" The glint of laughter she noticed in his eyes made Champa flare up, "You try to make fun of us! But let me tell you ... about the miseries we must face! I ... my father's land was taken by the factory owner. Oh yes, he gave us some money. But how long would it last? Babuji was given work by the factory people ... but the payment was never enough, and never in time. We had to keep borrowing to pay the *bania*. You don't know how humiliating it was! The insults we poor must suffer!" she ended accusingly.

"Hush, Champa! We all have our problems. Didn't I tell you how my own relatives grabbed my property with the connivance of the concerned officers? It was so unfair!" added Vijay.

"Everything is unfair in this world. The stories I have heard! From Usha, Munia, Ganga and other girls. It will open your eyes, Shri Manas Guptaji!" declared Champa.

"But violence is not the way to solve the problems of the poor," protested Manas, "There are rules, laws, courts and judges. The government has started so many schemes to help the underprivileged."

"It is all eyewash. Government money goes into the pockets of the corrupt. Rules and laws are made to be broken by the rich and the powerful ... don't we know it? No, there is no other solution.

The haves, with their greedy, grabbing ways must be destroyed, completely annihilated, before policies to benefit the needy can be made!" declared Vijay.

"There is another solution. Vote out the government which does not help the poor. Bring in the people who will," argued Manas.

"Come on. You know they are all alike. Just replacing one set with another will not help. The whole system has to be done away with. Revolution. That's what we need. Revolution! And that is what we will achieve!" cried Vijay with an air of finality. He had had enough of the immature argument being put forward by the young man. He did it just to evade the important issue of ransom.

"Are you leaving?" asked Champa, following him to the door, "But he hasn't answered your question!"

"I must report it to Commander Sir." Vijay explained. He gave Champa a tender look and gently touched her hand. She held his eyes and whispered, "Don't go. How I wish you could stay with me forever."

"I will, one day," whispered Vijay, before walking out. When he reported the conversation to the leader he was surprised to find him looking amused. "You are right. The boy is ignorant and immature. No wonder … leading a sheltered life surrounded by rich relatives– he has never seen the other side, never experienced the helpless despair of the poor. What does he know of the real world?"

"What must we do? If his relatives have informed the police …?"

"If they have … you well know what must be done. He won't live to see another day. That's all," Bhaskar's voice turned hard and uncompromising.

"Yes, Commander Sir," said Vijay with a smart salute. He turned to leave, but the leader called him back, "Wait, comrade Vijay. We will execute him when the time comes. But in the meanwhile … I would like to explain the Maoist ideology to him. He is an intelligent young man. As I said before, we need talented, qualified young men in our organisation. Why don't you leave some of our literature with him? He might find it interesting."

"Yes Sir." Vijay, who never questioned his leader, hurried to get the books and documents. Bhaskar himself picked out the material he wanted Manas to read. "Here, take this. It will give him better insight into important issues. There are many intelligent and educated young men in big cities who believe in us and in our philosophy. Students from JNU, for example, and from other colleges and universities. They may not join us here in the jungle but they help us in several other ways."

"You are right, Sir," said Vijay.

"And comrade, we must get the ransom. But we cannot contact the Guptas from here every time. The police will trace our call. You must go to the city now and ring up from somewhere. I leave it to you."

Vijay thought for some time and then looked up. Why not go to the city with Champa, who had helped him carry out a successful mission earlier? When he sought the leader's permission, Bhaskar smiled. "I presume the girl's presence is necessary. Not only for your mission, but also for the company she will provide, isn't it, comrade?"

"Yes, Commander Sir," mumbled Vijay, lowering his eyes shyly, like a girl's, and nodding gravely.

28

The twosome set out for the city the next morning, dressed in civilian clothes that would not attract attention. Vijay looked a typical city youth in a natty, mustard coloured T-shirt and jeans. Champa, in borrowed feathers consisting of a colourful sari and matching blouse looked pretty, with her long hair loose on her back. They looked very much a couple in love, which they actually were, recently married, which they were not, out on a jaunt to the city. One of the comrades gave them a lift on a motorbike, and dropped them just outside the city. They looked like a couple from the village, out on a pleasure trip to the town. They walked into the crowded, dark hall of the cinema showing the latest Hindi movie. Combining pleasure with work, they watched the romantic scenes in a film embellished with fast music and sexy dances.

Vijay noticed the obvious delight that brightened Champa's face. She had never seen a movie before. "I can't believe it," he said wonderingly. He caressed her cheeks in the darkness and pushed an arm against her soft, yielding breast, "You've really never seen a movie?"

"Who would take me? My father had neither time nor money, and my mother … oh no, never!" She gently pushed his arm away and instead caught the hand that was touching her cheeks.

"I watched so many films with Sudhir," mumbled Vijay, remembering his college days, his eyes misting over at thought of his friend's exit from his life. Pangs of grief and pain crept afresh into his heart at memory of those days not so long ago. How could he sit here and enjoy a girl's company, watch a movie when he had lost his dear friend? Guilt, sorrow and regret filled his heart. He felt suffocated; the song the hero belted out seemed to pierce sharply through his brain. With a suppressed cry of anguish he covered his ears with both hands and closed his eyes.

"What is it? What happened?" Champa, absorbed in the film, reluctantly disengaged her attention and turned towards him.

"Sudhir. I wish I hadn't come. How could I? It was a silly plan. I wish the Commander had stopped me," cried Vijay in a tortured voice.

Champa quickly took both his hands in hers. "It is alright, comrade. Life must go on. You must carry on, do your duty. I am sure that is what Comrade Sudhir would have wanted too, don't you think?" She whispered, trying to comfort him. She laid her head against his shoulder and affectionately stroked the back of his hands.

"Maybe you are right," Vijay responded with a sigh. Though he could not enjoy the film any longer, the warmth of the girl's body pressing against his in the darkness, the loving touch of her fingers on his hands, aroused a tender, gentle passion in his own. He laid his head on hers and felt the soft, silky strands of her hair caress his face, soothing away the pain.

Soon the movie was over. It was time to finish the task assigned to them. In the crowded foyer of the cinema hall Vijay located a phone placed on the counter of the food stall. "Can I make a call?" he asked the man serving the customers, "Here, take this money!" He handed over a note that was far in excess of the actual cost for a call. Quickly he picked up the receiver and dialled the number he had got from Manas' mobile and committed to memory. The man at the counter shrugged his shoulders, and, without a word, pocketed the money and turned to his customers. His eyes fell on Champa. She flashed the man a charming smile and asked for a packet of Kurkure and a glass of lassi. A smirk on his lips, the man became busy serving her, the young, attractive customer.

Vijay grabbed the opportunity. He snatched up the receiver. He spoke low so that none would hear. He quickly muttered, "Who is it?"

"Ram Prakash Gupta," answered a voice.

"Oh, Dadaji? I've a message for you. We had asked for something for your grandson. He is with us. You did not bring it as promised. It must come soon or …"

"Who is it? Who's speaking?" interrupted a sharp voice.

"Same place, same time, as instructed earlier. Sunday, understand? This Sunday … pucca, or … you know what'll happen to the boy! He will be beheaded! And if you talk to anyone … the police … too bad!" hissed Vijay into the phone.

"Hello, hello, who are you?" voices snapped back but Vijay banged the phone shut. "Have you finished, Champa? Come, let's go, shall we?" He flung an arm protectively around his girl and escorted her outside. It was a relief to get it over with. Hissing dramatically into the phone like the villains he had just watched in the movies gave him a strange feeling. He certainly did not wish to seem as crude and cruel as those onscreen.

Just as the two, satisfied with the success of their mission, were about to step out they heard a shout, "*Arre*, it is Champa! Champa, where have you been?"

Vijay felt the shoulders of his companion stiffen. Her steps halted. He turned to her. He saw she looked startled; her face had paled. Champa soon managed to recover her poise and turn a smiling visage towards the couple who faced her. "Gouri, what a surprise! What are you doing here? And how are you?" She caught the girl's hand and hugged her in delight.

Gouri stepped back to stare at her old friend in surprise. "I am well enough, Champa. But you? Where have you been? I learnt that you had disappeared, gone away. Where? The whole village has been talking about it. Where were you?"

"Umm … m! I was … am … with him. Vijay, my friend," murmured Champa quickly, pushing her young man towards the two others.

"*Accha*! And this is my .... *Him*!" giggled Gouri, pulling a lanky youth forward. "And he? Is he your … ?" She looked curiously towards Vijay who had become busy studying the film posters on the wall.

"N … no!" stammered Champa, "I told you, he is a friend," she repeated, wondering what the girl would say to that. She had never expected to meet anyone she knew, for her village friends hardly ever visited the town. To meet Gouri, of all people, was a shock she was still trying to get over. She was relieved to see that the answer was accepted without any further questions. "But what are you doing here, Gouri, so far from home?"

"He wanted to celebrate," said Gouri shyly, patting her gently rounded stomach. "God has been so kind to us. You know … there's to be another member in our family soon."

"*Sach me*, Gouri … oh, is that so? Lucky you! When is the happy event?" asked Champa, looking relieved at the change in the subject.

"In three months from today. Soon," said Gouri, "And before it became … difficult to go anywhere, *he* wished to take me to see a *fillum*! That's how I am here."

Vijay gently tugged at Champa's arm, making urgent signs to her to hurry up. Champa knew it was dangerous for them to stay there so long. She turned away, "*Achcha* Gouri, *ab chalein*? I must leave," she said.

"I met Jhumki some days ago. She is also getting married," eager to give her all the news Gouri chatted on, "All our friends are getting married, one after another. Oh, and I wonder if you know, your father is back home. So Jhumki told me. Does he know about him?" she gestured towards Vijay who was trying to pull Champa's arm, whispering something urgently.

"Come on, it is late! We have a long way to go," mumbled Vijay turning towards the exit gate.

But Champa was gaping at her friend, her face a mixture of surprise, delight and wonder. "Back? Are you sure, Gouri? Is my father home? When did he come?" She caught the girl's arm and shook it in great excitement. "Oh, I must go home! I must meet him!" she cried.

"Yes, yes, we will, Champa. Let's go now. We have to go to the market also to buy a few things!" insisted Vijay pulling her away. "Namaste. We will meet again," he firmly told the other two and hurriedly walked away, almost dragging the girl in his haste.

"*Baap re*, that girl talked so much! We must get out of here fast, before we meet someone who recognises me!" said Vijay, as soon as they were out of earshot. "People may not know you, but I may be recognised." He covered his mouth and half his face with a scarf he had brought with him. Luckily it was getting dark.

Reluctantly, the girl followed him as he led her past the honking cars, the cycles and the rickshaws that crowded the main road. With the shops, full of crockery, fruit, garments, toys, plastic goods and sundry other goods hugging the side paths, it was difficult to walk. Somehow they zigzagged their way through the traffic, the pedestrians and the litter that lay on the road and reached the medicine shop for which Commander Rekha had given them a list. Other items of daily use which could not be found in the forest also needed to be bought. The two hastened through the shopping chores.

With Champa all decked up in a sari by his side, Vijay had a taste of the domestic bliss that could be his in the future. In spite of his nervous haste he found the time to lead the girl to the bangle shop and buy her a set of bright red bangles. It was thrilling to give her the little gift and to watch the blushing delight that spread on her face at the sight of the bangles.

At the crossing they found a rickshaw to take them to the spot where the motorbike awaited them. Once they had stepped into the rickshaw and were well on their way Vijay remembered his responsibilities.

"Finished at last!" Vijay breathed in relief, "You shouldn't have talked to that girl. She was asking all kinds of questions. It is not good for us."

"But did you hear? Babuji is back! I want to meet him. He must be so worried. He doesn't know where I am, I must tell him," cried Champa. She had not got over her excitement.

"Yes, yes, you will. But not now. We are here on a job, remember? And we must hurry back into the jungle before we are seen," Vijay reminded her.

Champa nodded silently. She was thoughtful and still beside him but he could sense the disturbance that lay just below the calm surface. Her hands in her lap were clenched tight in tension and her body felt straight and stiff against his own.

As the rickshaw drove along a lonely, quiet road with high walls on either side, Vijay pointed to a yellow and red building inside. "Look, Champa, that's the school I went to, rather, lived in! After Babuji died my mother got a job here. We lived in the hostel where she was the Warden!" He was thankful that it was a quiet area with hardly any people on the road otherwise he could have been seen. They soon passed the residential area with its silent, enclosed bungalows behind their high walls. He pointed out the old, sprawling home where his father had resided. "And see … that house with the yellow walls, with all that land around it? It was my grandfather's. My father also lived there." And he told his companion how he and his mother had been dispossessed of their share in their grandfather's property. Champa, who had dwelt in her two-roomed thatch and mud hut all her life stared wonderingly at the grand house, her eyes round in awe. "Lucky you, to live there," she enviously murmured.

"Yes, but then we had to leave it," Vijay reminded her. "And look, that is Sudhir's lawyer father's mansion! Isn't it a fine place? Think! He left that luxurious palace for the jungle camp. What a great man! And there, that gracious old building is our old College. Sudhir and I were there in the same class!"

Vijay found Champa listening to him with wide, wondering eyes. As they passed the main police headquarters she abruptly turned her head the other way. He remembered she had mentioned something about some terrible incident that had taken place there, though she had not elaborated further. Now she spoke softly though bitterly, "I agree with the comrades. Just because Babuji was poor, weak and helpless they could keep him in jail for so long. And attempted to do what they did with his daughter. If he had been educated and wealthy, would they have dared?"

"Never!" agreed Vijay wholeheartedly. He took her hand gently in his and spoke soothingly about other subjects to help divert the agitated girl. After a long time he felt her relax at last, to his relief. By now they had reached the motorbike parked at the edge of the forest. Its driver took them as far as he could into the jungle. The rest of the distance to the hideout had to be covered on foot. As they walked through the now dark night, Champa snuggled closer to Vijay.

"I am so glad you are here, comrade. I can talk to you. You help take my pains away. Will you always comfort me when I am sad?" she asked, her voice soft and pleading.

He put his arm gently and protectively around her. "Of course, my dear. We must stay together for each other," he tenderly whispered.

"I am so happy Babuji has returned. But how can I go back? I have you now. I want to be with you, always, forever," she said, looking up into his face with eyes turned large and luminous.

The glance made Vijay tremble; he felt his whole body melt into nothingness. Quite in a daze, he nodded, without a word in answer, though he gently tightened his arms around the slender body. "And I with you!" he mumbled a few seconds later. He fumbled in the dark to take out the box of bangles that he had bought her. Holding her hand gently in his he pushed the bangles onto her wrist. "Let's promise each other we'll stay together always. These bangles are proof of our everlasting love."

Champa jingled the bangles on her wrists, breaking the spell that had wrapped their two selves together in a magic cocoon. She laughed happily. Then she became silent again. "I want to see my father and brother … so much it hurts," she said wistfully. "But the thought of separation from you is even more painful. And I have come to like my new life too."

Vijay, in a blissful mood himself, laughed and said teasingly, "Make up your mind, girl. You can't have both."

"I think I already have!" Champa's voice rang out joyfully in the dark. She threw her arms about him and shouted, her voice ecstatic, "You!" she cried out loud and her voice echoed against the black hills again and again, "You! Yes, you! It's you I want to be with!" she cried. "Hush," Vijay put his hand across her mouth and drew her face closer to his.

They still had a long distance to walk but the two, wrapped in each other, forgot the whole world as they took their own time to complete the journey that night.

29

Bhaskar Reddy

It was a shock to Bhaskar to see a mission fail, a raid simple enough not to require any great planning for success. It was difficult to explain the failure, considering that years of experience in carrying out raids, ambushes and attacks were behind him. It was an even greater shock to lose someone as talented and committed as Sudhir. Bhaskar realised he had come to depend a lot on the enthusiastic and energetic young man who was the only one who could question him fearlessly, helping him to clear his own doubts at times. The long, animated discussions that they had often had in the evenings had been intellectually stimulating. He wished he could continue those sessions.

When Vijay returned from the city and arrived to report to him Bhaskar looked up eagerly, "So comrade, you are back? Did you contact the Guptas?"

"Yes, Sir." Vijay gave him an account of his trip and waited for further instructions.

"Did you give them the time and place for handing over the ransom?"

"Yes, Sir, I did. They must do it this Sunday," replied Vijay.

"Good. Our men will be present at the spot and inform us as soon as the party contacts them."

"Yes, Sir," replied Vijay.

"If they still do not respond the boy will lose his life. It will be tragic. An intelligent and qualified student will be lost in the prime of his youth."

"Yes, Sir. You are right, Sir," answered Vijay.

"The country needs technical professionals. The Party appreciates them and would like them to serve the people instead of wasting their talent by joining a capitalistic company," continued Bhaskar in a regretful tone.

"Certainly, Sir!" agreed Vijay, nodding his head.

Bhaskar wished the lad would say something more besides meekly agreeing to whatever he said. Sudhir would certainly have been more articulate and forthcoming. A lively discussion would have followed. No doubt Vijay was pleasant and eager to carry out his every command. But he never had any opinions to contribute unless specifically asked to do so. Even then he was so diffident about expressing his own views.

A student like Manas, however, with an independent, free thinking mind, would be an asset to the Party, provided of course, that his mind could be converted to Bhaskar's way of thinking. A good replacement to the talent that he had so unfortunately lost!

Meanwhile, he must make do with the material that he had. Vijay had to be converted into a more effective revolutionary.

"We did not succeed in the raid. We are still short of ammunition and finance. The ransom has not come either. What do we do?" His aim was to draw out the young man rather than to search for an answer. Bhaskar well knew what must be done. He now searched Vijay's face to see his response.

There was silence in the room for a few minutes.

"Maybe we should carry out another raid, Sir," said Vijay hesitatingly after a few minutes of contemplation.

"Oh no! Not just now. Not so soon after the last one, comrade!" Bhaskar cried vehemently. His eyes shrewdly watched the expression on the other's face, which fell at the rejection of his statement. Vijay did not dare to venture an opinion after this.

Bhaskar lowered his eyelids to hide the triumph in his voice. "No, definitely not! Not another raid." And then he played his card. "But tell you what? Here is a list of contractors working on the roads and the railway line. We must ask them to pay us levy, or we will stop the construction work. Get that levy!"

Vijay jumped to catch the bait. He was ready to do anything now, to please his leader and to make up for his tactless suggestion. Bhaskar felt pleased. Very correctly he had sensed that Vijay was not comfortable participating in activities he considered to be blatantly wrong. The kidnapping and the shooting was reluctantly done, at Sudhir's persuasion, he guessed. Though Vijay was eager to please, his heart was not always in the job assigned to him.

A revolutionary must necessarily be tough. To be effective in his new role Vijay must shed his inhibitions, forget his conscience. Bhaskar nodded grimly. With Sudhir gone, there was just Vijay left as an educated, intelligent and loyal follower. He had to mould the young man into a bold, committed and hardened soldier, ready to fight every battle for the sake of the Party.

"So, comrade, will you do the job?" he asked, watching Vijay's face with narrowed eyes. He saw the struggle on his face, even though he had lowered his eyelids to hide the tension in his mind.

Vijay gulped and set his lips into a firm line. "Yes, Sir. I will. I'll certainly contact the contractor," he said determinedly.

"Excellent, comrade! I knew you would! You may begin with the people constructing the bridge on the NH 33. You know the old one has broken ... a new diversion is being built, along with a new bridge. Here is the name of the company, its engineers and the contractor."

"Yes, Commander Sir," Vijay brought his heels together and saluted the leader. Bhaskar smiled, pleased with himself.

He had forced the youth to stride further down the thorny path–of full commitment as a Maoist. Once he became involved in unlawful activities like extortion, demanding of levy, kidnapping and later, perhaps, killing, it would be difficult for him to return to a normal life. He would have to remain forever a fugitive hiding from law.

Vijay was steadily climbing up the peak to becoming a Maoist, he was glad to note. The youth was certainly malleable and easy to convince. Unlike the stubborn Manas, a tough nut to crack.

Triumphantly, the leader outlined his plan for the operation he wished Vijay to undertake. The two wrote out in bright red the posters that would be put up near the construction site. The spot where the levy was to be handed over and other instructions were given to Vijay who listened carefully and nodded silently from time to time. Then Bhaskar called in three other men who were to work with Vijay and gave them further directions.

Bhaskar turned to the other matter that needed his attention. That Manas boy too had to be indoctrinated, drawn into the fold. He planned to have a long discussion with him. Young men at this age were enthusiastic and idealistic, he well knew, and ready to take up causes. In fact, the Central Committee of the CPI-Maoist planned to expand its base by inducting new members from the cream of society, especially well-educated youth who were dedicated, principled, selfless and hard working. A student who had passed out from the IIT was bound to be intelligent and hard working. His qualifications would be useful to them in modernising their weapons and their technology for land mines, bombs and other material needed for the armed struggle.

"And Comrade," Bhaskar called out as Vijay was about to leave, "I'd like to talk to Manas Gupta before he is sent back home. Is he in better shape now? You may join us in the discussion!"

Manas definitely looked healthier and more comfortable as he sat on the bed, sipping a glass of tea. The girl was there and Bhaskar was quick to notice the glance that passed between her and Vijay as she stood up to greet the visitors.

"Well, young man. How do you feel today?" Bhaskar said in a friendly tone.

"Better, Sir. I hope you will allow me to leave soon …?"

"That depends on your people. As soon as the ransom is received we'll see that you are delivered into their hands safe and sound."

Manas shrugged his shoulders in a careless gesture as if to show that he did not really care.

"I must admit I am impressed by your courage. You are a brave young man," remarked Bhaskar, trying to soften the boy through flattery. "Aren't you scared? We can kill you, you know? That is, if your people don't deliver."

Manas answered again by twisting his lips in a defiant gesture and shrugging his shoulders. "Your decision," he muttered.

"Admirable, truly," nodded Bhaskar, "We need young men like him, don't we, Comrade?" He turned to Vijay for confirmation.

"Yes, Sir. We do." Vijay gave his usual reply.

"But I have no intention of joining the violent bandwagon. I am not impressed, not even by those," Manas indicated the papers and documents lying around him on the bed.

Bhaskar smiled to himself. At least the boy had taken interest, gone through the literature. "I see that you have read our material. I hope you found it of interest?"

"Oh yes," interrupted Manas, "Very. It is a call to act against your own nation, your own people, your own Constitution. You wish to wage a war against your own country!" he raised his voice accusingly.

"Yes. Why not?" asserted Bhaskar, his voice loud and passionate. "If you read those books you will understand. Our aim is to fight for the welfare of the common man. It is a battle for a just and worthy cause. We wish to overthrow the government and usher in a new one. What's wrong with that?"

"Everything's wrong. Your way is not the right way. Look, I have already browsed through these three documents– "Hold High the Bright Red Banner of Marxism-Leninism," "Programme" and "The Strategy and Tactics of Indian Revolution". And I am not impressed … I don't agree with your methods!" declared Manas.

"Well, at least you read them," Bhaskar toned down his voice and smiled.

"Because there was nothing else to do. I thought I might as well utilise the time … find out what makes you guys tick! And let me be frank–I am horrified! Really and truly!" emphasised Manas.

“That is the usual bourgeois reaction. I should have expected it from a capitalist like you. I believe you belong to a very rich business family, one of those who suck the poor to fill your own coffers. I am very disappointed … I thought you would be intelligent enough to understand,” said Bhaskar, deciding to go on the offensive.

“Not only that,” Vijay butted in, his voice agitated, “Didn’t Comrade Sudhir tell us–the family made its riches by selling smuggled coal and spurious liquor … fooling the poor?”

Champa, who had been listening attentively, absorbing the new ideas, decided to join in. “I remember … several young men in our village died after drinking the fake liquor made by you. Wasn’t it from your shop?” she turned indignantly towards the injured boy.

“Of course not!” Manas declared angrily, “Don’t I know where the liquor is made? In so many earthen *handis* in so many village homes? That too by women, including old ones! From rice or from *mahua*! Don’t blame my family for it!”

“Then don’t blame the poor either! What else can they do?” challenged Champa indignantly, “They have to earn money. After all they have to fill their stomachs! It was not their wine which killed … everyone knows that the killer wine came from your factory!”

Bhaskar, realising the discussion was not leading anywhere, decided to end it. Though disappointed by the boy’s ‘immature’ reaction, typical of the class he belonged to, he knew it was not easy to break the years of brainwashing he had received in his own social milieu. The ransom was to be handed to them on Sunday. So there was still time. Maybe he would talk to him again before sending him back.

“You must rest. But we’ll continue our talk later, when you are better,” Bhaskar said in his reasonable, friendly manner, before returning to his room.

30

Supervising the drill was one task that Bhaskar always enjoyed. It gave him great satisfaction to see the disciplined manner, the precision and the briskness with which the squad moved. The boys and girls had been soundly trained; their actions were well coordinated, deft and fast. The girls, he found, were quicker and smarter than the boys. A majority of the trainees were uneducated, unemployed youngsters recruited from the tribal villages close by. Coming from desperately poor families, they were glad to join the guerrilla army for paltry salaries, sometimes only because by joining the squad they got enough to eat. Once trained, they were as good as soldiers belonging to any army, noted Bhaskar with justifiable pride in his achievement. Yes, he had every reason to be proud of the training he had provided his soldiers.

The Commander was out in the open, sunny fields with the trainees, next to the *saal* and *sakhua* grove. It was early morning. The air was fresh and invigorating, lending energy and enthusiasm to the boys and girls. Bhaskar took them through their exercises–running, jumping, falling on their knees, crawling on the ground, climbing over rocks and up trunks of trees–in quick smooth movements. Satisfied with their performance, he finally led them to the spot under the trees where they would be able to rest for a while. As was the usual practice, the drill would be followed by talks and lectures.

Vijay had left camp to carry out the task he had been assigned. Sudhir was gone. So Bhaskar and Commander Rekha were handling the trainees today. Bhaskar gestured to Rekha to address the group.

"Comrades," she began, "Today I will tell you more about the weapons that we use." She went on to lecture the students about the differences between pistols and revolvers, guns and rifles, and how they must be maintained and taken care of. She showed them how to handle them, which ammunition to use, and where.

After that it was Bhaskar's turn. He gave the trainees a short lecture on the history of Maoism and the more important elements of its ideology. In the end he motivated them by repeating, once again and in very simple language, how it was all for their own good, and how the Maoist Party would liberate them from the grinding poverty under which they were forced to live, bringing them freedom through equality.

He found Champa, free now that the injured lad was better and there were no other patients, listening breathlessly, hanging on to his every word, nodding now and then in agreement. Earlier she had participated just as eagerly in the exercises. Bhaskar felt especially pleased to note the change in her personality. From the uncertain and ignorant village girl that she had been earlier she had graduated into a confident and committed guerrilla soldier. So far he had sent her only on soft missions but now, he decided, she was ripe enough to undertake warfare which included actual firing. Maybe next time she could be sent on a raid along with her friend Munia.

Satisfied with the performance of the trainees Bhaskar was in a good mood as he walked back to his room. "One minute, Comrade, I wish to talk to you," he heard and turned to find Rekha hurrying to catch up with his long strides. He waited for her, a warm expression of welcome softening his hardened face. She was breathless when she reached him. "I want to talk to you about that boy, Manas Gupta," she said, trying to match her steps with his.

"Oh, Manas? What about him?" Bhaskar slowed down.

"He is well enough now to move on his own. What do you want me to do with him?" asked Rekha in her business-like way.

"We need to keep him here. We have given his family time till Sunday. Till they send us the ransom he stays with us," replied Bhaskar.

"I understand. But you know he is now in a position to walk, though he limps. Won't he try to escape?"

"Keep him well guarded, of course. I can trust you to manage it, can't I?" asked Bhaskar giving her a glance that clearly pointed to the intimacy that existed between them.

"Yes, you can," laughed Rekha, her gaze caressing his face for a few fleeting moments. "I must go now, see what I can do with your prisoner." She swung off in the direction of the sick room. Bhaskar watched the slim, straight figure, with the crop of short hair that had turned steel grey much before time, march briskly and vanish around the corner. He felt a glow of warmth fill his heart–it was a comfort to have a relationship with a person like her, who understood and believed in the Maoist cause and for whom it mattered as much as it did to him. They shared the same ideals, the same goals and could together dream about the revolution that would one day bring justice and order to the people and the country.

A short, dark man was waiting for him when Bhaskar reached his room. He recognised him at once. Dipu Oraon lived in the tribal village close to their camp. He had come there often, bringing some news or a message or a request for help from the villagers. "How are you, Dipu?" asked Bhaskar, patting his shoulder with a friendly air.

The old man bent and touched the Commander's feet. "*Theek hatho*, Commander sahib," he answered, "We are alright … as much as we poor folk can be. But not all is *theek* for you and your people."

"No? How is that? Is something wrong?" asked Bhaskar, his voice turning sharp, his eyes screwed up as he searched the man's face.

The villager nodded and lowered his voice to a whisper. Realising that he had something confidential to say Bhaskar drew him into his room and closed the door. "Now you can talk. No one will hear," he assured the man.

But Oraon continued to speak in a low voice. "*Raat ke pulis ayile ho*. The police came to our village yesterday … wanted to know where the jungle folk hid. They asked others in the village; then they went away, saying they will come again. That's why I came ... to tell you, something is going on ... " said the man.

Bhaskar was immediately alert. Had the police discovered their hiding place?

Oraon lowered his voice still further. "They are searching for the boy, comrade ... that boy from the *aam ka bageecha*. I heard the police talk. They said his people were so rich. They know all the leaders. It has made the police very active ... it is not good for you, comrade."

"It is nothing. But listen ... keep a sharp eye open and tell me if you get any news," said Bhaskar lightly. He had his informers not only in the village, but also in the police. As soon as the villager left, Bhaskar turned to the task. He contacted his people, the secret informers who worked for him in the administration and the police department. It led to an alarming revelation. Dipu Oraon was right. The police had laid the blame for the kidnapping on the 'jungle folk'. They had already discovered the location of their secret hideout and were planning an attack on the Naxalites. It was not the time to try and find out how they got the information. They must act immediately, urgently. The camp must be abandoned at once before the police arrived.

Always ready for such an eventuality, Bhaskar had earlier discovered a safe spot on the other side of the mountain. It was well hidden in a fold between two hills, unknown and unvisited even by the locals. He had come upon it while exploring the area to make a detailed map of the region. He noticed that close by was a stream which gurgled unseen under bushes and behind rocks. If he had not heard the gentle tinkle of the falling water he would never have realised that it even existed. It was a perfect spot for their new hideout.

"Time to shift!" Tersely, Bhaskar issued his orders. There was a practised drill to be followed with which the camp inmates were already familiar.

There was no confusion, no panic as everyone set about dismantling the camp and clearing away all signs of their existence. The temporary mud walls were hastily pulled down. The tin sheets serving as roofs were piled up to be carried to the new spot. The girls rolled up the canvas and the tarpaulins and pushed them into sacks. The Commander's precious possessions, the books and documents, were packed into boxes, along with the dismantled machines and the gadgets.

The Commander rushed them along. Rekha supervised the whole affair, urging everyone to hurry. They must leave the site immediately, for the police could be there any moment. Thanks to the efficient planning and the instructions given by the two leaders the job was accomplished within just a few hours. The temporary camp, together with its makeshift toilets was completely erased from the scene with hardly a sign left to tell the tale.

As soon as they were ready Bhaskar ordered everyone to assemble for his final address. "Comrades, as you know, we are transferring our camp to a safer place for the police have got wind of our hideout. There is no need to panic or be afraid. All will soon be normal. We will begin again and life will go on as before. But now, all must leave. Only those who are carrying our material to the new camp will follow me. Commander Rekha will give instructions to the others."

Rekha hastened to first reassure the younger recruits who looked shocked and bewildered by the sudden development. "Comrades, you must not fear or worry. This is only a temporary change. It is time for all to vanish. Walk away in twos or threes. Disappear in different directions. Some of you have friends or families in neighbouring villages. You may take shelter in their homes. Or hide in the jungle, if you know of any safe place. When it's okay for you to return we'll send out a signal. Again, come back in small groups as soon as we inform you about our new location," she explained.

Finally she turned towards the Commander. "What about the kidnapped boy?" She pointed towards Manas crouching in the shade under an overhanging rock, his mouth gagged, his hands and feet tied to prevent him from escaping.

"He comes with us. Blindfold him!" ordered Bhaskar, "And untie that rope around his feet!" Champa, carrying a folded tarpaulin sheet across her back hastily put it down and ran to help. She was joined by the two men who had been ordered to guard the prisoner. Together the three cut the ropes around his ankles and supported him as he staggered unsteadily to his feet. The boy was still in a bad shape, observed Bhaskar, but shrugged off the matter. He would have to walk for there was no other alternative. Manas tried to say something to him through the cloth around his mouth but Bhaskar chose not to respond to it either. The two men tied a black scarf over the prisoner's eyes. They clutched his arms and pulled him forward. Manas walked unsteadily, looking drunk and dazed.

Bhaskar and Rekha watched the men leave the site. Members of the squad he took so much pride in, the young trainees, walked off towards the trees in the distance. Before long they had all disappeared, as instructed, in twos and threes. The shadows that lay dark beneath the leaves had swallowed up the various small groups. After his army had vanished, the Commander turned to the few who waited to accompany him to the new hideout. "Alright comrades, time to leave! Let's march forward!" There was no emotion in his voice, no sign of any regret at having to leave a place that had been home to them for so long. Bhaskar was beyond any such soft feelings. It was just a tactical move for him, a retreat to another hideout from where he could strike out again to continue his battle another day.

Once settled in a fresh hideout he would plan his next moves. He was confident he would always score over the police–for he was clever enough to counter their every move. The thrust and parry of battle was a challenge to the shrewdness and intelligence he knew he possessed and was proud of.

However, there was one fact that disturbed the confident leader greatly. Where was Vijay? He had been sent to collect levy. Instead, had he gone to the police and informed them about their hiding place? Had he finally succumbed to his conscience and decided to confess his role to the police?

It was a disturbing thought.

But no, were the police on their trail because of the boy they had kidnapped, as Oraon had told him? The first ransom demand was made on phone from their hideout. Had the police been able to trace that call? When there was nothing but silence from the Gupta family, Vijay had called again, this time from the food stall of a crowded cinema hall. There was no way the police could have traced the second call. Then how? Was it because of the first call from the hideout? The questions whirled round and round in Bhaskar's brain. But wise and intelligent as he considered himself to be, he could not solve the mystery.

The Commander was puzzled. But he knew he must wait until truth revealed itself.

In the meantime they must make haste to proceed to the new hideout.

31

The little group had traipsed for more than two hours in the scorching heat. The nullah and the valley across which it flowed had long disappeared from sight, along with its familiar surroundings. Bhaskar trudged mercilessly on, neither resting himself, nor allowing others to pause, even for a moment. He could see that the girls were looking tired and breathing hard, the prisoner with his injured leg was on the verge of collapse, and those carrying the boxes and other heavy stuff were stooping low. It was an exhausted, worn out, drooping squad that trudged silently behind its leader. The only person who still walked straight side by side with him was the grey-haired, energetic second leader, Rekha, who tried her best to inspire the tired soldiers to carry on.

Bhaskar had a reason for hurrying the marchers on. To arrive at the new spot after the sun had gone down and then begin setting up a shelter for the night in the midst of an unfamiliar wilderness would have been dangerous and foolhardy. He knew they must reach their destination well before nightfall. It was still afternoon and in this treeless zone, the sun beat harsh; yet they must make the most of the daylight.

"Come on, comrades, not far to go now," Rekha urged the drooping travellers. She turned to Bhaskar with an appeal in her eyes, "Let them pause. Just for ten minutes," she begged.

"Alright, let's halt for five minutes," conceded Bhaskar. There were sighs of relief as loads were quickly dumped to the ground and aching shoulders were rubbed or massaged. Champa unloaded her burden and helped the prisoner drink water from a bottle. Others relaxed in various postures, sitting perched on rocks or stretching out on the grass. Rekha offered Bhaskar some water from a flask that she carried, which he drank in big gulps, the cool liquid flowing down his throat, soothing his whole body. He gave her a grateful glance. She returned it with a smile and took a long sip from the same flask after he was done.

Refreshed after the short halt the travellers seemed to move faster. The rest of the journey was completed well before sunset. As the bright orange orb, surrounded by its pale yellow halo, sank behind the hills the travellers hurried to set up temporary shelters to house them for the night. Two large tents, one for the males and the other for the females, soon raised their heads above the flat ground cleared of the scrub and the thorny bushes. Bhaskar showed them the brook that gurgled nearby. They refreshed themselves by splashing the cool water on their hands and faces. Quickly they munched the dry *chura* and *gur*, the *sattu* they had brought with them and drank the water from the brook. Finally, snuggled close together under the tents the exhausted travellers fell asleep.

It was only the next morning that the camp could be set up properly. The group worked according to plans practised earlier. Everything was accomplished efficiently and fast. By next evening they were as well settled as they had been at the earlier location. It was with great relief that Bhaskar surveyed his room at the camp, now restored to its old, comfortable condition. His books and maps were in place, the folding table before him, his chair by its side and his camp cot on the other side. The kerosene lamp cast its soft glow on the map laid on the table. His gun and pistol were laid carefully in their usual places. Earlier he had taken a stroll around the camp and walked off to survey it from a distance. He was well satisfied with the location selected by him.

It was impossible to spot the camp from a distance. It was only when one turned a sharp bend around a green, heavily vegetated hill slope that the white tents of the camp came into view. First of all, nobody would come around the bend and even if some stranger did, it would take him several minutes to discover the camp hidden behind the wooded slope, under cover of the thickly canopied trees.

Bhaskar wanted life to become normal as soon as possible. He sent out a signal immediately, asking his folk to come to the new spot. A trusted person was sent back to guide them there. Soon enough, the camp fell into its normal routine.

Bhaskar carried out all the activities with an outward calm that did not reveal the thoughts that disturbed him. The nagging doubts had become sharp thorns that pricked him every time his mind was unoccupied. He had to pay attention at last to the suspicions that he had harboured all the while but pushed aside, busy as he had been. How did the police discover their hideout? Had Vijay betrayed his trust and informed the police? And where was he, for heaven's sake? Should he not have returned with the levy from the contractor at the construction site? By now he should have learnt about their abandoning their hideout. He must also have received information from one of his men about the new location. So where was he and why had he not returned with the levy? Why had he not turned up yet?

When the girl, Champa, walked up to talk to him after class, Bhaskar gave her a grim nod. "Yes, what is it?" he growled, frowning.

"Please, Commander Sir, have you any news of Comrade Vijay Lall? Does he know we have shifted? How will he find the new place?" she asked breathlessly, all in a rush.

"You don't have to worry," said Bhaskar coldly, "We have our ways. He should know by now."

"Then why hasn't he come?" persisted Champa.

"He will," murmured Bhaskar shortly, turning away from her and walking off. But the girl was not to be shaken off. He felt light, quick steps follow him and wheeled around to find her right behind. "But where is he, Sir? Is he in any trouble?" she asked, anxiously.

"I told you, he will be here soon," said Bhaskar, striding on. To his irritation the girl continued to follow him. He swung around to frown at her, his black brows drawing together and his eyes glaring at her,

"Why do you follow me? Don't you have anything to do? How is the patient, Manas? He looked quite unwell during the journey. Weren't you supposed to tend to him?" He fired questions at the girl and without giving her the chance to ask any more, ordered her to continue with her work. "Go! Do not stand there staring at me! Find out how the patient is doing." With a grunt he moved away before the impetuous Champa could react to his scolding. Her face paled to hear the anger in his voice, but the next moment she shrugged her shoulders and whipped back in the direction of the care centre.

Bhaskar grunted in satisfaction. It was important to maintain discipline and display his authority over the youngsters from time to time. He did not want them to stray or take undue interest in affairs not related to the cause. The girl had acquired confidence and skills, no doubt, but she was yet to imbibe the discipline, the respect and obedience towards authority that must be an integral part in the makeup of a good soldier. Being close to senior comrade Vijay did not mean that she could take liberties with the commander as well. That free spirit that she often displayed had to be curbed.

To check whether the girl had followed his orders Bhaskar walked over to the care centre. She was already there, pouring out tea from a blackened kettle she had just brought in from outside. The prisoner, who had fallen back into helplessness after the arduous journey, lay on the cot. Bandages covered his injured leg. His face looked as pale and colourless as it had when he was an invalid. He was awake, however, and reading a book sent to him earlier, Bhaskar was pleased to note.

"I am glad to see that you are recovering, after that long journey," he remarked, smiling at the boy.

"The wound reopened. I lost a lot of blood," said Manas in a matter-of-fact tone. Looking calmer and more composed he now seemed to be resigned to the situation.

"You will be alright soon. Comrade Rekha is a good doctor," said Bhaskar pleasantly.

"I guess so. And Champa a good nurse!" smiled Manas. Bhaskar was happy to note that he was now in a more receptive mood. Maybe it was a good time to talk to him about the Maoist doctrine. He made himself comfortable by settling down on the stool next to the cot. "I see you are about to have tea. May I join you?" he asked.

"Of course!" said Manas readily.

The boy seemed to welcome his presence. Obviously he was willing to talk. "Champa, will you make an extra cup for me?" Bhaskar asked the girl.

Champa hurried to pour some more water into the steaming pot. "Yes Sir, Commander Sir," she said.

"So you are reading Mao … do you find it of interest?" Bhaskar picked up the book the boy had been reading and asked in his best conversational voice.

"Well, it is a very different philosophy. I had read about it, of course, but never studied it in detail. You know I am a science and engineering student. I have not studied politics or an art subject before. That is why I find it so fascinating," replied Manas in a voice more serious and much less flippant than earlier.

"Neither had I. Until I met people who believed in his philosophy. It opened my eyes. There is so much to learn. That book will give you a good idea about other possibilities, other ideas. You must complete it," suggested Bhaskar in his amiable voice.

Manas looked at him quizzically. "It is such a thick book. Do you mean to say I must stay here that long?"

"Your family must send the ransom on Sunday, so there are only two more days to go. But … " he shrugged his shoulders, "I have not heard from your people at all. It is up to them, of course."

"I see. Does Marxism encourage kidnapping and ransom? I would not believe so," Manas spoke slowly, musingly, as if really wondering what Marxism meant.

"Let me inform you. Violence is only a means to achieve your goals," emphasised Bhaskar. He spoke clearly, laying stress on each word that he said. "If the ultimate goal is to benefit the helpless and downtrodden, any means is justified. Even violence, of which kidnapping for ransom is but a very small part."

"This is where I don't agree!" Manas put his cup on the table and gestured with his hands, his expressive eyes with their thick lashes glittering in excitement, "It is okay if you want to help the downtrodden. I fully agree with that wish. No, I definitely do not have any quarrels about that! But … and I strongly believe it … it should never be at the cost of other lives. Never!"

Bhaskar caught a glimpse of Champa's eyes, sparkling and alert, fixed on the boy's face, engrossed in their conversation. She must also learn, he decided, and raised his voice for her benefit. "Believe me, I know more about life than you do … sometimes there is no other way, no other solution, except to employ violent means. I have seen it. I know."

"Seen what? What makes you so sure?" asked Manas.

"When the rich become so powerful that they bulldoze their way through everything, when corruption is so well entrenched that cash is the only king, then what else can you do? Violence is the only way to check it! Destroy it all. Create a new world where there is equality for all. There comes a time when you must reach out and grab power with both your hands, yes, even through violence if need be," explained Bhaskar very patiently, pleased to find the boy taking interest.

Manas frowned, as if trying to understand. He did not scoff or make sarcastic comments as he had done earlier. Instead, he asked, curiously. "Well, for a moment I will believe you. Yes, the world is not fair towards the weak. They are exploited by the rich and the corrupt. They stay hungry while the rich gorge themselves till they are sick. The capitalists consume everything, leaving nothing for the poor. They use them as their servants and cast them away when they are of no use. I agree. I also agree that a new world order must be created where there is no exploitation and no inequality. You are very right about it all."

"Good. Now you understand, don't you?" Bhaskar asked, leaning forward eagerly, his face aglow with excitement. The boy had seen light after all, understood the reason and logic behind his explanation. He stole a glance at the girl to see her reaction. She, too, was nodding her head, clearly approving the boy's statements.

"Of course I understand!" replied Manas.

Bhaskar felt triumphant. At last, at last, the boy was coming around, changing his views.

Manas raised a finger and smiled. "But ...!" he smiled pleasantly and paused. Then he straightened up and looked Bhaskar in the eyes as he firmly asserted, "But ... where I do not agree with you is when you say that violence is the only solution. I do not agree because I believe in democracy. I believe you can change the situation by voting in another representative, another government!"

"Democracy?" Bhaskar sat back, disappointed, and snorted in disapproval, "It is a solution advocated by the weak. They think they can take the easier way out! Just cast a vote and the required change will come! But has it helped the past many years? We are in a worse situation than ever before. No! You must have the courage to shed blood, only then will you create a different society!"

"That seems to me to be too drastic ..." murmured Manas only to be interrupted by Bhaskar.

"Not at all! Those who are committed, like we are, have the courage to shake up society ... through any means! We don't duck behind the shield of democracy and elections. We reach out and grasp what is needed. Yes, at the cost of blood and death. By creating fear. It is the only way to bring about change," Bhaskar declared. It was indeed a challenge to convince Manas, intelligent and clear-headed and as unafraid to argue as the other student, Sudhir, whom he missed so much. But there was a difference. Sudhir was sympathetic towards the Party's cause; this boy believed in ideas totally opposite to theirs.

Manas shook his head vigorously and glanced at Champa to ensure that he had her ears. "How wrong you are, Sir! I do believe the youth of this country has the capacity to change the world. We are educated, we have the skills, we are as good as anyone in the world!" he said and stared intently into Bhaskar's eyes, trying to make him understand. The commander remained dumb as the boy confidently and firmly asserted, "Let me tell you, Sir, we too are idealists! We too, want to improve the condition of the have-nots! We'd also like to change things … not by killing, Sir, no, but through our hard work and our education … yes! Yes!" Manas banged his fist on the table next to him and repeated emphatically, "Yes, Sir, through our efforts and our skills! In management, engineering, medical or education! We can change the world, Sir. Yes Sir, we can!"

With a corner of his eyes Bhaskar caught Champa listening to the boy in rapt attention, the expression on her face eager and curious. He did not want her to get swayed by the impractical ideas being fed into her mind. At the same time he found himself interested in the argument. "Comrade Champa, will you get me a glass of water? After that, you may leave," he commanded, and waited for the girl to go, which she did with a reluctant pout.

"So you think it is easy to do it?" he asked as soon as the girl had left.

"Yes Sir. I have been thinking about it. It is you who made me do so. You are right, Sir. We do need to get out of our grooves and try to change … not by guns and rifles, Sir, not through mines and bombs. But through our brains, our intelligence! We will create a better society. Let me go back home, Sir, and I will show you."

Bhaskar shook his head grimly, a smile of sarcasm twisting his lips. "You can do it only by joining us, young man. You just cannot construct a road unless the stubborn rocks obstructing your path are blasted away. Destroy the decrepit old before you create the shining new–that's the way to do it!"

"No, Sir. Let me tell you, there are other youth like me, full of ideas and enthusiasm. We should try and mobilise them to do something constructive instead of leading them astray on the path of violence. We can do it Sir!" There was a challenge in his voice that Bhaskar did not miss.

"No, you cannot, young man," said Bhaskar coldly, shaking his head, and wagging a finger at his adversary. "The greed for more money, for lavish living and for acquiring goodies is too deeply entrenched in the youth of today. They will never lift a finger to help. They will never deign to spare a thought for those who have not had the advantages that they have had. For them the poor do not exist, except as loyal servants. Tell me, have you done any good so far to anyone at all? Ever?"

Bhaskar noticed that Manas flinched and remained silent for a while. So the question did make him think! He felt a sense of triumph.

"Maybe you are right," admitted the boy slowly, thoughtfully.

Bhaskar smiled to himself. It was just a question of time. If he persisted, he would surely succeed in indoctrinating this boy. He watched Manas closely, waiting for his reaction.

At last Manas glanced up. "You have a point, Sir..."

Bhaskar perked up. So had he managed to convince him? At last!

"But don't you think, Sir, for doing good to the society or the individual, we must first make that money. We must work hard, take up jobs, let our businesses and trade flourish, before we can help others ... so in the end the old system will work!" Manas emphasised.

He just does not understand, concluded Bhaskar with a sigh of frustration The more he tried to convince him the further did the boy sink into the depths of the capitalist quagmire. It was pointless to try and talk sense into his head. He was too stubborn to think beyond his own wretched, decadent life, and impossible to convince. When he had seen him reading Mao's thoughts, he had thought Manas was changing his mind. He had hoped wrong. Yet, at least the boy had agreed that society needed to be changed. But it was too small a triumph for Bhaskar.

For a long moment the older, harder leader gazed at the prisoner who stared back eagerly, hope shining in his youthful eyes. The mature, experienced warhorse who had seen the worst in his life and embraced what he felt to be the right doctrine to counter it, and the enthusiastic student who was yet to begin his life's journey–faced each other, each searching in the other's eyes for assurance and belief in his own different ideology. At last both men sighed in despair at the other's obstinacy and turned their faces away.

No, the boy was not prepared to change, or to believe in what he, Bhaskar, advocated so strongly. In fact he could influence others with his ridiculous ideas. He had already seen the light in the girl's eyes. She must be removed from proximity to the boy and sent on active duty instead of being cooped up there for long periods. It was not good for her. He would have to think of something for the girl.

Bhaskar rose abruptly and without any more pleasantries, left the prisoner's side.

32

Champa

Champa was thrilled. Commander Rekha had announced something momentous that morning. Munia and she, along with a few boys, had been chosen to raid a police *chouki* that night. A gleam of anticipation lit her eyes as she ran to hug her friend. She was happy to note the sparkle of high excitement that suddenly replaced the tragic expression darkening Munia's face ever since Sudhir had passed away.

Actually the two commanders had planned the raid together. Bhaskar had decided that it was time the battle was brought to the doorstep of the police, if only to divert their attention. Besides, they needed the weapons and ammunition. Also, both felt it was time Champa faced some real action and Munia got rid of her grief. Rekha outlined the action plan in great detail. Munia listened carefully, as it would be the first raid undertaken under her command.

A little before the sun withdrew behind the tall trees and while there was still light, the girls donned their uniforms and picked up the weapons assigned to them. Along with six others, they marched towards a village situated on the other side of the hill. The lonely hamlet, close to the coal mines, had a police outpost. A few policemen were stationed there to guard the area from criminals, coal thieves as well as Naxalites. They were sure to have arms and ammunition too.

As usual, darkness fell as soon as the sun dipped below the horizon. They could hear the birds chirp noisily as they flew towards their nests leaving a hush that lay grim and sullen over the now black forest. The squad, led by one of the tribal boys who had explored the area earlier, crept down a rough slope dotted with rocks and scrub. Soon they could see the lonely village tucked far away in a dark, narrow valley. The huts were scattered, a few well isolated from the others and surrounded by fields. The night sky above seemed darker and greyer because the village lay covered with the dull, grey haze of coal dust that arose from the surrounding mines, mixed with smoke from the coal burnt by the villagers. Their guide pointed in the direction of a pucca structure standing some distance away from the huts. "That's where the police are stationed!" he told them.

Munia was the leader of the *dasta*. She had been assigned the duty in view of her experience and seniority, the others being much younger. Some were mere boys with barely any hair on their chins and cheeks. Now she issued quick, clear instructions to her team members, assigning each a role. Champa and another boy were to advance first and hide at the back of the police *chouki*. The rest of the group would follow, sneaking close and quietly surrounding the *chouki* from all four sides and then, at a signal from the leader, swarming to the front door and breaking into the two-room house.

"Comrade Champa, you are with Tirki! And Comrade Tirki, you must go that way," pointed out Munia. Similar orders were issued to the rest. "Lal Salaam and good luck to you! Let's return with a great haul of arms and a grand victory!" she wished the others and blew softly on her whistle.

Champa and the rest of the team quickly tied the black scarves they had brought with them over their faces. They slung their rifles over their shoulders and made sure everything was in place. Champa and Tirki scrambled cautiously downhill, ducking low behind rocks or bushes at times and running forward to take shelter behind tree-trunks at other moments. The excitement of the running and the hiding sent the blood racing to Champa's head, her heart thumping so loudly she could hear it beat against her chest.

Soon they had slipped down the slope into the valley where the huts were huddled. The two crept stealthily down a dark road, black with coal dust from the mines. Black silhouettes of electric wires suspended untidily overhead and their tall poles, interspersed with the odd hut or two, stood out against the sooty grey sky. The lonely, silent place was like a ghost village shrouded in eerie darkness. It made Champa shrink back for a moment. Then she braced herself by taking a deep breath of the air that came mixed with dust and the smell of burning coal. She had to shake off the black dust and gravel from her bare sandaled feet every few moments. Reaching closer, the two walked cautiously on tiptoe to prevent any sound from reaching the guards.

"Quick, we must get to the opposite side!" whispered the girl as they stared at the drab yellow walls of the building before which they stood. A low brick wall, crumbling down at several spots, guarded the *chouki*. They sneaked around its sides until they saw the ramshackle wooden gate in front of the building.

"Not through the gate. We'll be seen," whispered Champa, peeping in. Through the open door of the building she had glimpsed the silhouette of a man standing inside with a gun. "Let us see …" They turned back and once more crept silently along the wall until they discovered a gap they could break through. "Look," she pointed out excitedly. A portion of the wall had collapsed there leaving a broad, gaping hole, the bricks lying in an untidy heap beside it. "Shall we go in through this?" The boy nodded and signalled to her to wait while he thrust his head in through the hole to see if all was clear. He drew back soon.

"Don't see anyone," he told her, "We may go in. But silently."

It was too dark for them to be seen, but on the other hand they could stumble in the darkness and give themselves away.

"Careful," warned Champa as her companion kicked a piece of coal cautiously aside. The sound slashed the silence sharply. For a moment she halted, holding her breath, hoping the scraping of feet against the coal and the bricks scattered underneath would not reach anyone's ears.

Fortunately the lantern that swung from the eaves of the thatched roof provided some light. Faint though it was, at least it was enough to prevent them from tripping over obstacles. There! Thank Shiva, they had reached the back of the little building. They crouched there in silence, waiting for the others to reach and for the leader to blow her whistle. For Champa the wait was nerve wracking. She had no idea how long it would take for the others to reach. Ears alert for suspicious as well as welcome sounds she felt her head throb painfully in tension.

A faint noise, of feet stepping over the soft dust, was enough to raise the hairs on the back of her hand. "Who's there?" immediately a voice rasped out from inside the building. She realised she was not the only one who was alert. The police were as sensitive to sounds as they were. Tirki stuck his head out to see, but Champa quickly pushed the youth down beside her. "Shh!" she warned, finger on lips.

There was no answer to the query from the building. She heard the policeman mutter angrily to himself as a hush fell around them again. She knew Munia and the others would be sneaking quietly to their assigned places in the cover of darkness. But not a whisper was heard, nor was there any telltale sounds from feet treading close.

"Who's there?" once more the call pierced the calm of the night, strident and aggressive. Again, it was answered by an uneasy stillness.

"Halt! Or we'll fire!" It was the last warning before the man raised his rifle. Someone fired out through the door, flung wide open by the gunman. The beam of light that spread out through the door was weak but enough to light up the scene outside. Champa could see the gravelled path and hear the click of guns and the stamp of boots. Just then the low whistle from Munia for which the group had been waiting reached their ears. "The others have reached! Come, quick!" Champa tried to pull Tirki but he had already jumped to his feet. The two rushed to join Munia and the others who had surrounded the police *chouki* by now. Together, all eight Naxalites rushed to the door where the lone policeman waited, his rifle raised. As soon as the policeman saw the armed guerrillas he took aim and fired. His companions, waiting inside, ran to take position beside him. Quick, sharp shots rang out from both sides.

Excited and nervous though she was, Champa knew this was the moment she had been preparing for, the moment when she must show them all. Heart pounding wildly, face on fire, she put her finger on the trigger and, for the first time in her life, aimed it at a real, flesh and blood, live, human being. The shot rang out, clear and sharp. In a trice the man had swung aside. She had missed her target. Before he could return the fire or she could raise her weapon again, there was another flash. This time the bullet found its target. It was Munia's rifle which had done the deed. The policeman crashed to the floor, blood oozing from the wound he had received.

And now there was confusion everywhere. The four armed men inside and the eight Naxalites attacking them fired indiscriminately at each other. Flashes of fire, shots at all angles, cries and moans filled the air as bullets met their targets. Champa had got pushed into a corner behind one of the boys who was firing into a group of policemen. In the melee she could not make out what was happening and who was hitting who. The smoke and noise spread around and she just stood and trembled there, her eyes almost blinded by the fire from the weapons. In just a few minutes all was silent. As the smoke cleared up Champa stared at the gory scene that was revealed.

There had been four men inside the room. Now three lay on the floor, one dead, two wounded and the fourth vanished from the scene, for he had fled, leaving the place to the attackers. Two of their own boys lay quiet and still on the ground. As the girls bent to examine them first one and then the other slowly fluttered his eyes open and Champa realised that they were both alive. They had received minor injuries. The rest of the team was unhurt except for glazes from near misses and scratches.

"Alright, comrades, gather up the loot! Comrade Champa, see to the injuries!" instructed Munia. Champa quickly noted that their injuries were nothing compared to the damages inflicted on the police who lay there unconscious and oblivious to everything, leaving the attackers free to gather up the weapons, which they did, quickly and efficiently.

The guns and rifles were slung on shoulders while the ammunition was hastily packed into gunny bags.

"I have taken my revenge!" exclaimed Munia, and there was a savage glint of joy in her eyes. "I'm glad I came on this mission. I have accomplished what Comrade Sudhir set out to do!" She raised her fist high and cried triumphantly, "Lal salaam, comrades! *Jeet mubarak ho*! Hurry now, we must leave before the escaped man returns with more forces! Pack up fast! Champa, you carry that bag! Now let's go!"

Amidst great haste, the eight raiders picked up their booty and ran from the site of the firing. They split into twos and struggled up the gentle incline of the hill. Loaded with heavy weapons, it was a difficult walk, but hidden in the dark shadows of the wooded slopes, they remained unseen during the return journey.

The mission had been totally successful. In triumph they entered the camp where the inmates still slept because the night was only half gone. Commander Rekha was the only one who was awake and waiting. She hurried out as soon as she heard the noises outside and waited to welcome them. The victorious *dasta*, led by Munia, proudly saluted her and laid the looted booty down before her. "Comrades, you've done a good job. Commander Bhaskar will be so pleased. Now stack that loot away and relax the rest of the night. You deserve it!" Rekha told them.

"For the first time I feel at peace," said Munia as the two friends lay side by side as usual, "After his martyrdom, I mean. But how did you feel, firing for the first time? At real people?"

"I couldn't hit him. You did!" Champa corrected her.

"Still, you fired at him, didn't you?"

"Yes, but ... " Champa lapsed into silence, her mind elsewhere. No doubt it had been an exciting experience. The race downhill in the dark, the hiding and the crouching had been thrilling. It took her back to her school days when she played games with the girls at her village. Now that the raid was behind her she remembered the first several moments with a smile of pleasure. But the other part, the attack–she shuddered in the dark–was a frightening, spine-chilling experience. How scared she had been when she faced the policemen with their guns. It was just chance that she had fired first, followed quickly by Munia, who had actually saved her, she now realised, for surely the policeman would have shot her dead the very next moment.

A shiver of horror ran through her. No, she did not feel brave, did not feel triumphant. She was just plain afraid. Anything could have happened. She was lucky that everything had passed off well and they had returned safely. She covered her face with her blanket and murmuring "Om Namah Shivaya-Om Namah Shivaya," an image of the deity in the Aamra Vatika temple before her, fell finally asleep, just as a pale dawn was breaking over the horizon outside.

33

The next day the whole group was presented before Bhaskar, along with the cache of valuable arms brought by them. The pleased smile on the leader's lips made it all worthwhile to Champa. The nervousness and fear vanished. Instead she felt the pride and the satisfaction of a job carried out successfully. The congratulations received from other comrades made her exult even more. The day passed in a blaze of excitement, praise and celebration, for Rekha had ordered pulao, alu dum and puris for their meal. These were rare items for those in the jungle, used as they were to *khichri*, *sattu* and other cheap, easily available stuff.

Much later, walking down the still unfamiliar surroundings Champa felt her joy being drowned in the anxiety of Vijay's continuing absence. He should have been back by now. The Commander had said so quite clearly. But he had not returned. So where was he? A picture of her lover lying wounded, alone, somewhere appeared before her for a moment, but she hastily rubbed off the image from her mind's retina. No, it could not happen, not to her beloved. She quickly strode towards the girls' shelter. Only Munia could distract her, she must find her and unburden herself before her friend.

The girls were in a relaxed mood after the long, gruelling days spent shifting, setting up camp, at the same time carrying out their regular activities. Last night's raid had added to their exhaustion. Champa found the girls sprawled on their reed mats or their plastic sheets. Some dozed; others stared vacantly at the walls while a few chatted in low voices. Commander Rekha was away on her own trip. Champa threw herself down on the mat next to Munia and with a sigh stretched out her tired limbs. "Sleeping?" she asked.

"I cannot. There are too many thoughts … they won't let me sleep," mumbled Munia, "Even when I am so tired I should just fold up."

"Thoughts? They trouble me too!" confessed Champa.

"Of course I feel much better after that raid. But still, sometimes I feel …" She ended her sentence with a little sigh.

"I heard some strange talk the other day," Champa tried to change the subject, "Between the kidnapped boy and Commander Sir. Both want to do things, but differently. Sir thinks shooting and killing are the best and only ways to change things, but Manas does not agree."

"Of course Commander Sir is right. I believe him. Don't you?" asked Munia, diverted, as Champa had hoped she would be.

"Umm … hmm. I should. Killing for putting things right and for improving the world may be a good idea. But it can backfire on you, too, isn't it?" she said hesitantly, a note of doubt creeping into her heart.

"What d'you mean?" asked Munia sharply, sitting up to face her friend.

"Your own loved ones may also get killed, won't they? Like comrade Sudhir was," asked Champa.

"How can you say that?" Munia's voice sounded indignant, "He sacrificed himself for others. He died a martyr. I am proud of him!"

"Oh yes, of course," cried Champa, immediately regretting her words. She rolled over to put an arm across her friend's slender waist. "Oh, I shouldn't have said that, Munia. It was so wrong of me."

The two lay close together, and in the warmth and comfort of each other's presence soon fell asleep.

The morning brought good news for Champa.

"I heard Comrade Vijay is back. Did you know?" Uma announced while the girls were washing at the brook. Champa was splashing the cool water from the brook onto her face.

"Back? When?" The girl, bent over the water, almost lost her balance in excitement. The neem twig she was chewing on dropped from her mouth. She steadied herself quickly and retrieved the twig from the water.

"Early this morning. It was still dark. Bijju was on guard duty. Could not recognise him in the dark and raised an alarm," giggled Uma.

"Then?"

"Comrade Vijay shone a torch on his own face and shouted out his name," said Uma, laughing. Champa giggled gaily, feeling happy once more. She dipped the twig in the running water, swishing it to and fro to clean it. She munched on it with vigour and gusto. The edge, bitten and crushed, soon turned into a stiff bristle for brushing her teeth. She quickly finished her brushing and washing and, impatient to meet her man, raced towards the Commander's room. She knew he would be there. Vijay was inside but unless invited she knew she could not enter. Impatiently, she hung around. A little later Rekha saw her loitering there and sternly ordered her to carry on with her own job instead of standing outside.

Vijay remained closeted with his leader for almost the whole day. When he came out at last Champa was back on nurse duty from where she could spot him by standing near the door. He had a bandage on one side of his head. She gave him a welcoming smile. But Vijay's lips remained shut in a grim, straight line; there was no answering gleam in his eyes. For a moment he stood unsmiling and uncertain outside, then decided to walk across to her.

Champa ran joyously forward to greet him. Vijay put his finger on his lips and gestured to her to return to the room. He followed her as she stepped back inside.

"Are … are you alright? What happened to you?" she quickly asked, stealing a glance at the patient who lay asleep, fortunately for the two.

Vijay nodded his head. "I'm alright." He drew closer and wrapped her in his arms. "Oh Champa, it's been so long. I wanted to see you … so much," he whispered.

"But … what happened? Where were you?" she asked, snuggling close, feeling the warmth of his body seep into her own, comforting her.

"I'm back. Isn't that enough?" he asked, lips against her ears. She nodded silently and they remained thus for a while, until the sound of Manas shifting position and sighing in his sleep made them separate hastily.

"I must get this wound treated. The men did a good job but it was all done so hastily. Can you fix it for me?" asked Vijay.

"Of course," Champa began removing the bandage on the forehead. Manas could wake up any moment and she must be seen attending to the injury rather than nestling in someone's arms. By now well trained as a nurse by Rekha, she worked efficiently and professionally.

"Oh, you are back?" Champa heard and found Manas blinking his eyes, his head half-raised and turned towards them. "Any luck with the ransom?"

"No," said Vijay shortly, "In any case I was on another mission. There is still time for the ransom. Today is Saturday, remember."

"Is it? I seem to have lost count. So tomorrow is the big day! Have you heard from anyone?" inquired the prisoner.

"No!"

"Kidnappings and ransom are not going to help ..." began Manas when Vijay shut him up with an angry glance. "I don't want to listen to the rubbish you keep repeating. I know what is right and what is wrong, so don't try to teach me!" he cried. Then he swung around and strode out of the room.

Obviously he was in a bad mood, realised Champa. She did not try to stop him but was left with the bandage in her hand and the scissors dangling from her fingers. She threw them down on the bed and glared indignantly at Manas.

The lad grinned back at her, not a bit regretful. "Your boyfriend is so bull-headed. Just like his leader. They don't want to listen to anything they don't agree with. They prefer to walk off rather than argue it out. They think every argument can be answered by a bullet in the back!"

"So you think you are the clever one, isn't it?" muttered Champa.

"Well, I am better than them. They have walked off so many times ... in fact whenever I try to discuss anything it ends in their leaving in a huff! Why don't they try to convince the other person logically and intelligently? Because they don't have any answers! They'd rather shoot down or bomb out all opposition! Hah!" said Manas contemptuously.

"You must believe what they say, like I do. After all, they are acting on behalf of people like me. We don't have everything like you do," protested Champa.

"What a nut you are! Just like those other poor fools! Don't you see, they are using you and other uneducated, backward youth like you? They want power, which they will get through believers such as you," replied Manas thrusting an aggressive finger towards her.

"Power, what do you mean? They are helping the poor … don't you see?"

"No … that's what *you* think!"

"Uh … huh … so what do you want us to do?" frowned the girl. She looked expectantly at Manas.

"I am glad to see you are willing to question … unlike others. Your mind is still open. Their brains are already filled with bull-shit."

"So what must I fill it with?" challenged Champa, sitting down on the stool next to the bed and fixing her large eyes on him.

"A proper education, to begin with! Have you been to school?"

"Yes, but till the eighth only. My stepmother stopped me. She wished me to stay home and help with housework," replied the girl.

"You should acquire skills. I think you will make a good nurse … " Manas said, thinking.

"Who will allow me to? And where do I get the training?"

"Dr Rekha has already trained you. Hasn't she?"

"A bit. But there must be more to learn … about medicines, injections, pills?" asked Champa.

"You are right. If ever I get out of here, I would like to help you. You have been really good to me."

Pleased, the girl smiled back at him shyly.

34

Champa heard the rest of Vijay's story that evening after the day was over for the camp inmates and the two could meet at last. It was a moonless night but the stars were out in their myriad sparkling hues in a velvety smooth sky. A light breeze rustled through the leaves and cooled the otherwise warm, summer evening. The gurgling of the brook a little further away provided a melodious background to the lovers as they sat close together on a flat rock.

Vijay related the story of his mission from the beginning to the end. "Boss was so upset when I told him everything," ended Vijay finally, on a regretful note.

"But why? You did bring back the levy money?" she asked.

"He said the police could be on our trail. He is right. It did not occur to me, of course. But he is so clever. He understood."

"Oh no!" Champa's voice quivered at the thought. "What will happen to us if the police catch us?"

"Commander Sir will know what to do. We know he will find a way out," said Vijay confidently, but his words failed to reassure the nervous girl.

"Will they catch us all?" she repeated anxiously, remembering how cruel the police could be and how, right before her eyes, they had treated her father so inhumanely. "Oh, Vijay, what does the future hold for us?" Champa's eyes were wide with fear.

"Don't worry, Champa. I am sure all will be well. The commander will take care of us," Vijay patted her shoulders. "Come, let's go back. It is late and I am so tired after walking all night ..." He got up with a long drawn out yawn and pulled her to her feet. Meekly, Champa followed him, but the fear and anxiety would not leave her, making her cling to his arm as they walked back.

Vijay sensed her anxiety and turned to her. He gave her arm a confident squeeze. "Why worry? We have placed ourselves in Commander Sir's hands. He knows best. He will do whatever is best for his people. We must trust him."

"Yes, but … " Champa wanted to confide her doubts and fears in him but did not like to add to his worries. She held her tongue and returned his squeeze with as much warmth as she could. She wanted him to smile, so that the dimple she loved to watch would dance once again on his taut skin. Though his mouth still had lines of fatigue around it, she felt satisfied to see his eyes light up at her touch.

"We are fighting for a cause, Champa. It may mean frustration and tension at times, but let's not worry about it just now. It's the cause that we should think of. Some day we will be victorious. Until then let's be patient. Remember, one day triumph and glory will surely be ours!" Vijay mouthed the words she had become familiar with by now.

"Yes," mumbled the girl, gazing into her lover's eyes as they shone with dreams of a brighter future. She felt herself lost as her glance wandered down towards his lips. There it was! Fascinated, she gazed at him as the tiny dimple in his brown cheek sprang in and out while he spoke reassuring words to her.

"You understand, don't you?" asked Vijay at the end.

"Yes, of course!" nodded Champa vigorously, eyes on his face but ears only half listening.

The next day was Sunday, the day fixed for receiving the ransom for releasing Manas. Champa met Vijay as he walked back from the Commander's room. His forehead was lined with anxiety and his face tight and drawn. He did not smile at Champa. "Any news?" she asked.

"No. Not yet. The men assigned to receive the sum from the Guptas are on their way to the appointed place. We'll know in a while if the money is received. They will inform Commander Sir through a coded signal."

"Oh, I do hope we get it. What will happen to Manas if they don't?" she asked with a worried frown.

Vijay only shrugged his shoulders. "He will deserve whatever Commander Sir plans for him." He burst out angrily the next moment. "What kind of people are they? Aren't they worried about their own child?"

"Poor Manas! I feel sorry for the kid!" murmured Champa.

"Kid? Come on, he is not a child. He is older than you. Don't waste your tears on that stupid, stubborn chap and his uncaring family. None of them deserve nor need your sympathy."

He is still in a bad mood, thought Champa, and refrained from asking any more questions. Much later, however, there was no need to ask, for in spite of all attempts at secrecy the news had spread. She saw the little groups that had gathered about, speaking to each other in hushed voices, looking over their shoulders to ensure no one was listening. Munia and the other girls stood deep in some discussion in a corner and she rushed to join them. "Do tell me!" she begged, "What is happening?"

"Haven't you heard?" asked Usha, "It's about the ransom."

"Oh! What happened? Did they get it?"

"Shh. Keep your mouth closed," warned Munia, "No. We got a message instead. No one turned up. Our men waited and waited. Nothing happened."

"What? What will happen to the prisoner?" Champa was filled with dread.

"Don't you worry … Commander Sir will know what to do," answered Munia. "There are other things to think about. Seems the family filed an FIR with the police. And the police has been trying to find the kidnappers ever since."

"Good we left the other camp," said Champa with relief, "They will never find us here!"

"Don't you be so sure," Munia gave a short laugh, "The police have their ways. For all you know, they kept watch over the men who were to receive the ransom. They will trace them out, that's our fear. And torture them until they reveal all!"

"*Baap re*! What will happen to us then?" Champa muttered.

Munia shrugged her shoulders and pointed towards the leader's room. "Commander Rekha and Comrade Vijay are there. They must be discussing what can be done now. It is a real emergency," she said.

Everyone waited with growing anxiety. Something serious was going on for the big ones were shut together for a long period. It was only in the evening that they learnt more.

Bhaskar ordered the inmates to gather together for an important announcement. Champa stood at the edge of the crowd, looking with anxious eyes at the three leaders, searching for signs of what was to come. The Commander had a stony expression in his black eyes, revealing nothing of his thoughts while Vijay's face was turned dotingly towards his leader. Commander Rekha looked over their heads at some distant spot, her face grim.

"Comrades, Lal Salaam to you all. Today we face another emergency. I want you all to listen carefully. We have received information from many secret sources that the police, after making enquiries, are searching for us ... No, no questions, please." He raised his hand to warn his listeners.

Champa gasped in dismay. She looked at the others to see their reaction and found that most had their usual, closed expressions on, revealing nothing of their feelings. Vijay nodded his head as the Commander continued, "I know it will mean another dislocation and all the problems of shifting. We are looking for another good place. We will know by tomorrow. Be prepared! We shift as soon as we find one."

No one spoke or protested. With fixed eyes they gazed at their leader for more information. But the commander had no further news to convey. "That's all, comrades. As I told you, be prepared for all eventualities." He swung around and left for his room, followed by

Vijay. Rekha stayed on to ensure that everyone went back to their tasks but she remained as tight lipped as the other two.

Later Champa went to his room to give Manas his dinner. Two youths had been assigned recently to guard and keep wary eyes on him all twenty-four hours of the day. Now that he was much better there was every chance that he would try to escape. The Commander had issued instructions for keeping a strict vigil over the prisoner. She found Manas sitting up eagerly, waiting for her visit and the food. "Any news?" he asked as soon as she entered. Champa understood of course what he referred to but did not think it wise to say anything. Lips tightly sealed she nodded vaguely.

"I get it," he cried, "It's no, isn't it? Or you would have told me! You haven't got the ransom. I knew it. I knew my people wouldn't give in to ransom pressure. Hats off to my grandfather! He has guts, the old warrior!"

"So do you!" thought Champa looking at him with admiration mixed with pity. How could he look so pleased when he knew he could be killed? Or did he not know the fate that awaited him? She understood quite well, of course. The Commander would not show any mercy at all, for had she not seen that hard glint of steel in those dark, heavy eyes?

35

Vijay Lall

The past few days Vijay had been on a roller coaster of emotions following the several ups and downs that he had faced.

At first, when he realised that the contractor had no intention of handing over the levy, he had felt great despair. The idea of returning to his leader empty-handed had depressed him greatly. Somehow he had gathered himself, determined to turn the failure into success. Vowing to get the money, Vijay had trailed the contractor and finally accosted him in the town as he walked down a lonely street. He had, quite coolly to his own surprise, thrust a revolver against his back and hissed at him, asking him to pay the levy amount, or else. The contractor had quickly handed over all the money his wallet contained, not a mean amount, for he had been on his way to pay his labourers.

Satisfied, Vijay had allowed him to go. Not long after, his team had received the second jolt. As they tramped triumphantly back through the forest they heard a shot. A police party had suddenly ambushed the returning group.

Immediately returning the fire Vijay and his men had vanished swiftly into the jungle. The police, not so familiar with the dense forest, failed to catch them and they had managed to flee with just a few minor injuries. Vijay marched confidently back to the camp with his men.

Then he had his third shock. The whole camp had vanished as if gobbled up by the ferocious, black jungle. For long, shocked moments he had stood there blinking his eyes in amazement. How did it happen? Where had they all disappeared? Had the police reached and caught them all? He could not believe it, no, it was not possible, not with Commander Bhaskar there to lead them. And then he had remembered old friend Dipu Oraon who lived in the tribal village nearby. He had rushed there to find the old man, who not only told him the whole story but gave him the exact location of the new hideout.

After another long, exhausting trek in the dark they had finally reached the new camp. With a triumphant flourish Vijay had handed over the levy to the Commander and waited for the words of praise he was longing to hear and was sure would follow.

The leader remained thoughtful and preoccupied, deep lines of frown frozen on his forehead. Vijay's face fell in disappointment. But soon enough he learnt the reason for the worry. Bhaskar explained that though he had abandoned the old shelter, bad news continued to dog him. The police, on the hunt for them since the Gupta boy was kidnapped had been seeking out and arresting his people. His fear was that the police would succeed soon in extracting information about their whereabouts.

"Oh no, Sir! But that would be most unfortunate for us," cried Vijay, his face paling to hear the news.

As concerned now as his leader Vijay stayed on and the two discussed plans long into the night.

And then it was Sunday, the day scheduled for the ransom. The long hours passed in a see-saw of mood swings. There was tension and apprehension followed by optimistic expectations of receiving the substantial amount of a few crores from the rich Guptas. The hope soon turned into despair when late in the evening they finally received the message. No one from the Gupta family had turned up at the appointed place. The party assigned the task of receiving the ransom had waited a long time and finally sent a short coded message informing them that the mission had failed.

The news had leaked until the whole camp knew of the matter. Finally, when the Commander addressed them Vijay was present too, along with Commander Rekha, Champa and all the others.

Later that night Vijay was suddenly summoned once again into the leader's presence. He found the Commander sitting up in his bed, the room in darkness, the lantern in the corner casting a small circle of light around itself on the ground. "Come, Comrade Vijay," Bhaskar looked up to see him enter. His voice was grim and heavy with worry, "Some more bad news for us."

Bad news again? Anxious eyes fixed on his leader's face Vijay waited with bated breath to hear the rest.

"A runner from Dipu's village came a few minutes ago. They have caught the old man. Now they will torture him until he coughs out the information. Poor Dipu!" muttered Bhaskar, gesturing with his hand to Vijay to sit on the chair next to the table.

Vijay was too shocked to do so. He remained standing, his mind going back to the village where he had met the old man only two days ago. He remembered the lined, grizzled face with the stubble of white beard, the broad nose above the dark lips and the yellow gleam of his broken teeth as he had smiled goodbye. "Tell the leader I am thinking of him. He has gone far from us but we villagers will remember him," he had said, grey rheumy eyes gazing into his, "He did a lot for us. Yes, he did. We will not forget."

"We must search for our next hideout," Bhaskar's determined voice broke into Vijay's thoughts.

"But Sir, we just moved!" he protested.

"Yes. Yesterday I warned our people to be prepared. But I was hoping that it would not really be necessary. Now it seems that it is. If they have caught Dipu they are bound to discover this place. Don't you think so, comrade?"

"Yes Sir, you're right, Sir!"

"So what d'you think we should do? Shift camp once again or face the police?"

"It's for you to take the decision, Sir. I am sure whatever you decide will be the best for us," answered Vijay, looking up at his leader expectantly.

"We must teach the administration and the police a lesson. They killed our man, Sudhir, and are now breathing threateningly down our necks. We'll have to show them! Or they will continue to put obstructions in our path," the leader spoke after a while.

"Yes, Sir. What shall we do then?" asked Vijay.

"I have decided!" Bhaskar stepped down from the bed and picked up the lantern, setting it carefully on the table next to the papers and the map. Vijay moved aside to allow the commander to take his place on the chair. "We must fight it out!" declared Bhaskar finally, sitting down and unfolding the map. "We don't want to run away like cowards. This time I intend to take a stand." He spread the map out and pulled a blank sheet of paper towards him. Pencil in hand he began to draw his plans.

"Look, we are here, well hidden behind this ridge. If we place our men here, they could keep a lookout … No, not men … the girls. We'll keep our girls here … to watch the forest paths and warn us the moment anyone appears … " muttered Bhaskar, outlining his plans for defence.

Vijay bent closer to follow the scribbles in the dim light. His eyes followed Bhaskar's fingers as they moved tersely over the paper. "After all how many of the force can penetrate so far into the jungle? It is sure to be a small squad. Our guerrilla soldiers will be more than equal to them. Yes, we will crush them! Teach them a lesson they will never forget!" the Commander's voice rose in determination.

The leader was absolutely right, thought Vijay, nodding his head in agreement. After all, if those days of intense training of the squad had not prepared them for a real confrontation what was the use of it?

"Comrade Vijay, we won't allow them to get away with it! They must be chased off, for good. Tell everyone we have decided … we will stay! First thing in the morning, ask everyone to assemble. I will issue the instructions myself." Finally he swept the map to a corner and drew himself up straight. His face gleamed even in the weak lantern light and his eyes seemed afire in anticipation and high excitement.

"Action at last! We need to fight, Comrade, not scamper off like frightened rabbits!"

Infected with the excitement he saw on his leader's face Vijay saluted him sharply and strode purposefully off. The panic that had filled his mind earlier on hearing the message, evaporated, and was replaced by visions of a brave fight against an old enemy that needed to be destroyed. The commander was a veteran of many an encounter handled successfully and Vijay was confident he would lead them once again to a glorious victory. He found himself looking forward to the thrill of experiencing something new, something he had never seen before, from which they were bound to emerge winners.

As soon as the camp inmates gathered for drill and lecture the next morning the young soldier rushed to join them. The Commander arrived soon after. As usual the men and women sat in orderly rows behind Commander Rekha, waiting eagerly for their leader to address them.

"Lal Salaam, comrades," Bhaskar greeted his people, his tone more serious than usual, his body stiff and straight, "Yesterday I told you that we may have to shift camp, since the police have come to know of it and will try to destroy it. But now we have other plans … we mean to stay here and defend our camp. We'll teach the police a lesson they'll not forget in a hurry. Please listen carefully now … " He outlined his plans to the guerrilla squad which listened stoically as the leader defined the exact tasks to be carried out. Vijay's searching glance swept over each face that gazed attentively at the leader. He found the listeners totally absorbed, intent, and knew that each would do his best for the task assigned.

Excitement broke out as soon as the leader left and the guerrilla army prepared itself to defend the camp. The girls who had not yet finished their training were to take up posts furthest away from the camp. Their job was to play the role of village girls out to collect firewood or graze their animals. They would be the first to rush back to report any unusual movement noticed in the jungle. The second line was of young shooters hiding in the forest, ready to fire on the troops advancing towards the camp. Then there were the land mines buried at strategic points en route, waiting to blow up those who reached closer. Thus with the approach route covered at every crucial point the camp would be safe and well prepared to defend itself.

How brilliantly had the leader conceived every detail, thought Vijay admiringly. No force on earth could harm them now. He was confident that they would have the upper hand and the police would be forced to retreat. It was with a triumphant smile that he met Champa soon after the meeting.

"See, didn't I tell you? Commander Sir will take good care of his people. As long as he is there to lead us we have nothing to fear," announced Vijay when he met the girl.

Champa gave him a small, uncertain smile. "If you say so, I'm sure we'll be safe," she replied.

"Of course. And you and I will get a chance to demonstrate our skill with weapons, in case there is an attack!" laughed Vijay. He put up two fingers in a sign of victory, "Action at last, as the Commander said. Don't you feel excited?"

Silence greeted his confident assertion. There was a distant look in Champa's eyes. "I was so scared the last time," she mumbled. "You were not there. The shooting was so … frightening. For a moment I felt I was about to die. But with you by my side, I won't feel afraid."

"There is no need to feel scared. Oh no, not at all. The Commander is too clever. He won't let any harm come to us. Besides, as you said, I am there too, to love and protect you!" Vijay gave her a reassuring glance and a gentle pat to her arm. He was relieved to see the shadow of uncertainty lift from her face. She smiled back at him, her eyes shining with the pride she felt towards her gallant protector.

Later, the Commander discussed more details with him. "See, we have mined the road that the police vehicles will take. They will have no alternative except to reach us on foot. Think! A march of twenty kilometres or so, through unfamiliar jungle terrain, where our men will be waiting, hidden behind trees, bushes and rocks. They have no chance! It's advantage Lal Sena, all the way," gloated Bhaskar, "And once we're done with them, they will never dare venture into our territory again!"

Bhaskar's eyes met his follower's adoring ones as he swung an arm in a high arc that ended in a sign of victory. "Lal Salaam, comrade. Our red flag will continue to fly high. Have no doubt about it!" he cried.

Vijay, too, raised his hand in answer before bringing it down to his forehead in a smart salute. "Right, Sir! May victory be ours!"

36

Those deputed to report on any unusual movement soon shed their battle uniforms and left for their posts, disguised as simple village girls gathering wood or minding their cattle. Several young men also slunk into the jungles to hide and await the police intruders. The rest of the squad, including Vijay, Rekha and the leader stayed on to make preparations for defending the camp.

They brought out the weapons and had them cleaned and checked for any defects. Explosives and ammunition were pulled out from their secret hiding places. Some had become damp and had to be set out to dry in the sun. Everything brought to shipshape condition, the squad members were at last sent to their shelters to have some rest.

The sun was just about to vanish below the earth when two excited informers, the girls in the forest, rushed back to camp to report on what they had seen. Sona and Rama were immediately escorted into the commander's presence by Rekha. "They've brought some news, Sir," she told the Commander.

Sona and Rama saluted their leader as Vijay crept closer to listen. The girls blurted out their story in excited, breathless voices. "We saw them, Sir. A group of men, moving single file through the forest. They were loaded with automatic weapons and ammunition."

"How many?" rasped out Bhaskar sharply.

"We counted, Sir. Twenty," answered Sona, the elder of the two.

Before long two other girls had rushed back to report, from the other side this time. "We spotted them down in the valley, creeping past the rocks lying near the stream. We ran to tell you, Sir," they reported.

"How many?" asked Bhaskar tersely.

"Twenty to thirty, Sir," answered the girls, "We saw quite a long line of armed men proceeding towards the hillock."

The comrades looked at each other in astonishment. "We thought that side was totally inaccessible," wondered Rekha, "How did they reach so close?"

"They are approaching from two different directions, obviously," summed up Bhaskar, "Not just through the one obvious route, as I had expected them to."

"Yes, from two opposite sides, Sir," said Vijay, "But not to worry, Sir, you had instructed us to guard both, and that is what we did. We are covered from both sides."

"True. Let's hope that's all. We are ready to defend both sides," nodded Bhaskar, satisfied that they were well prepared.

A little later another pair of girls ran up, breathless and excited. They had spotted a line of troops advancing from a direction they had never thought would be approachable. The men were still far away, about two kilometres or so, but there was no doubt about it. They were headed in the direction of the camp. Bhaskar got up abruptly, and began to walk up and down in the room. The other two looked on with anxious faces. What was happening?

More news was to arrive soon. By now the comrades in the camp had understood. The police had taken them by surprise, for they were reported to be advancing from different directions, and would soon be closing in on them. They would be surrounded by the troops on all sides.

"They have turned out to be more intelligent than I gave them credit for," admitted Bhaskar ruefully on receiving reports from other messengers. "How did they manage to cover such difficult terrain? I thought it would be impossible for them to reach!"

"Yes, Sir, that's exactly why we chose this place as our hideout! Because it was so inaccessible!" exclaimed Vijay, as astonished as Bhaskar was.

"Exactly. Hmm. I did hear that the new SP was very tough, adventurous and daring. He seems to have done a good job. However, comrade, brilliant as the enemy may be, they can never be as tough, or as clever as we are. Don't worry. I can outwit them with another strategy if this one has failed," claimed Bhaskar, as sure of himself as before.

"We trust you, comrade. We have full faith in your abilities," Rekha spoke softly, her glance caressing her friend's face with fond admiration.

Bhaskar acknowledged her feelings with a slight nod in her direction. "Thank you, comrade. Don't forget, I have chosen this site very carefully. It is strategically situated. We get a good view of approaching soldiers from the top, but they may not see us." He raised his head and his voice was sure and confident. "Comrades, they may advance from any and all sides," he declared, "But defeat will still be theirs. As I said I've chosen well. Once they are closer to us they will all have to cross a narrow gorge before finally reaching. They may not know it, but I am fully aware. That spot will be their death. That is where my counter strategy will win over theirs."

Vijay let out a relieved sigh. He knew he could trust the leader. He was sure to be cleverer than all the others, thought Vijay, a sense of pride swelling his heart.

"We are sure it will, comrade," Rekha's voice reflected her confidence and pride in the leader, "We know you'll succeed, as always."

"Good, thanks once again for the trust you have placed in me. You will not be disappointed," answered Bhaskar, smiling at her, "Here are my instructions. Vijay, you will take command of the defence!"

Vijay clicked his boots together, and waves of hope flooded his heart. The Commander was no fool, and much too shrewd for any police officer to beat. They were sure to win. He felt proud that the master had placed so much confidence in him and made him the leader of the squad. He would not let him down, ever.

Meanwhile Bhaskar had turned to Rekha. "Comrade, send four of the best girl shots with him, along with ten of the toughest boys. Comrade Vijay, look, this is the position you must take." With quick, sure fingers the leader made his new plans, pointing out the various spots on the map. "See this hillock here? The one overlooking the approach to the camp? This is where you take position."

Hurriedly he began to explain the details of the new strategy while Vijay listened carefully, nodding from time to time. Rekha, who had rushed to carry out Bhaskar's instructions, was back by the time he had finished. Munia, with Uma, Sita and Ganga, all armed and in uniform, accompanied her. For a moment Vijay felt disappointed, for Champa was not part of the group. But there was no time for regrets.

With the directions fresh in his mind, he stepped out to assume command. "Lal Salaam, comrades. Follow me." And he ordered them to march forward.

It had turned quite dark by now. Night had completely wrapped the hillock in its black veil. The squad walked in silence, torches and flashlights showing them the way. It took them an hour to reach the spot marked out for them in Bhaskar's map. He had chosen it well. Below them was a narrow, deep gorge which all troops would have to enter, whichever direction they arrived from, before they could reach any closer.

"Now pay attention, comrades," Vijay's voice was an urgent whisper. "Comrades Munia and Uma, you must take position on the opposite side of the gorge. Hurry up and leave, take the other two girls also with you! And remember, fire only when I give the signal!" As the four crept off, fast, to cross the valley and hide on the other side Vijay turned to those left with him. "Listen, comrades. Spread out and hide, wherever you can. Remember to fire only after I signal," he repeated, "Until then hold fire! And remember, each shot must be aimed to kill. Not a single shot must go waste!"

Silently the men crept forward to take positions behind rocks and trees from where the approaching police party could not see them. The idea, Vijay realised, was to frighten the policemen into thinking that they were surrounded by the enemy from all sides, though he knew his own squad consisted of only ten men and four girls. The bullets raining suddenly on them from above would confuse them into thinking that they were totally surrounded by a big army. Brilliant, he thought, mentally taking his hats off to his leader who had devised the intelligent strategy.

Everything was in place soon after. The girls flashed a torch from the other side to signal that they had taken position. Vijay glanced around to make sure that the boys on his own side were well hidden. With a nod of satisfaction he hastened to proceed to the vantage spot from where he could glimpse the approaching enemy. The valley lay in semi darkness, patches of white sand glimmering softly where the moon cast its silvery beams. The crickets and other insects had stopped their humming; the beasts of darkness were strangely silent, as if waiting in a breathless hush for something to happen. Above him, leaves and branches hung unmoving, for the air was still and heavy, pervaded with a sickly smell of over ripened, rotting fruit, though Vijay could not guess which.

He saw and felt it all with a sharpened sense of awareness, his eyes piercing the darkness, ears acutely tuned to catch the softest sound. It seemed to him that he had stood there for an eternity in the deep silence and the nothingness around. But when he looked at his watch he found that the arm on its face had dragged itself, impossibly slowly, through just fifteen minutes. Impatiently he swung his arm about, hoping to make the watch go faster, but it continued to move in its own steady, slow rhythm. Vijay sighed in frustrated impatience and fixed his eyes determinedly on the valley below.

Emptiness met his penetrating glance once more. The expectant hush reminded him of those days long ago, when exam results would be announced at school assemblies. He remembered the silence that fell as the otherwise noisy lines of unruly boys watched the headmaster arrive on stage and stand before his table, result papers in hand. He would gaze at the suddenly quiet, disciplined lines in the Hall, a smile, grim and grave, playing on his face as a thousand hopeful eyes stared back at him. How tense he felt, how he wished that when results were announced his name would top the class list. Before *Pitaji* died and even after his death, Vijay's only desire was that he should not let him down, ever. And he never did, scoring the highest, remaining almost always at the top in his class. No, he had never let his father down.

Throwing back his head to stare at the stars above Vijay made a pledge to himself. He would never let his leader down, either.

Somewhere in the distance he could hear the hoot of an owl. It brought him back to the present and he peered down at the valley once again. Far away on the opposite side, down below in the valley, he had sensed some movement. Immediately he was alert. Was it an animal or were they soldiers? Eyes glued to the spot he waited, examining the moonlit sands for the slightest flutter disturbing its serenity. Yes, he was right. There had been some movement there. Black shadows were creeping stealthily, silently, appearing into view, slowly becoming bigger, clearer and more visible. Yes, they were moving figures. As he focused his eyes on the shadows they began to acquire definite shapes. Soon he was sure. The troops had arrived. It was time for action.

He sprang up, the leader's instructions ringing clear and sharp in his head. He waited for the men to advance until the moving heads were just below him. Quickly he raised his arm to swing his torch. It was a signal to the girls on the opposite side to fire into the valley. As the first shot rang out from the girls' side, it was immediately followed by a series of shots from his boys. He could see the commotion it caused amongst the troops down in the valley. The men fled in different directions, some back the way they had come, others staggering to take shelter on the steep slope or racing ahead to the other side. Smoke filled the valley. It covered the men and hid their figures, helping them to run and take shelter.

Soon the men had taken cover behind the rocks and bushes that littered the sands. Gunfire echoed now from the valley. The police were returning the fire, their guns aimed upwards. But the guerrillas, well hidden above, definitely had a vantage view, and could pick up those in the valley one by one, destroying them. It was not long before the gunshots from the valley died down, once again leaving the place in a deathly silence, broken at times by soft groans and low moans.

Vijay lay there a long time, still and unmoving, waiting for more action in case there was any. The leader had warned him not to take any chances, for the enemy was not to be taken lightly. For all they knew they would be attacked, perhaps from behind or from some other direction, if they were intelligent enough to have alternate plans.

Only after he had made absolutely sure that the enemy had retreated without leaving any men behind that Vijay dared to breathe. He rose slowly to his feet, still uncertain, still waiting, for anything could happen even now. Gradually, as there was peace all around, a slow flood of relief began to fill his heart. He realised that there was not a breath of movement down below. Nothing stirred, nothing moved. Once again he waited, just to make sure the enemy was not there anymore. His ears were alert for sounds. All that he heard was his heart thumping loudly in the silence that reigned. Yes, he was confident now that all was well. The enemy had definitely retreated.

He jumped up, exultant in his triumph and victory. They had made it! They had beaten the advancing enemy!

However, caution was still to be maintained. The first step would be to make sure that the girls on the other side returned to camp safely. He remembered that he had instructed them to remain hidden until he gave the sign. With the loud shrill call of the wild fox that roamed the jungle he signalled their victory. It was a secret coded message sometimes used by the guerrillas. He knew they would now head back to the camp, taking a different route from them. At last he and his boys were ready to leave, triumphant at the resounding defeat they had given the enemy. There had been no casualties amongst his boys. Not one of his squad had been injured.

It was still dark when they reached home to report their glorious victory. The Commander, waiting in his room, received the news with a warm smile and a pat on his shoulder.

"Congratulations, Comrade, for a task successfully completed. That was good work!" he said, making Vijay flush with pride.

"I salute you, Sir. It was due only to your careful planning. I do admire you," murmured Vijay, bending to touch the leader's feet.

"No, no, no need to do that. But I wish I had more followers as dedicated and intelligent as you are. We need many more young men such as you." said Bhaskar.

Vijay lowered his eyes modestly to hear the praise. He felt proud to see the smile of happy confidence on his leader's face and to remember that he was responsible for it.

"Maybe that Manas boy could be persuaded to join us," continued Bhaskar, thinking. "His parents did not respond to our demand for ransom. We should actually get rid of him. But on the other hand I feel it will be a real waste to destroy that talent and experience. Maybe we should try again to indoctrinate him … "

"Ours is such a worthwhile cause, Sir. He should see reason. Specially as it will give him a new chance, a new life. You are right, Sir. We should talk to him once more," suggested Vijay hopefully.

"A chance to be born again. Yes, that's what it will be for him, as otherwise he faces certain death," Bhaskar ruminated, "I must speak to him again with an offer he dare not refuse! But it will be his very last chance!"

37

Manas Gupta

So they had not received any ransom. When Manas learnt this from Champa he found himself struggling with conflicting emotions. At first he was proud that his family had refused to bow down to terror tactics and pressure. He had always known his grandfather to be a strong man, unbending in his principles. His father also was too stubborn to give in to bullying. If anything the threat and pressure would have made the two all the more determined not to buckle down.

The very next moment an image of his distressed mother stole into his mind and his eyes misted over with sudden tears. Poor, dear Mamma, she must be in a really terrible state of shock, fear and anxiety. He remembered how, whenever he left for his hostel, or went abroad with friends, she would ring up every day just to make contact and to reassure herself that he was fine. The very thought of his mother in pain plunged him into the deepest depression.

His parents had left Delhi a few days ahead of him. His own visit was delayed because of a friend's birthday bash, but he had promised his mother he would follow immediately after the get-together was over.

"*Theek hai*, *beta*, but come soon. Meanwhile I will make sure that your grandfather has made Aamra Vatika comfortable for you," she had promised, "There are so many problems to be faced there; half the time there is no electricity! Being cut off from town makes it so lonely and insecure. I must also ensure that the TV, the internet connection and the phone lines are working. You shouldn't feel out of touch with friends the two months you are there."

"That's OK, Mamma. I enjoy being with you all. I love Aamra Vatika, and of course, there will be lots of mangoes to eat. This is the best time to be there. I'm looking forward to it," he had grinned, hugging his mother.

And now here he was, in the midst of nowhere in a jungle, surrounded by hostile Naxalites who could kill him any moment. His mother would have had a fit to see the terrible condition he was in. Wounded, lying in a dirty bed, unshaven and unclean, eating food even his servants would have refused to touch, and guarded by armed men as if he was a criminal. Mercifully, the woman Naxalite, Rekha, who claimed to be a doctor, had arranged some nursing service for him in the shape of that village girl, quite an amateur really but still, someone who provided care as well as company to him.

He still could not believe it. There was a strange sense of unreality, as if all this was happening not to him, but to someone else. He was a spectator, watching with interest the various players acting out their roles. He enjoyed baiting the Naxals, criticising their strange ideas and their beliefs and arguing with them. It brought some excitement into his prison life when the village girl's lover, along with the big man, the leader, struck up a conversation with him. Their talk about their 'cause', their ideology and the 'revolution' amazed him. Did they really believe that their violent ways could benefit anyone, leave alone the poor and the underprivileged?

Often, as he lay there, alone except for the dour and silent guards, or the ignorant village lass, he thought about it all and wondered. How could so many young people–the guerrilla soldiers he had seen, the tribal youth and even boys like Sudhir and Vijay, with their educated backgrounds–become hard core Naxalites prepared to give up their lives for their 'cause', as Sudhir had done?

Puzzled, he had once asked Champa why she had joined the 'jungle folk,' the name given by villagers to the Naxalites.

"As if you'd understand!" she had scoffed at him, "You rich folk can never understand."

"Tell me!" he had said and something in his voice must have reassured her, for she had replied by relating to him her own story. She had spoken about her labourer father, landless because he had been cheated by the factory owner, poor and illiterate and thus weak and exploited, her nagging and selfish mother, the unthinking, power crazy policemen who had taken away her father and molested her when she went searching for him.

He had found her story moving and had felt sorry for her. "But how are you helping your people?" he had asked just one question.

"Help? First of all, I am with folk who understand us poor people. The jungle folk have taken up the fight because they want people like me to have a better life. They are on our side, they are for us!" she had declared vehemently.

"So they claim. They go and kill innocents and then they say they are helping … d'you believe it?" he had asked, his eyes searching her face.

"Of course. I believe in whatever the Commander, our leader says. He is such a good man, so kind and so brave. He has taught me so much that I didn't know," asserted Champa.

"Like? What has he taught you?" he had been persistent.

"Like … he has taught us to fight for ourselves, to be strong and defend our rights … oh, there are so many things. We have lectures and classes and learn so much. You must hear our leaders when they explain their views. It will open your eyes," Champa had declared.

"But have they taught you any skills to help you earn your bread and butter? Have they taught you what your rights as the citizen of a democratic nation are? Has he told you that as a citizen of this country you can choose your own government, not by using bullets but by voting at elections?" he had fired questions at her.

Champa had listened, open mouthed. "Voting? I remember the elections. Some men came that night to our village … Babuji returned home drunk. 'See this picture? Put your thumb here … near it'. He told my mother. But she showed him the hundred rupee notes in her hand.

'No, no, here!' she said. They fought … I don't know what happened after …" she had replied, "So what has voting got to do with us?"

"That's how you change things. Not by chopping off heads, like your friends here!" he had said scornfully, though he had felt disturbed by her words.

"How dare you say that? You don't know them!" protested the girl, angry at the accusation.

"I do, girl. They believe they can achieve their goal through violence. That's not the right way … you must admit," insisted Manas.

"What else? That's the only way anyone will listen to our woes," insisted the girl.

"No! There are other ways. Go to the police …"

"Hunh! What good will that do?"

"How will killing help?" countered Manas.

Champa stared at him. Then she had tossed her head and cried, "I knew you would not understand!" and had flounced off before he could say anything more.

Manas had felt disgusted. Such ignorance! The villagers must learn, they must understand how the world functioned. Surely they could not remain in darkness all their lives, he had sighed impatiently. He wished he could do something to remove the ignorance that surrounded him. But what, he had wondered …

And now, since the ransom had not been paid, he knew the Naxalites would no longer wait. Any time they would strike, ending his life by shooting him or cutting off his head. The thought filled him with fear and dread. He did not want to die, but sooner rather than later, they would drag him away, take him to some lonely spot and finish him off.

Images of his own killing floated across his vision often when he was alone. No matter how he tried to shrug it off or think of more pleasant matters, the knife that swung forever above his head dug its way deep into his thoughts again and again. Every moment he expected the door to open and that terrible monster, their leader, to enter and drag him to his death in the jungle.

At other times he felt deeply resentful. Why had fate done this to him? Why had he been gifted a wonderful life, filled with all the luxuries, been given all the opportunities to develop into a competent engineer, only to be dragged into the wilds to receive a bullet in the head?

Sometimes furious anger against the Naxalites gripped his heart. They had snatched him cruelly away from his cosy environment just for a few crores of rupees. Then he corrected himself. What was just a small amount to him could mean a big change in so many lives, if spent to help them.

But no, that was not what his captors planned to do. They had their own motives, which did not include benefits for others. No, it was meant for buying weapons, guns, revolvers, bullets, bombs. Yes … all that caused death, destruction and loss. That was what the money was needed for. The thought made him furious. He wanted to attack, to smash the bullying mouths arguing with him into a million fragments, or to chop off their limbs as they themselves would have had no hesitation in doing.

But no, he was different from those uncouth villains. For them violence may have been the way to attain their goals. But how could he accept the cruelty and barbarism that only turned a human being into a demon? No, he was a cultured, civilised person, with the right morals imbibed through good education. He could never stoop to their level, nor could he give up his sense of what was decent–including his polite, courteous manner–no matter what they did.

So, with supreme effort he controlled himself and attempted to speak civilly. But he could not help it; sometimes his feelings did get reflected in the derisive, sarcastic comments that escaped his lips in conversations with them.

As his mind drifted on, the door suddenly opened and to his great astonishment he found the two villains of his thoughts, Bhaskar and Vijay, walking in. "Time for my execution?" he cried. As usual he made light of the terrible event he knew was bound to follow.

"Not if you listen attentively to what we say," answered Bhaskar gravely much to the doomed prisoner's surprise. Behind him Vijay nodded seriously. Manas could not help noticing that the young man's face had lit up, for just then his girl, Champa, had also entered the room, carrying a kettle and glasses with her. So there would be tea before he was sent to the gallows, he thought wryly. He faced his executioners squarely and said in a belligerent tone, "Alright, shoot. What do you have to say?"

"Now listen carefully, IIT friend. We respect your intelligence, education and your training as an engineer. We do not wish to destroy it all so indiscriminately," said Bhaskar, watching the young man's face closely.

"Great. Thank you for appreciating my qualities." though greatly astonished and suspicious Manas replied as politely as he could, "So what d'you want from me?"

"I'll put it as plainly and simply as I can. And remember, it is the last time that I speak to you," warned Bhaskar.

"Sure. Go ahead, I'm all ears," answered the prisoner, wondering what was coming.

Bhaskar glanced at Vijay who was listening intently. Champa too hovered in the background. She had already served the tea and was waiting to remove the glasses. She had inched closer, kettle in hand. Bhaskar bent and gently touched the young man's hand. "As I said, we have regard for your learning and experience. We would benefit greatly if you supported our cause," he said in his most gentle and persuasive tone.

"Is that so? How?" asked Manas, wondering.

"You could assist with all things technical. We need your expertise for our gadgets–weapons, ammunition, computers, wireless and other mechanical stuff," explained Bhaskar.

"I see. And in return I get to live?" asked Manas, guessing the rest.

"Yes. You join us. Become one of us," offered Bhaskar.

Shocked at the unexpected proposal offered to him by the Naxalite leader, the prisoner, sentenced otherwise to die, kept his lips pursed for a long, tense moment. Join them? Surely they did not believe that he would give up all that he thought was decent and correct and become someone like them? As he glanced at Vijay's expectant eyes he could feel his face flush with anger and his head throb as the blood rushed to it. How dared they? "Do you want me to be like you?" he threw the words at the young man, trying hard to keep his cool but not succeeding, "To kill innocents and pretend I'm doing it for a cause?" Then he turned towards the older one, the leader and the brain behind it all, "I told you I didn't believe in your theories or your ideology! Yet you make this ridiculous offer!" he ended angrily.

"Careful, young man. You don't know what you are saying. I can finish you off in one second!" warned Bhaskar, his brows drawn together in a scowl and his eyes like burning coal.

"I don't care. Not anymore. You can do what you like. But I must have my say!" Manas raised his voice higher, "Let me tell you what I think–the have-nots are better off without you! They are better off receiving good education that will put them on their feet! Definitely not by learning the art and science of killing! They are better off acquiring skills that give them jobs! Not by setting off mines and bombs! D'you understand, you jungle beasts?" He had completely lost his cool by now and with it the control he had kept over his tongue. This was the man who was the cause of all his misery, he remembered, lashing out at him with all the anger and fury he had kept in check all this while.

Bhaskar's lips twitched in anger. He raised his fist at the furious Manas and muttering, "You've brought it on yourself, IITian," stomped out of the room.

"You … you fool!" cried Vijay as soon as his leader had left, "You've made him furious. No one can save you now. You are doomed!" He quickly followed Bhaskar out. Champa was left standing there, the kettle still in one hand, her mouth hanging open in amazement as she stared at the defiant Manas.

"Why did you do it? You had a chance … you messed it up!" she said gently, her voice soft with sympathy.

"Oh, shut up! How can you even think that I would join that … that killer of men? Don't I have a conscience?" shouted Manas. He threw his glass at her, angry at the silly fool of a girl who was stupid enough to believe in the villains.

Champa's eyes widened in shock as the glass shattered against the mud floor. In silence she swept the broken pieces and picked them up. "I can understand your anger. But why take it out on me?" she asked before walking out, leaving a fuming Manas to fall back on his chair.

38

Bhaskar Reddy

Bhaskar, cool and intelligent though he was, had never felt so humiliated and insulted. He was furious. It was the same rage that had so burnt him when he had lost his dear sister. He could feel his facial muscles tremble with the hot anger that coursed through his entire being. He gritted his teeth, remembering the boy's insulting words. No, he had had enough. No more. Before the day ended they must get rid of the youth. There was no point in keeping him alive. He had to be exterminated.

Not wanting to lose control the Commander hastily strode towards the haven that was his room. He would calm himself by listening to the soothing music on his tape as he often did when he was in a bad mood. Or he would lie on his cot and close his burning eyes for a few moments. Perhaps that would make him feel better.

Hearing the sound of steps he turned back to find Vijay trailing him, followed by that girl, Champa, who had witnessed his humiliation in the sick room. He was about to tell them sternly not to follow him when he saw Rekha walk towards them. What a relief it was to see her warm, pleasant face and to note her brisk steps as she reached closer. "Yes, Comrade?" he enquired eagerly.

"Did you hear it?" she asked as soon as she drew near, and now he noticed the alarmed expression in her eyes

"Is something the matter, Comrade? You seem disturbed?" he threw an anxious glance at her.

"Perhaps you did not hear the sound … the drone of a helicopter. It flew past our camp a little distance away from it on the left side; hovered for a while, as if trying to locate something. Then flew off …"

Bhaskar frowned, wondering what it denoted. "Maybe it flew off course on the journey to its destination."

"Could be, but there's another possibility. The police retreated after their defeat in the encounter with Comrade Vijay and his squad. But they got a good idea about our position. They also realised that the land route was not advantageous for them, so ..."

"I see now why you look so alarmed. You fear they may attempt to target us from the air?" queried Bhaskar, sharp enough to imagine the rest.

"Exactly, Comrade! That's why the helicopter flew close to our camp. To reconnoitre," nodded Rekha.

"You are right. We must take it seriously. Alert the people, Comrade Rekha. We must be prepared for all eventualities!" ordered Bhaskar, his voice tight now with a sense of urgency. His mind raced fast. Did the arrival of the helicopter indicate something, as feared by Rekha? Or was it just an occasional, random flight overhead?

As Rekha whirled around and left to carry out his instructions Bhaskar turned to Vijay. "Comrade, let's not make a mistake by ignoring the incident. We must foresee what may follow." Anger evaporated, his face was now grave.

"Yes Sir. We wait and watch. But you are right, we should be ready for all possibilities," agreed Vijay.

"Exactly, Comrade, we cannot afford to rest. Who knows, there really might be an air attack!" jested Bhaskar lightly with an amused smile. Not really believing it could happen, Vijay laughed along with him. Both knew it was too far-fetched an idea. Besides, they were so well tucked in under leafy canopies and shady rocks that it would be difficult to spot them from the air. It was also dangerous for helicopters to fly too low. All in all, though they must remain alert, they knew in their hearts that an air attack was quite unlikely.

In spite of his doubts Bhaskar summoned Vijay to his room. He unfolded a map that he had prepared after surveying the area thoroughly, and drew his fingers over it. "Look comrade. Fortunately the area is studded with boulders and dotted with bushes and spreading trees. We are well hidden. Still, we should have an evacuation plan as well. If the attack really takes place, it may not be enough to take shelter, we may have to make a run for it."

Vijay could understand his anxiety. Of course they did not expect it but what if an air attack did take place? It certainly would not be easy to face an enemy that targeted them from above. The Commander, however, looked confident enough to challenge the unexpected and would surely devise a strategy to face even that contingency.

Bhaskar was silent for a long while, concentrating on the map. Soon he was ready with his plans. He explained it all to Vijay, his voice sure and assertive. Step one involved taking cover immediately any danger in the form of flying machines appeared in the sky. Step two would be to vacate the place immediately thereafter, hiding behind cover of trees and boulders. The inmates must all leave, as they had done earlier also, and reassemble later at a designated spot. Vijay was given command of the guerrilla soldiers while Rekha was to assume responsibility for defending the rest of the camp inmates, including girls, older women and others who were not in the fighting squad. Bhaskar himself took overall command of the whole operation.

The first task was to issue instructions to his people and to keep up their morale. "Comrade Vijay, will you get everyone here? In just two minutes. I want all to assemble outside my room!"

Before the two minutes were over the space outside was filled up by orderly rows of men and women, some in uniform, others in informal dress. Rekha, looking grave, accompanied them, along with all the girls, including Munia and Champa. Bhaskar faced them with a grim smile. "Comrades, as you know, the police has been looking for us ever since that boy was kidnapped from town. His people refused to pay the ransom we demanded. Instead, they informed the police. We were well hidden in this remote place, but the enemy managed to discover our hideout. They attacked us. We gave them a resounding defeat, as you well know. But that has not stopped them. They may attack again. We must be prepared."

There was a hastily suppressed sigh of disappointment but Bhaskar disregarded it to continue, "Many of you saw the helicopter. We suspect that it was searching for us. It may return to attack us. In case it does, you should know what to do." He went on to outline his line of action. The usual stony silence greeted him but Bhaskar knew that his orders would be well followed.

"Any questions?" he inquired.

"No, Sir. Your directions are so good. We know what we must do," answered Vijay, "But what about the prisoner? Is he to be left where he is? Or do we take him along if we evacuate?"

"No, not at all. He must be executed!" asserted Bhaskar, "for bringing all this trouble on our heads!"

Bhaskar instructed Vijay to roll up his maps and safely pack his laptop, gadgets and other precious papers and instruments before doing anything else. In fact everything in the shelter was to be kept ready for being removed hastily if the situation so demanded. He could see the girl Champa glance at him, a question on her lips. He frowned at her. He did not wish anyone to question him. "Comrade Champa, you take care of the medical stuff. Isn't that your responsibility?" He growled at the girl, who pursed her lips and nodded.

Before his listeners could leave to carry out their allotted tasks, Bhaskar heard a sound, low and clear. It was the steady drone of a helicopter flying high above their heads. The startled men and women stayed rooted, craning their necks upwards to see. For a few seconds Bhaskar could not believe it. He shook his head, muttering, "No no, it's not possible ..." before looking up, his hands shading his eyes as he stared at the dazzlingly bright sky. A few fluffy clouds floated above in small, scattered groups. A tiny, winged speck had just emerged out through the clouds into the blue sky. It approached them from the south-west, expanding in size as it reached closer. There were no longer any doubts now. The little speck had metamorphosed into a silver coloured helicopter headed in their direction. The crowd stood transfixed, staring in wonder at the flying machine. The whirr of the wings grew louder until it could be heard clearly by those down below.

To Bhaskar it was like a loud drill rotating inside his ears, the wings twisting and turning inside his brain, churning up waves of alarm. For a few, terrible, fleeting moments, images of the devastation that the flying monster could let loose on them, flashed before his eyes. He watched it swoop lower until he could clearly read the words painted on one side.

"It is a police helicopter, Comrades! Run, take cover!" he shouted, "You've got my instructions! Don't fear. We'll get over it! Just do as I told you."

As the men and women began to run in different directions to take cover Bhaskar glanced at Vijay. "As soon as you have finished the packing, Comrade Vijay, execute the prisoner. It's your responsibility!" His cheeks flushed in fury as he remembered the insulting words the boy had flung at him. Even in the midst of the emergency he could not help thinking–the boy deserved the worst for having wasted all his time, with not a rupee to compensate in ransom. Not only that, if the police was attacking them, it was because of him.

"And Comrade Vijay … Remember to do it slowly … chop off his limbs first, one by one. The IITian must be punished severely!" he ordered, loudly and viciously, "Lastly, slit the neck. Let him die a painful death. He deserves it."

"Y … yes, Sir!" Bhaskar noted the reluctance in his voice and decided to ignore it. That Vijay lad was too soft, he must learn to be cool about killings or he would never make a good soldier.

Vijay's face had paled. He wiped his perspiring forehead and looked at his leader, "Sir …" he began, but Bhaskar had deliberately turned his face aside.

He glanced instead at the helicopter again. It indeed seemed to be hovering in the sky above, like a great big bird looking for prey. Obviously the men inside had not spotted them yet for they were searching the ground, their binoculars fixed towards the greenery that effectively hid the guerrillas and kept them out of view. Clearly visible to those on the ground, Bhaskar, however, could even make out the weapons in the hands of the men inside. He realised they were well prepared; it was a planned attack.

Eyes screwed into narrow slits, forehead deeply creased, Bhaskar gazed at the helicopter looming closer towards them. "Now to tackle the menace above!" he hissed. "Everybody, rush for cover, wherever possible!"

The next moment they heard the first crack of gunshot. It sent all those who still hung around scurrying for cover. The shot confirmed their fears, removed their doubts. The men in the helicopter were indeed taking aim at them.

Vijay raced inside his leader's room to carry out his orders to pack his belongings. Rekha and the others ran towards their own shelters to gather up their stuff. Champa, as instructed, was about to scamper off too. Before leaving she glanced backwards, her eyes searching anxiously for Vijay.

"Go, girl! Don't just stand there!" Bhaskar waved her off, "Hurry up and finish your own work. Let him do his!"

She scurried off. Bhaskar remained outside, surveying the scene. The sounds of firing were louder now. He caught sight of the bursts of fire, mercifully still at a distance. The strikes dazzled his eyes even through the tree cover and the smoke that rose in the air. Suddenly, a screaming grenade landed somewhere in the neighbourhood, sending a spiral of fire and smoke up through the trees. A bullet cracked not too far away from where he stood, making him race, helter-skelter, to duck quickly under a rock.

The air attack had begun.

39

Champa

Champa heard Bhaskar's instructions for the execution of the prisoner. Stunned, she just stood there, frozen with horror at the vicious cruelty of the order. Yes, yes, she knew he must be punished. The Gupta family had not sent the ransom money. There was absolutely no reason why the son should stay alive. He had shown no signs of remorse either, uttered no pleading words to be spared, nor had he ever begged for kindness. His behaviour had been just too rude. How could he expect the leaders to show mercy towards him?

Everyone was racing to take cover. But the girl lingered behind uncertainly. The words of the Commander shocked her. She stole an anxious look at Vijay. Would he really carry out the execution as directed by the leader? But Vijay had already vanished into the room and she could not catch his eye. When the Commander shouted at her to go she swung around and sped towards the sick room. Glancing up hurriedly, she saw the helicopter swoop down, thankfully quite off the mark. It seemed the men there did not yet know the exact location of the camp. She watched it fly off upwards again, and begin taking a wide circle. It would be some time before it returned to continue its attack.

She slowed down, anxious, a worried frown on her forehead as she remembered the prisoner. She felt a sneaking admiration for the boy creep into her heart. It was really brave of him to argue with the leaders. If he did not believe in their cause it was only right that he should stand up for his own beliefs. From what she had seen of him she felt he was not the type to give in just to escape execution. Oh no, he wouldn't! But it required real courage to take a stand.

Reaching the sick room, she stopped, surprised. The door was open. The two guards had vanished. Neither was the prisoner on the cot. Had they all fled? Or had he already been executed? A stab of grief smote her at the thought. But then she heard some noises and peered into the far corner. There he was. The prisoner lay sprawled on the floor, his mouth gagged and his hands and feet tied up at the back. The guards had not taken any chances and fled only after tying him up tightly.

The sight of the young man trussed up like an animal brought back the fact sharply into her mind, forcing her to confront the reality–he was about to be killed, after being tortured. She shuddered. The very thought of a human being treated in that gruesome way was terrifying and abhorrent. Would Vijay be able to do it? Surely not?

"Glug-glug, glump hrrmph," she heard and ran over to see. The prisoner was trying to attract her attention by making noises against the cloth tied around his mouth. Should she remove it? She rushed over and pulled down the cloth to allow him to speak.

"Whew, that was terrible. Thank you!" muttered Manas as soon as he could, "Water, I want some water. I'm so thirsty!"

Champa ran to quench his thirst with water from the earthen *surahi* in the corner. He gulped down the liquid, fast, and gave her a grateful glance. "Thank you once again."

"*Baap re*–all tied up! How long has it been?" asked the girl, her voice sounding concerned.

"I guess my time is up. They are preparing to–what do they say? Annihilate me ... I mean, to kill me" answered Manas in his cynical way.

"You may be right. I heard the commander give some orders," replied Champa, trying to avoid the boy's eyes.

"OK. What did you hear?"

"Something. No need to tell the exact words."

The silence hung heavy between them for a few seconds. "We're under attack, from the air! I must rush to pick up a few things!" cried Champa, jumping up. She did not want him to ask more questions.

Besides, she must hurry and leave. She quickly tied up the cloth around his mouth again and ran to finish her work. But she could not prevent herself from glancing back at the prisoner. His plight filled her with pity. "No, no, I must not look at him," she told herself sternly, but could not help doing so. She had taken care of him, tended to his injuries, bandaged his wounds, and fed him all these days. He was her patient and she was duty bound to look after his needs. It was the responsibility of a nurse to protect the person under her care, so Commander Rekha had told her. How could she then allow him to die? But then she was also a soldier in the guerrilla army and duty bound, once again, not to flout any order given by the Commander of the army.

Thoughts chased each other swiftly, wildly, in her mind while her fingers hastily packed the bandages, medicines and other sick room stuff into a box. She would soon flee, run to take shelter somewhere. But what about him? All her protective instincts rushed to the fore at thought of the boy's fate, her mind overwhelmed by growing compassion. Poor boy, after all, what crime had he committed? He had not killed nor harmed anyone, yet was being punished most cruelly, for no fault at all. First kidnapped, then shot at, and now about to be put to death for some petty cash–was it right? No, no, no, her heart, mind and her conscience protested vehemently.

Once again Champa's eyes darted towards the helpless victim lying on the floor. Like a beast led to the slaughter house, she thought indignantly. Feeling her glance, he looked up and met her eyes. She blinked and looked away but her feelings must have shown on her face. He immediately responded to the emotions her eyes revealed.

Once again the curtain that usually veiled his feelings was torn apart. She caught a split second glimpse of the dark terror that lurked deep in the prisoner's eyes. It was the same stark terror she saw on Gopal's face when the jungle people pulled him, screaming, from his room, gun against forehead, the same terror that she sensed in the bleating of the goat before his throat was slashed. And it was the same terror that she felt when the policemen pulled her, alone and helpless, into a lonely room to rape her.

The sheer fear and dread revealed in the prisoner's eyes wrenched at her heart. She could not just watch, nor ignore it. She no longer cared what happened to her. No, it did not matter anymore.

Before her was a helpless human being. She would not be human if she did not rescue him from the inhuman death awaiting him. Feelings of compassion and charity, natural in anyone belonging to the human species, swept aside all her fears. She forgot every other danger.

The girl rushed to the prisoner, a pair of scissors in her hands. With quick, deft movements she snipped at the rope that bound his feet and hands. She pulled away the cloth tied around the mouth. "Come on, get up! Hurry, come with me!" she cried, pulling the prisoner to his feet. She supported him as he staggered unsteadily after being tied up for so long. "Hurry, before they come and kill you!"

Champa clasped the prisoner's hand and dragged him out through the door. She threw wary glances all around, crouching low so she would not be seen. She could hear the sound of the helicopter far above and knew it would be back soon. Meanwhile, in the rush and chaos all around it was not difficult to flee unnoticed, especially as she knew her way about. She dragged the prisoner towards a lonely spot where she thought it would be safe for him.

"Look, that's your escape route! Be careful! There won't be anyone there! You'll have to find your way back. Go! Before anyone sees you!" she urged the prisoner who gaped back at her in astonishment.

Manas did not move. He still seemed to be in a daze. Champa gave him a little push. "Go on, run!" she cried. At last he seemed to wake up. The light of gratitude shone in his eyes.

"You … you are rescuing me," he muttered, doubt in his voice. "But why?"

"I … I just feel bad for you," murmured Champa, "Now go!"

"They will kill you for setting me free. You must leave too!" urged Manas, realising the danger the girl faced.

Champa pushed him aside. "I can't! I won't!"

"Why not? Leave the jungle people. Go home. You have a family, you told me. Go back to them," Manas insisted.

"No! I can't leave Comrade Vijay. I love him. I will be with him until I die," cried Champa.

"But you will be killed in the attack. Or get caught by the police. They will punish you. And if you are lucky enough to escape the police, the jungle folk won't let you live!" warned Manas.

"You don't understand. I can't leave him, whatever happens. I will live and die with him!" the girl declared passionately, "Now you go, hurry!" She gave him another push and then fled, before Manas could utter a word. She was confident that he would be alright. He would be able to find his way back, and survive somehow. At least it was better for him to wander in the jungle in the hope that the police would discover him. They would be glad to find the missing boy. Yes, Manas would be alright.

It was with a feeling of great satisfaction that she turned back towards the camp. She remembered that she had to pick up the sick room stuff and ran to get it. She walked in and stood still in shock and surprise. Vijay was standing there, along with the two guards who had returned.

"I came to carry out the Commander's orders. But where is the prisoner?" Vijay asked as soon as he saw her. "Where were you?"

"Went out to see … what's happening, Vijay?" Champa asked, trying to gain time to gather her thoughts before she replied. She was still breathing hard after her rescue act.

"They are still firing. I packed up the Commander's stuff. Now I must do my job … finish off that boy! But where is he? D'you know?" asked Vijay. Champa felt his eyes bore hard into hers, as if suspecting her hand in the boy's disappearance, her guilt laden mind told her.

"You mean you were ready to kill, by … by … first … cutting off … as I heard him say?" her voice trembled; she could not bring herself to say the words.

"Of course! Commander's orders!" said Vijay shortly.

"But … you don't like unnecessary violence, do you?" asked the girl.

"No, but I must obey him. Learn to be tough, as he says. Where is the boy?"

The girl could only stare at him with bewildered eyes. Was he ready to do anything, even something so contrary to his nature, something so barbaric, just to please his leader? Vijay did not meet her questioning eyes. "Where is he?" he repeated, looking away.

"How do I know? He was not here when I came to pack up," fibbed the girl. "Ask them," she pointed towards the two guards, "It was their duty to guard the prisoner, not mine."

Did he still look unbelieving? Champa glanced sideways at Vijay, trying to read his feelings. He was looking the other way. She wondered what was in his mind but did not dare to ask. About to leave, all that he said was, "I must inform the leader. He will decide what to do. Let's go!"

Champa quickly suppressed the sigh of relief that had almost escaped her lips. She was not sure if he believed her or not. But deep in her heart she knew and understood. Even if he did suspect her role in rescuing the prisoner he would keep the suspicion to himself, for he loved her. She would not reveal the secret either. Vijay would never forgive her for disobeying his leader's order. No, there was no need to tell him. Let the doubts remain in his mind; she would neither confirm nor talk about it.

40

Champa and Vijay

Bent low under a shady thicket of trees Vijay crawled towards the rock where he knew the leader sheltered. Champa stayed close. To their consternation they found that he was no longer there.

"Where is the Commander? I must tell him something!" Vijay looked around to search for him. Another soldier who now hid there pointed to a banyan tree a little further away. "Look, there he is, under that tree." Vijay could see him now. Bhaskar was partly covered by the thick roots that hung from the tree's branches. Vijay and Champa bent low to avoid being targeted and ran to join him.

"What is it? What will you tell him?" asked Champa, panting behind him.

By this time they had reached the tree where the leader stood.

"Comrade Vijay, I'm relieved to see you. Is the job done?" asked Bhaskar.

"I have a question, Sir. Shouldn't we fire back at the men in the helicopter? Why must we remain sitting ducks for them? Let us give it back, bullet for bullet!" Vijay had clearly set the question of the prisoner aside, Champa noted with relief.

"Comrade, once again you make a mistake. Firing back will only give our positions away. They will know exactly where we are," answered Bhaskar. His voice did not have its usual sharpness, Vijay noted with surprise. It made him look at his leader again. Was something wrong?

There was an expression of great weariness in Bhaskar's eyes. His face seemed drawn and strained, the lines on his forehead stood out sharp, and his lips seemed to droop. The other two had never seen the leader's face look so grey before, and the eyes so bleak.

"How is everything, Commander Sir?" asked Vijay, shocked to see the change on the Commander's face.

"Not good, comrade," replied Bhaskar. His voice sounded hoarse. "We … we seem to have lost a valuable colleague. Will you tend to her, comrade Champa?"

Her? Who was it? Champa's heart thudded with fear and anxiety as she crawled over to the spot where he pointed. Dear Shiva, let it not be anyone she knew. She could see the figure that lay on the ground in the shade of the wild jamun tree. Munia and a few other girls crouched around it. Champa's steps turned heavy, her fists clenched in tension. She still could not guess who had received the fatal bullet, though she could see the khaki cap covering the face. So the firing was not always off target. It had succeeded in claiming at least one victim. She turned over the cap and gasped in shock and surprise. She had never, in her wildest thoughts, imagined that they would lose the brave and confident soldier who lay there in a heap, eyes closed. No, she could not believe it. It was not possible that kind, caring and efficient Commander Rekha was no more. The old warrior had been hit by a bullet which had pierced her heart. There was no way she could have been saved, and death had been instantaneous, realised the stunned girl.

A huge lump rose in her throat for she had grown to love and respect the leader, who in her own quiet way had helped them all. Rekha had taught her not only the skills of war but the art of caring and nurturing as well. Champa owed the lady soldier a great deal, for she had been a friend, teacher and guide.

It was not the time to grieve, however, for Rekha was not the only one pulled under the shade of the old jamun tree. There were a few others, some injured and a couple barely alive. Champa rushed to help the badly injured, medical kit in hand. She heard the cries and calls for help and tried to do her best, but it was a difficult job, much beyond her knowledge and experience. She knew she was no expert. Without Dr Rekha to direct her she felt nervous and totally helpless.

Ganga, Munia and other girls tried to help, but were ignorant about tending to injuries. She found herself supervising the work and marvelled at how she, a half educated villager, could take the responsibility. But it was an emergency and she had to cope with it somehow.

The enemy had a distinct advantage, firing as they did from above. She feared they fought a losing battle. It was only Bhaskar's unending confidence and courage that made them carry on. The leader was not about to give up. With his lady love gone, there was none to question him either. Vijay rushed to be at his side. His heart grieved with his leader for the lady who had been almost like a mother to him. He clenched his fists in anger at those who had done this to her.

It was already late afternoon. The sporadic firing slowed down after a while as darkness began to shroud the jungle, hiding and protecting the guerrillas from their enemy. Soon it stopped altogether. Nature had forced the enemy to withdraw, giving the Naxalites valuable time to carry out their plans. Looking up, Vijay saw the helicopter flying back the way it had come.

"Comrade Vijay," Bhaskar called out from his hiding place. "It is time to call our people back. Will you give out the orders?"

"Yes, Sir!" said Vijay. He sent out the message and as the squads retreated back to camp he stood around to gauge the damage. He realised that the loss had been immense, much more than they had at first thought.

Later, when he met him in what remained of his shack, the Commander looked exhausted and sad. Dark rings circled his eyes. "Time for us to leave," he said finally with a sigh. "There is no point in defending what can no longer be defended. Tomorrow the police would be here again. We must leave before that."

"Yes, Sir. We'll all disappear before they arrive. Like last time. But where do we go once we assemble again?" asked Vijay.

"The government has become overactive in this area. We must find ourselves another place in another state. May be return to Andhra Pradesh. Jharkhand need not be our home forever. There are other places, surely," Bhaskar muttered his thoughts out loud.

"Yes, Sir. We can go to Odisha, Chhattisgarh, or Andhra Pradesh. Or why not Nepal?" asked Vijay

"Anywhere … but we'll be back soon, once we have regained our strength. The war against the capitalists must continue. We must fight for the power to bring change in our country!" declared Bhaskar, his voice once again regaining the earlier strength and confidence.

"Yes, Sir, we must!" Vijay nodded his head vigorously in agreement.

"But for now, we leave at once. Comrade, get it organised. And make very special arrangements for … for Commander Rekha. We must bid her an honourable farewell." His voice about to break, Bhaskar abruptly stood up and gestured to Vijay to leave.

The young man strode out immediately in deference to his leader's grief. As he walked out he remembered that with Rekha gone, he was the next in command after Bhaskar. It was his responsibility now to carry out the orders the Commander gave. With a catch in his throat he resolved to himself that he would come up to the expectations of his beloved, heroic and committed leader. He would shoulder his duties now with greater dedication than ever before.

Champa was tending to the wounded and injured soldiers in the dim light of a lantern. Vijay rushed close, looking for her. Champa was busy with a wounded figure which lay on a cot. Somebody had pulled it out of one of the damaged shelters. Drawing closer, Vijay glanced at the bloodied and pale face of the injured person. It was a woman, he noticed, and felt his heart sink. Another victim of the firing. There were too many of them, for the bullets had found their targets, even as the comrades fled and hid beneath trees and rocks. Champa ran to him as soon as she saw him. "What shall I do for Comrade Munia?" she moaned, wringing her hands, "She seems quite bad to me. I don't know how to help her. Oh, how I wish we had a doctor around," she cried desperately.

So it was the brave and sprightly Munia, realised the stunned Vijay. She with the infectious charm and friendly warmth, who had already suffered a tragic loss when Sudhir was killed, was now gone herself. Vijay remained silent in his shock and grief. He shook his head and wished that he could help, but there was nothing that he could do.

"I've come to take you. It is time for all to leave, as the Commander had told us," he said instead.

"But what about all these injured folk?" asked Champa.

"Give them First Aid. Tie bandages and provide some support. We must go. The police will attack again," Vijay said, "We must escape. To continue our fight, as we must, for the Party!"

Champa returned to her work. Soon a line of bandaged, wounded soldiers began to creep, or hobble, swiftly out of the camp. The girls tied bandages on wounds, applied medicine and helped carry out the wounded on makeshift stretchers. Absorbed in her task, she hardly heard the soft, gentle voice when it called out, "Comrade, come closer. I wish to speak to you!" It was Munia. Champa rushed to take her friend's hand. The injured girl's dusky skin was grey like ash, the blood drained out of her. Her hand felt cold. "I'm about to join him, so I'm not afraid." Munia's voice was so weak it could hardly be heard. Champa bent closer. Her friend was looking at her with big eyes grown even larger.

The sight of the strong guerrilla soldier lying there in that pathetic state made Champa's heart sink. She tightened her clasp over the cold hands. "Shh … why do you say this?" she gently murmured.

"Because it is time for me to go. But I told you. I have no fear because … you know why! Lal Salaam, comrade. May our cause triumph!" Munia's eyes were calm as they looked straight into her friend's tearful eyes.

"But who is letting you go? You will be alright soon, Munia," Champa laid her other hand on the girl's forehead and began to caress it softly. As she did so, the wounded girl's eyes drooped close over her cheeks. Champa watched her face anxiously. It was some time before she realised that Munia was not going to wake up from her sleep. Her friend was gone, forever. Champa covered her face with both her hands and broke into sobs. "My only friend, my best friend, Lal Salaam to you," she cried, over and over again.

For a long time the girl remained stunned and in a daze, though her hands and feet continued to function. The last of the injured were leaving the shade of the tree. She knew Vijay was busy too, organising the exodus and making preparations for everyone, the wounded as well as the dead, to move out.

Finally, after the last person had left, Vijay ran towards her. Champa was winding up. "Come, hurry, let's go!" he cried, holding out his hand towards the girl.

"But where?" asked Champa.

"Wherever the Commander leads us. I am ready to follow wherever he takes me," explained Vijay.

To Vijay's surprise Champa shook her head and did not move. She did not take the hand he had stretched out towards her.

41

"What's the matter? Aren't you coming?" asked Vijay, withdrawing his hand slowly. "Come on, let's go. Hurry!" His questioning eyes probed her face for an answer.

Champa did not meet his eyes. She stared at a spot way behind him and remained thoughtful for a while. "We are not sheep that we must follow him wherever he goes," she said finally in a low voice. "Vijay, we need not go with him," she added, almost in a whisper.

Vijay looked incredulous and unbelieving. "What do you mean, Champa? He is our leader. He is the one who knows what is best for us!" declared Vijay.

"He does not, Vijay. We must decide for ourselves. And … and don't you see, we are not slaves. We are being used for their own gain …!" Manas's voice, accusing the jungle folk of using boys and girls to gain power for themselves, echoed in her agitated mind.

"Stop it! Champa, how dare you say that? How can you utter those blasphemous words? Do you realise what you just said?" Vijay sounded totally scandalised. His face flushed in shock and disbelief.

"I am sorry … didn't mean to upset you, Vijay," the girl hastily apologised. "I know you worship him, and I do think he is doing it all for our sake … for people like my father … but …"

"They have made so many sacrifices for us, Champa. Remember Sudhir! Why did he die? For us! Why did Bhaskar Sir leave his job and home to dwell in the jungle? To get rid of the rich and the selfish! Why? So that better policies can be made to suit the poor! Don't you understand?"

"I do, Vijay. I know. Only I don't like … the … the … killing! It is so cruel, so … so … inhuman. Is violence the only answer?" murmured the girl, her long lashes sweeping her cheeks as she looked down at her feet rather than at him.

Vijay stared at her, hardly believing his ears. "What d'you mean, Champa? Is this the time to discuss these things? The police is about to attack and kill us. Are we to sit here and argue about what is good and what is not?"

The girl raised her eyes at last. There was a strange look in them, an expression that could not be fathomed and which he had never seen before. It frightened him. He caught her hand in a desperate gesture and tried to pull her along. "Come on, we must leave! The Commander has already left. Let's go!"

"Vijay … I can't," said Champa "All this blood and death … it is not worth it. Where will it lead us? How does it help anyone?" She did not realise it, but Champa was again mouthing the very thoughts that Manas had once expressed.

"There's no time to discuss … but you know very well, Champa. We fight for a great and worthy cause … a glorious future. For the time when we'll have the power … to help the underprivileged and the exploited! Oh, come on, girl, the Commander has explained it so many times. Why question it now?" Vijay was getting impatient. He knew the commander would be waiting, wondering why he took so long. With his companion Commander Rekha gone, the leader depended solely on him. He had to stay by his side.

"Besides, I love you, girl. And so do you, Champa. Or don't you?" cried Vijay. The girl's obduracy was making him desperate.

"Of course I do," Champa hastened to admit. Her eyes lingered tenderly on Vijay's face. Quickly she reached out and touched the dimple which had attracted her so much. Then she laid her head on his chest and rested against his lean, hard body. It had always made her feel so protected. "Vijay, don't go," she pleaded and clung to him.

Vijay's arms tightened against her for a few moments of togetherness. Then he bent to murmur softly, "I must go. For me the Commander is the father I never had … my guide and my guardian … I can never desert him! Specially not now, when he is in trouble," he set his lips in a determined line.

"But you are my one and all too!" protested Champa, "I need you too."

"And I believe in our cause," continued Vijay, as if she had not interrupted, "Absolutely. It is my goal in life now. So must it be for you!"

"It is, it is! I do believe in the cause! But I really feel it is not right to kill, nor to hurt anyone. Specially the innocent who has not committed any crime. After all, we are human beings, not barbaric beasts!" Champa burst out. The picture of a helpless prisoner, his hands and feet tied as he waited for the guillotine flashed before her eyes. She turned her face away. Gently but firmly, she separated herself from Vijay and drew back several steps. Her face was set in determined lines.

Vijay tried another track. "Do you realise, Champa, you are walking into danger? Where will you go? You think anyone will welcome you when you return?"

"I have not thought of that," admitted the girl, "But I am sure all will be well. Lord Shiva will take care of me, as he did once before. I will go to the temple …"

"Enough! I must leave … are you coming or not?" Vijay asked, impatient now and exasperated at the girl's unreasonable stand. Even listening to her words seemed like sacrilege to him. He closed his ears with both his hands and cried, "Champa, I must!"

"Vijay, don't go," pleaded Champa once again.

"I must!"

"It is easy just now. Nobody will notice in the confusion. Let's escape!" urged the girl.

"I told you I can't!"

"But I know you don't like the killing either …?"

"I'll do whatever the Commander wants …!"

"No, please ..."

She gave him an imploring look. How can he, she wondered. Was the leader, then, everything to him? Was he ready to give up his own beliefs, ideas, his thoughts–himself too, and lay it all at the feet of someone else?

"I must. It is time to leave, Champa!" Vijay swung around, ready to race off. But the girl stood there, large eyes fixed expectantly on his face, sparks of hope still shining in them.

"Are you coming with me or not, Champa?" There was a frantic, desperate note in his voice.

The girl tried to smile. "I can't. I do not like ... I know you don't like the bloodshed either! Don't go!"

"I have to," said Vijay gently, touching her cheek in a tender gesture, "If you don't join me I must walk alone. Behind my leader."

The next moment he had slipped out into the dark night. Champa stood there, sad and forlorn, gazing sorrowfully at the spot from which he had vanished. They had both chosen, made their decisions. Though heartbroken, she knew she was right. The heartless killing and the violence could not be justified, whatever the reason.

It was all hushed, quiet and dark. The helicopter was gone. No doubt the attack would commence again, as soon as there was light to see. The police would then invade the Naxalite camp. They would find it abandoned, except for one solitary girl.

The police? The thought made her immediately alert. It was because of them that she had fled her village. Would she fall into their hands again? Alone? With no jungle folk to protect her she would be easy prey. She remembered the filthy acts they were capable of performing.

No, no! She must quickly escape ... slink away before the police arrived.

With a pang of regret she wondered–would she ever see the man who would reign forever over her heart? Maybe yes, maybe not. The thought of never meeting him again was like a knife twisting deep into her heart. But no, she had decided, she would not let it put her down.

She had gone through a lot in her young life. It had made her strong enough to face whatever Fate might bring.

Yes, she had grown up.

Manas was right. Violence could not be the solution. People like her must become strong enough to care for themselves. Strength came with education. Somehow, some day, she would grab that education, not just for herself, but for her little brother as well.

Decision made, Champa raised her head high and with firm, determined steps set off on the long trek through the jungle, away from the home she had found, and away from the man who had found a place in her heart.

42

Manas Gupta

The temple bells at Aamra Vatika were pealing loudly. And why not, the beloved grandson of the owner, Mr Gupta, had returned home. After everyone had given up hope, the kidnapped lad, Manas, wandering wounded and alone in the jungle, had been discovered and rescued by the police. By the grace of god he was back in the arms of his family.

There was great rejoicing by the Guptas who held a puja at the Shiva temple. Later, the elder Mr Gupta called Manas to his room where the whole family was gathered. "We are so happy you are back, Manas. Now you can return to the US and take up your job. When would you like to go?"

Manas remained silent, deep in thought. His mind was far away, in the midst of a dark, dreadful jungle, surrounded by the fierce, armed criminals who had shot him, captured him and kept him imprisoned.

Only, they were no longer cruel and merciless villains. Instead, they were lost and misguided boys and girls fighting for a cause they believed in. They had taken up arms to protect themselves from a harsh, unjust and uncaring world.

"I am not going, Dada. I changed my mind. I will stay here."

"Stay here?" asked his grandfather, astonished. "But why?"

Various faces were framed in his mind's eye. There was a handsome young man who had sacrificed his life for a cause.

There was a brilliant professor and an efficient and caring lady. The two together believed they could change the world for the better.

There was an educated youth who blindly followed his leader.

And there was a girl, strong, intelligent and kind, who had handed him back his life.

How could he forget the people he had spent so many days with?

"There's so much to do … right here at home, in this place!" breathed out Manas, at last.

"What do you mean?" asked the elders, puzzled.

Someone had dared to gift him his life, at great risk to herself. He must return that kindness, or be accused of selfishness. What could he do to show his gratitude?

Help others, of course!

Manas's eyes lit up, his face glowed with an inner knowledge and a new excitement. He knew now what his aim was, the goal he would strive towards. Yes, he had found his mission in life. "I mean … well, this is what I'd really like to do …" he murmured.

"What?" asked father and grandfather in one voice that dripped with curiosity.

"I would like to … do something that will benefit others … yes, I will set up institutions for those who can't afford good education! Free!" His voice rang loud and firm in the stunned silence that followed his announcement.

"Free? What do you mean? How can you do that?" asked his shocked elders.

"Yes, why not?" Manas raised his head high. There was a mocking gleam in his eyes as he asked, "We do have enough resources, don't we, Dada … Papa? Enough to spare for others?"

His father and grandfather stared at him with guilt laden, startled eyes. They had no answer to give.

Acknowledgements

Grateful thanks are due to,

my husband, Yashwant, for taking time out of his busy schedule to go through my writing, correct mistakes and give suggestions to move the story forward,

daughter Sharmila, an author herself, for reading, appreciating and adding to what I wrote,

Nita, Nilima, Rani, Indira, my friends in AWIC, (Association of Writers and Illustrators for Children), for continuing to encourage me, despite the rejections,

eminent author Amitav Bagchi, for his positive criticism and advice,

Kanishka Gupta, my agent, for helping me find a publisher,

my publishers Niyogi Books and their team for turning my thoughts and words into the beautiful book that is now in the reader's hands,

and, most of all, I am deeply grateful to Gita Rajan, my editor, who understood and appreciated the story, and provided great inputs that added value to the novel.